T0123321

From USA Today *bestselling author Anabelle Bryant comes a thrilling novel of unexpected passion—and its surprising consequences . . .*

"Your philandering ways need to come to an end. I'll not have my heritage die by your foolish neglect." Lord Jonathan Cromford, Earl of Lindsey, is not surprised by his cold-hearted late father's will and the numerous conditions for claiming his inheritance. But requiring that the rogue first produce an heir is beyond the pale. Still, there was nothing for it but to sacrifice his desires for the sake of his well-being. Temporarily, at least. Yet when Lindsey accidentally meets Lady Caroline Nicholson, he finds that his life is suddenly full of the unexpected . . .

Recently returned to London from Italy, Caroline won't allow the questionable circumstances of her family's hasty departure to overshadow her desire to marry well. With the help of her society-savvy cousins, she intends to be engaged before the season ends. But even her best laid plans do not prevent her from becoming tongue-tied upon meeting legendary rakehell, the Earl of Lindsey. She can only hope their instant attraction won't devastate her future, much less her reputation. Still, as chemistry and fate throw them together, both Caroline and Lindsey may have to choose between comfort and pleasure, fear and truth, security and risk . . .

Visit us at www.kensingtonbooks.com

Books by Annabelle Bryant

London's Most Elusive Earl
London's Late Night Scandal
London's Best Kept Secret
London's Wicked Affair

Published by Kensington Publishing Corporation

London's Most Elusive Earl

Midnight Secrets

Anabelle Bryant

LYRICAL PRESS
Kensington Publishing Corp.
www.kensingtonbooks.com

LYRICAL PRESS BOOKS are published by
Kensington Publishing Corp.
119 West 40th Street
New York, NY 10018

All Kensington titles, imprints, and distributed lines are available at special quantity discounts for bulk purchases for sales promotion, premiums, fund-raising, educational, or institutional use.

Special book excerpts or customized printings can also be created to fit specific needs. For details, write or phone the office of the Kensington Sales Manager: Kensington Publishing Corp., 119 West 40th Street, New York, NY 10018. Attn. Sales Department. Phone: 1-800-221-2647.

Lyrical Press and Lyrical Press logo Reg. U.S. Pat. & TM Off.

First Electronic Edition: October 2020
eISBN-13: 978-1-5161-1092-6
eISBN-10: 1-5161-1092-7

First Print Edition: October 2020
ISBN-13: 9978-1-5161-1093-3
ISBN-10: 1-5161-1093-5

Printed in the United States of America

Prologue

William Cromford, Earl of Lindsey, was laughing in his grave. Edward Barlow, the late earl's personal solicitor, was certain of it. Ensconced in Kingswood Manor, Lindsey's grand country estate in Bedfordshire, Barlow had decided it best to disclose the contents of the earl's will and its many contingencies in a tranquil pastoral surround, and thus had summoned those named in the document to the sprawling bucolic property. Barlow assumed the beneficiary wouldn't find peace with the deceased's legacy, and it was his intention to use the return trip to London to diffuse the anticipated shock and anger evoked when the gentleman heard his respective inheritance instructions.

Barlow glanced at his pocket watch to note the hour and settled his gaze on his leather satchel. Inside were confidential packets of information. Specific, life-altering, rule-dictating, document bundles that detailed exactly what the heir would claim were the requirements met. Today he would begin a process with myriad outcomes and far-reaching repercussions, not all of them pleasant.

He strode to the mullioned windows of the library and watched as an elaborate equipage rolled to a stop in the gravel drive. The distinctive gilded emblem shimmered on the carriage door and declared its owner. Jonathan Cromford, the rightful heir and *new* Earl of Lindsey, inherited a title and expansive compilation of land and investments with confidence and aplomb, despite he never experienced the same within a relationship with his sire.

Pity the late nobleman considered his son a wastrel. Far worse, the rightful heir hadn't ever given a damn what his father thought. From what Barlow had learned, the new earl was an uncompromising sort, whose rakish reputation and scandalous escapades kept the tongue-wags busy while the social elite turned a blind eye, all too quick to live vicariously through his exploits rather than censure his activities.

Still, the automatic possession of title and funds which occurred upon the sire's death were nothing but a modicum of the inheritance. So much more needed to be accomplished. Best to serve this medicine swiftly. Barlow reclaimed his seat after Lindsey entered, their handshake brief yet firm.

"Nine months seems an exorbitant waiting period for the contents of my father's will, but I'm not surprised at the delay," Lindsey commented. "I'm sure there are numerous conditions included in the document. He was a complicated man, and by no reason would he abandon that particular quality for something so inconvenient as death."

Barlow nodded, unsure a response was necessary. Instead he broke the seal on the packet before him and pushed his spectacles farther up his nose so he might continue the process. "Your father granted me an ample length of time to assemble the necessary documentation and ensure matters were in order before his instructions led to this day." He couldn't offer more in way of explanation and busied himself with the task of brushing wax crumbs to the left side of the blotter. "He also included a letter for me to read to you aloud."

"Like a child hears a story before bedtime? He chose his death to perform a paternal kindness? Perhaps that decision before any other finally stopped his empty heart." Lindsey barked a laugh that held no humor. "Indulge my impatience. I'll have that letter and be on my way, Barlow."

"I'm afraid my reading it to you is a condition set forth by the binding contract of his lordship's last testament. The instructions are detailed and specific. I must insist on following each one with exactitude to uphold the integrity of the probate process." He cleared his throat, his usual calm demeanor unsettled at the intensity of Lindsey's stare. "Unless I read the contents aloud and observe you've received the news, I would never be sure you'd actually opened the packet and hadn't thrown it into the flames of the nearest firebox."

"Get on with it then." Lindsey's voice held a sardonic edge as he waved his hand in a gesture of dismissal and settled deeper into the wingback chair. His eyes sparked with anger kept on a short leash.

Barlow bypassed the first two sheets of foolscap before he extracted the note written in the late earl's hand, the black ink on the page the last bequest for his son, albeit a sly situation nonetheless. He cleared his throat a second time and began to read aloud.

"Jonathan,

By now you've gained the title and taken control of the earldom, a right you claimed by birth as a peer of the realm. Though we haven't spoken in years, I've known of your habits and tolerated your excessive indulgence without complaint. You spare no expense on tailoring, horseflesh, and property, your roguish lifestyle enabled by the precedence and unquestionable power of the Lindsey heritage."

Barlow heard the young earl's grunt of complaint but he kept his eyes on the page and continued to read, unwilling to be lured into a disruptive conversation.

"As with many things, time alters life with indelible impact. The day one is born and begins to live, one also begins to die. Yet we are hardly prepared when the time is upon us. Therefore, I've set ink to paper in a formal legacy overseen by my solicitor to ensure you have fulfilled specific conditions before collecting the remainder of the settlement. There are but two requirements.

Restore the fiscal solvency of the earldom. You will be supplied with the accounting of an unfortunate situation. The coffers have suffered and so will you if the monies are not recovered. Wealth, like life, is not unending. You will understand more fully when you receive the records from my man of business.

The second condition is of a personal nature. You must produce a legitimate heir as soon as possible. Your philandering ways need to come to an end. I'll not have my heritage die by your foolish neglect.

Until these conditions are met, Barlow will limit the funds made available for your expenditures. As each month passes, if my legacy remains unfulfilled, the allowance will narrow significantly. This is meant to hurry along the process. There are others who benefit from my passing, and your success impinges upon their livelihood. Make haste. Mr. Barlow will oversee the particulars.

William Cromford, Earl of Lindsey

Chapter One

London
Two weeks later

Lady Caroline Nicholson withdrew into the shadows of Lord Albertson's study, a peculiar place to pass the time considering the first event of the season was well underway. At least two hundred guests were shoulder to shoulder amidst the festivities in the ballroom, dining room, and adjoining halls.

She wasn't lost, though. More the opposite. She'd purposefully snuck across the expansive estate and slipped into her host's private sanctuary in search of solitude. Which in itself made little sense when Lord Tiller, *the most desirable bachelor in London*, remained in the ballroom, no doubt dancing with a flirtatious, unmarried female.

As intended, Caroline had gained an introduction, offered engaging conversation and a not-so-subtle desire to dance, and yet the gentleman hadn't requested her card or lingered longer than etiquette required.

Apparently, she'd failed to impress. She raised her linen handkerchief to her nose and solidified her emotions with a valiant sniff. A few minutes of solitude would restore her confidence, and then she'd return to the ballroom with nothing more than mildly bruised pride and a lingering twinge of disillusionment. Suitable gentlemen were plentiful. It mattered little if the one who first caught her eye found her lacking. There were others who qualified as outstanding husband material.

Across the room a clink of the latch snared her attention and she swung her focus toward the entrance, where the door cracked open and two people swept inside. Concealed by the shadowy depth of the corner, she'd likely go unnoticed, though she had no cause to stay hidden. Propriety demanded she make her presence known. The last thing she needed was to be caught in an embarrassing scandal when she'd set her heart on making a match this season. Contemplating how to negotiate the impropriety of the situation, she squinted her eyes and peered into the dim interior. This part of the house was not included in the festivities, and the room was lit by only one box lantern and the waning flames of a dying fire.

Upon recognition, the irony of the situation struck her with brilliant clarity. Lord Jonathan Cromford, Earl of Lindsey, notorious rakehell and, in her opinion, *least desirable bachelor in London*, lured a lady into the room. His infamous half-smile was rumored to set London's fairer population into an automatic swoon. Having never experienced the impact, she doubted the result, although one could never be sure. At times, women made a fuss over the silliest fascinations. It would be interesting to witness such a phenomenon. She shook her head slightly at the inanity. Then again, her cousins had managed to educate her on every member of society who crossed her path or attended a function, and she appreciated their attention to detail. It enabled her a smoother entry into society here in London.

Half a room away stood a prime example of an unrepentant rogue, even though the marriage-minded set dismissed his bold exploits as daring and appalling. Certainly, the female in tow seemed enamored by the scoundrel's legendary charms.

Caroline watched as the earl lent the room a cursory glance, his attention riveted to the lady at hand. Had the scene before her not progressed with slapdash speed, she would have assembled a few polite words and made her presence known, but hesitation proved her downfall. Intrigued and inordinately curious, she took a miniscule step backward into the recessed alcove. Her bottom pressed against the wall. There was nowhere else to go.

The moment to object had passed. She was trapped by her own prevarication. Hopefully the couple would complete their assignation with a brief kiss and return to the ballroom. Any more time wasted would be unjust punishment. The music was scheduled to end soon and all opportunities to dance would be lost. How foolish to have allowed the earl to distract her, but distract her he did. She'd have to wait it out in utter silence. One shallow sniffle or misplaced exhale would bring about her discovery and inevitable ruin.

* * * *

Things weren't going as planned. Jonathan Cromford, Earl of Lindsey, tugged Lady Jenkin into the silent darkness of Lord Albertson's study. The lady had never played such a persistent game, and while he was after something specific, he hadn't imagined she would be equally as particular.

"Kiss me now, Lindsey." Her voice held just enough demand to be petulant. "You've led me on a chase all over this estate and I haven't yet been rewarded. I can't wait another moment."

"I couldn't very well kiss you while you stood at your husband's side. You shouldn't fault me for the impossible." He stripped his gloves and dropped them to a nearby chair before he gathered her close.

"He doesn't deserve my attention. All he cares about is his precious collection, kept in a private gallery for his eyes only. It makes for tedious conversation night after night. He allows no one to view it, yet he can speak of nothing else." She smoothed her palms over Lindsey's shoulders and encircled his neck, her lips drawn into an alluring pout.

"And is that what you want from me? Interesting conversation? Small talk and niceties?" He kept his mouth above hers even though she angled her chin higher.

"Never." Her answer was nothing more than a breathy sigh. "I want much more, and I shall have it. Now kiss me. I've waited all night to taste you."

He tightened their embrace and her gratuitous décolletage crushed against his chest. Then he captured her mouth in a brief, teasing caress. "Is that better?"

"No," she objected in husky complaint. "Not nearly enough. Why must you torture me? Kiss me again."

He kissed her hard, deep, stealing her breath and drawing her closer still.

"Do you always get what you want, darling?"

"I want you and your wicked kisses."

"Not your husband's attention? Not his precious fortune in paintings?"

"No. Your kisses are more valuable." She shifted slightly and twined her hand between them. "This…" She slid her hand downward. "This is priceless."

Startled by her boldness, he smothered the urge to pull away as her palm pressed against the placket of his trousers, her fingers tight around his cock. The lady was shameless, and apparently more than determined to have what she wanted. Two qualities that would lend themselves to his cause. He nuzzled several kisses along her neck and bare shoulder, all the while enduring her audacious strokes along the ridge of his erection. At least his body had cooperated.

"No man should long for oils and artwork when a woman as breathtakingly beautiful as you can be his greatest treasure." He eased his hand over the curve of her hip and around to grasp her firm bottom.

"I don't want to talk about paintings. I don't want to talk at all." She loosened the ribbons at her neckline with her free hand and lowered the scraps of lace that composed her sleeves. The plump swells of her breasts pressed high above the edge of her corset. "I need to feel you touch me. I can't wait any longer."

Knowing he'd never achieve his goal if he didn't first appease Lady Jenkin's appetite for wantonness, he trailed kisses across the top of her bosom, dipping his tongue into the silky vee of her cleavage, all the while concentrating on the most advantageous approach to the more important subject.

"I think about you every night alone in my bed."

Her chest rose and fell with the confession as he continued to lavish attention to her body. He stroked his thumb across her nipple, and she shuddered with his touch.

"And what do you imagine, darling? What naughty deeds do you pretend we commit together?" Tempering his impatience, he lifted her by the waist and placed her on the corner of Albertson's walnut pedestal desk. A clatter of accessories fell to the floorboards. *Sorry, old boy.*

"I want you stripped of all these bothersome garments, skin to skin, touching, tasting, the endless passion we'll find together."

The lady would not be deterred. She tightened her grasp on his breeches and he shifted, disguising his escape in a maneuver to reposition her as he bundled her skirts in his fist. She shivered when cool air caressed her exposed thighs.

"Would that it wasn't just fantasy? You deserve so much more than a quick moment of gratification on a hard wooden desk in the dark. I can't worship your magnificent body like this. I'm left to envision your beauty hidden from view." Somehow or another all that foolish poetry foisted on him at Eton proved useful in this moment. He'd tell her anything she needed to hear if it assisted in his objective.

His words gave her pause. Her hand stilled, abandoned of purpose, and she inhaled sharply.

"It doesn't have to be this way, Lindsey. I want you in my bed."

"What are you saying?" He pulled away, effectively distancing himself although he still held her skirts. "You'd have me take you in your bedchamber in the middle of the night with your husband's bedroom next door?"

And his collection of priceless paintings ten paces down the hall in his private gallery?

"Yes." She arched into him, seemingly bereft by the separation.

"You're as brave as you are beautiful then." He leaned in and pressed a kiss to her neck. "Unbridled passion is a quality not often found in refined ladies of the ton. Perhaps I've happened upon the one woman who is my equal in all things sensual and pleasurable."

"Tomorrow evening." She answered eagerly, covering his hand where it still grasped her skirts. "I'll be alone. My husband is attending some exclusive auction late into the night. You must come to me at my home. Together we'll be as wicked as two secret lovers, as daring as Romeo and Juliet."

He could only assume she wasn't aware of how that story ended. But he wouldn't dwell on it. Not when success was in reach. "That's a rather brave proposition, my lady. Are you certain?" One thing Lindsey knew with surety: he wouldn't be climbing down a trellis like some green lad caught with his pants around his ankles. The prize he was after had nothing to do with bed sport. "Your courage is inspiring."

Lady Jenkin shimmied off the desk and straightened her clothing, tying the ribbons at her neck and rearranging her sleeves, as if dressing in a hurry was one of her practiced lessons at finishing school.

"I'll be counting the minutes until I have you in my bed." She pressed a hard kiss to his mouth before she scurried from the room, her parting words a suitable exit line.

The door clicked shut and he released a long breath of exasperation. Then he wiped the back of his hand across his mouth, straightened his evening clothes and glanced at the mess of papers and spilled ink on the floor beside Albertson's desk.

A suitable and somewhat vile expletive curled off his tongue. Then another. He was angry and restless, but it wasn't the broken mess on the floor which caused this reaction.

Damn his bloody father for putting him in this predicament. Damn the man's bloody negligence. How dare his future be dictated by a dead man. Damn him to hell!

Mollified somewhat, he strode across the room and tipped a crystal decanter of brandy to fill his glass, savoring the smooth burn of the liquor. He replaced the empty snifter and stepped toward the door. Already exhausted by the necessary façade he would perpetuate once he returned to the ballroom, he reached for the door latch, the cool brass beneath his fingers fast to remind he'd forgotten his gloves. He pivoted and stilled.

Across the room, in the shadows, something had moved. It was dim in the interior, the low light cast by the declining fire hardly adequate, yet he could have sworn he saw a shimmer reflected, no more than a flicker of movement. He waited and listened. Was that the rustle of fabric or the condescending hiss of a coal in the grate?

He stalked across the Aubusson rug, his bootheels nearly silent, his pulse a steady thrum, which taunted he would discover nothing besides Albertson's lazy housecat where it slept on a raised bookshelf.

But with each stride he became assured of his suspicion, each step less quiet and more determined, until he stood before the most unlikely voyeur. He would have laughed if any humor remained in him. Instead he matched the lady's wide-eyed stare.

"Now who do we have here?"

Chapter Two

Caroline stared at the Earl of Lindsey, her throat incredibly tight while her heart rushed blood to every cell of her body. She had no answer for his question. Mayhap she'd forgotten her name altogether. And not because she'd been caught in an unseemly and utterly embarrassing situation. No, her pulse galloped triple time in response to the scandalous tryst she'd just witnessed.

At the start, she'd told herself to look away. To turn her back or stare at the tips of her dancing slippers. She'd demanded her eyes to close, but her body hadn't listened. Her brain had ceased to function, possessed by some unmanageable curiosity which overpowered better sense.

Much like now, when she couldn't produce her own name.

His voice, husky and warm, reminded of the first time she'd tasted brandy. Her entire body heated from the inside out, the effect both wicked and dangerous. Now she had no explanation for her reaction other than she'd become fascinated, entranced, and simultaneously mortified. Thank heavens the room remained cloaked in shadows.

"You can speak, can't you?"

His sarcastic remark shook her sensibilities loose and a lick of indignation replaced what was once embarrassment.

"Of course I can," she snapped, appalled at her tone, as he'd prompted her to anger. She stepped away, silently pleading for composure. A strange undercurrent had taken hold as soon as he'd approached, and she didn't like the way his presence threw her off balance. "How dare you insult me after what I've already been forced to witness."

"Forced?" He laughed, and the deep rich sound rippled through her to cause an unwelcome prickling of goosebumps across her skin. "Forced seems an overstatement. You could have interrupted at any time," he answered, his voice silky and assured.

"What would you have me do?" she countered, uncertain she made sense. Nervous rambling was so unlike her usual levelheadedness. "Politely announce myself while you…" She faltered, her mind in a frantic search for the appropriate word.

"While I what?" His eyes sparkled with merriment, no matter the room was dimly lit.

"Never mind." She moved toward the door, unwilling to remain in his company one minute longer. "You're despicable."

"Oh, you can do better than that. I've been called much worse."

"I don't doubt it." She bit her lower lip at the impolite reply. What an irksome man. She should extricate herself from the situation before further damage could be done. Any whisper of gossip or disparaging word from the earl would ruin her chances at marital success. Society loved a scandal, and she had no plans to become one.

"Although, the same could be said about you, when one takes the time to consider it."

"Pardon?" She stilled, knowing it was a fool's decision and reassured only by the fact the festivities were held on the other side of the estate, far and away from where she'd sought respite. The faintest strains of the orchestra confirmed discovery remained unlikely.

"Despicable. The same word could be used to describe someone who takes pleasure from watching others."

She spun to face him again, her eyes as round as her gaping mouth. "I took no pleasure from watching your…" She sputtered, but for only the briefest instant. "Activities."

He cleared his throat with what might have been an aborted chuckle. That he found amusement at her objection was added insult.

* * * *

Lindsey assessed the outraged female before him and noted every detail of her becoming appearance. Her plump pink lips were flattened into a disapproving line, and despite her claim of finding no pleasure in the scene that had transpired, even in the shadowy interior he could see a rosy blush stained her cheeks. She was likely a debutante who'd lost her way, although that wouldn't completely explain why she was hiding in the back corner of Albertson's study.

Could it be she waited for a liaison of her own? Perhaps instead of her interrupting his interlude with Lady Jenkin, he'd interloped on a prearranged private moment. Not one for puzzles, he abandoned the riddle accordingly. Besides, no one had shown on her behalf. It didn't matter that he'd locked the door once he'd entered. Anyone hoping for a few minutes of loveplay with the mysterious lady before him would certainly rattle the latch.

"I wasn't watching," she insisted, her expression more insulted than shocked.

"You closed your eyes then?"

"No, but..." She stopped, as if realizing the futility of her reply. "I had no choice but to see it." She gestured with her glove, a flash of white in the darkness.

His suggestion seemed to unsettle her. Damn if that wasn't refreshing.

"No choice? Life is composed of nothing but choices." *Unless one has a noose around one's neck as a gift from their dead father.* "Every time you reply I find myself further invested in this discussion."

For a moment she didn't move, though she raised an elegant brow, then with a sharp intake of breath and a swirl of pale blue silk she pivoted, her heels tapping an eager rhythm to the door. He let her go. The distraction she'd lent him had reduced his fury to nothing more than annoyance. He couldn't change the conditions of his father's will any more than he could ignore them. He was duly trapped, and no doubt the old bastard knew it, even now where he lay six feet underground.

Lindsey retrieved his gloves from the chair, his mind at work in a better direction. Why didn't he recognize the dark-haired beauty who'd secretly observed his interlude with Lady Jenkin? And why hadn't he acquired her name? That oversight could be easily remedied. For no more than curiosity's sake he would rejoin the festivities and direct a few tactful questions to the right people. He prided himself on the most current inventory of information, especially when it involved an intriguing female.

Now returned to the ballroom, he might have never stepped away, the usual festivities across the dance floor enough to entertain the crush as the orchestra prepared for the final musical numbers. The dinner hour was near. He nabbed a brandy from a passing servant's tray and strode to an area aside the French doors, where several gentlemen of his acquaintance conversed about horses, wagers, and the usual variety of male pursuits. His tendency lent more to listening than participating but tonight he had a different purpose.

One of his closest comrades Jeremy Lockhart, Viscount Dearing, was absent this evening. Dearing spent most all his time at home of late, his first son born recently. His friend's enthusiastic embrace of domesticity remained a matter beyond Lindsey's comprehension. In fairness, Lindsey had known little kindness in his childhood and hardly claimed to understand familial bliss. His mother died in spirit long before he'd come into the world, and his father instilled in him a skeptical view of life right to the bitter end. *Beyond, actually.* In that manner, a handful of friends were his family more than any blood relations, and he found the arrangement suited his lifestyle.

"She's a bit reckless, even for your taste, unless you're foxed."

Lindsey slanted his head, pleased to see Lord Mills approach, his waggish grin in place as he continued his commentary. Gregory Barnes, Viscount Mills, was a good friend and fellow scalawag—if men of their age could be categorized as such.

"Lady Jenkin is devouring you with her eyes. If she keeps it up, she'll have no appetite at dinner. Meanwhile, her husband may be obliviously lost to dull conversation, but the gabs are not so easily deceived. Have a care."

"I am nothing if not discreet," Lindsey replied.

A quick glance across the tiles confirmed Mills spoke the truth. In the study, Lindsey had already learned Lady Jenkin was anything but subtle. Still, he wouldn't allow an unwelcome scene when he was so close to achieving success. Were Lord Jenkin to suddenly pay attention to his wife or hear one whisper of conjecture, tomorrow evening's rendezvous would be in jeopardy, and now that Lindsey had located the painting he sought, he would suffer whatever role necessary to leave with the prize.

He silently cursed his father in an overused habit and turned toward Mills. "We should continue this conversation on the terrace. Stretch your legs?" He didn't wait for a reply, assured Mills would accompany him, and without hesitation opened the French doors to step into the bracing night air. They strode wordlessly across the granite until they were as far from the house as the landing allowed.

"Have you anything to share concerning the Decima?" Lindsey had confided in Mills in reference to his search for three particular paintings, including a few familial details that instigated his actions in the first place. Mills was a museum enthusiast, as well as a collaborator with the artistic lot who loitered about the alleys near the British Museum. The dichotomy of knowing the cultural elite and possessing connections to the fencers and thieves who perpetuated the black market was a priceless gift in itself.

Lindsey's father claimed the oil paintings had been stolen and charged his son with recovering the valuable collection of nudes known as The Fates. Nona, the spinner of time, was currently awaiting his attention in

Lord Jenkin's gallery. Decima, the weaver, was next on his list. He hadn't given a thought to Morta, the final painting, because it seemed pointless until he could make the foremost progress.

"I haven't heard a word, though an associate has mentioned he may ferret out a lead before the week's end."

Lindsey huffed a breath of annoyance. The bundle of documents and receipts he'd received after his father's solicitor read that infernal letter aloud proved useless in his search. "I appreciate the effort on my behalf."

"Anything for a friend." Mills eyed him with concern. "Your father would have the monies held indefinitely?"

"Apparently. It's his guarantee the conditions are met."

"But he'd dead, isn't he?"

"I assure you, he is, but his cruel control knows no boundaries, including an eternal dirt nap."

Mills didn't reply. With a nod toward the glass doors, the two men returned to the ballroom. Lindsey had hardly stepped over the threshold when his eyes were drawn across the room, where the dark-haired beauty from earlier stood within a cluster of guests, her profile limned in gold from the chandeliers above.

"Do you know the lady in pale blue silk beside the refreshment table?" He didn't look away, as if by willing it she might turn in his direction.

"That didn't take long," Mills answered in a droll tone.

"Explain." Short on patience, Lindsey refrained from further comment.

"Lady Caroline Nicholson, the only daughter of Lord Derby and his wife, recently returned from several years in Italy. Originally, they'd resided in Lincolnshire, although they sold the property before moving abroad and have only just taken residence in London. It's been mentioned Lady Caroline wishes to acquire a husband and that goal motivated the recent change of address, although a few murmurings suggest Derby needed to leave Italy under the threat of impending scandal."

"Excellent, Mills. You should work for the Crown." *She's magnificent.*

"I'd rather loiter around the ballroom with you. Prinny would never approve of your debauchery in fear the antics you drag me into would bleed upon his already tarnished reputation. And too, I value our friendship."

"You know too much for your own good." Lindsey couldn't help but smile as he continued to observe Lady Nicholson. *Why didn't she glance in his direction?*

"Perhaps," Mills continued. "Though I seem to have lost your attention."

"Send me a message if your associate discovers anything worth investigating." With a slant of his eyes he watched Mills step away. "I have a pressing matter of my own to investigate at the moment," he murmured. Lady Nicholson hadn't noticed him as of yet. She laughed at something shared by the older woman in her company, and he wondered when she would feel the weight of his stare. Under the light of two hundred candles, her flawless beauty spoke to his appreciation of the female form.

He'd noted her gown of pale silk earlier, but now with assistance from the ample overhead lighting he could admire how it hugged her body in perfection. The design was fashionable and gathered tightly around her trim waist, made all the more alluring as his eyes moved upward to the creamy swells of her breasts. She possessed an innate poise and grace that eluded young ladies by comparison. Her hair, dark as his morning coffee, was gathered in gentle ringlets, several curls left to cascade down the open neckline at her back, where a tempting expanse of silky skin was exposed. He moved his attention to her heart-shaped face. Glittering gems circled her neck and danced about her ears, and while she might have been offset earlier, she certainly looked comfortable in her surroundings now.

At last she scanned the room with a smile upon her lips.

And then their eyes met and that smile fell away.

Chapter Three

He wouldn't stop looking at her. Caroline struggled to stay focused on the conversation, but the weight of the Earl of Lindsey's stare was too challenging to ignore. Why did he watch her so? Hadn't she experienced enough humiliation at his expense? And still, as she exchanged words with her mother and each reply left her lips, she was aware of his notice, as if the heat of his attention reached across the ballroom and stroked against her skin. An unbidden warmth crept up her neck. Somewhat nettled, she refused to allow him to disorient her further.

She'd come to the Albertson's event armed with an encyclopedia of information supplied by her cousins, with whom she took tea regularly. Their knowledge of the social register was invaluable. Her goal this evening was to determine a prospective husband, not draw unwanted attention from London's most notorious scoundrel. It would prove daunting enough to find a gentleman willing to accept the limitations of her situation, but that was a consideration left to the future for now.

She dared a fleeting glance from beneath her lashes and answered her mother's query at the same time, although she wasn't exactly sure which words came out of her mouth. Her attention was divided, and even though the Earl of Lindsey stood clear across the sizeable ballroom, he might have been beside her the way his eyes held hers.

Here, unlike the dim interior of Lord Albertson's study, she was able to observe his appearance more easily, and God help her that they didn't stand in direct sunlight, the impact so unsettling. Her heart jolted into a wild tumult, as if to urge her to get on with the inspection.

He stood taller than the men around him, his raven-black hair worn longer than the style, though every strand was in place, as if they dared not disobey their master. His eyes, if not hypnotic enough, appeared outlined for emphasis, which she realized belatedly was the effect of his long dark lashes. She wondered at the color of his irises but dashed away the thought just as quickly. The Earl of Lindsey's personal characteristics were of no interest to her. Still, she noted his straight nose and angled jaw, the slightest shadow of new whiskers there as the hour grew late.

He was engaged in conversation with another gentleman now, and she perused his physique with caution. His evening attire was impeccable. His tailor must have a devil of a time. Previously too mortified by the immoral scene she'd been forced to witness, she hadn't realized how broad his shoulders were. The strong expanse of assertive masculinity narrowed down to a trim waist. He certainly hadn't allowed himself to go soft in the gut like so many other lords in the ballroom. Even Lord Tiller had a rounder middle by comparison.

Her exploration continued to his hands, one wrapped around a glass of brandy. The same hands he'd used to raise Lady Jenkin's skirts. To lower her neckline. Caroline felt blood rush to her cheeks, her memory too quick to supply the images. While she didn't wish to envision it, she couldn't stop thinking of the way he'd kissed Lady Jenkin, the woman desperate for another caress. What must it feel like to be touched, tasted, and adored by a man as enigmatic as the Earl of Lindsey? A distinct warning rang in her ears. Men like Lord Lindsey were dangerous. His very presence exuded virility and other potent masculine traits that would only lead to no good. No doubt he held the ability to charm the world before teatime. She noted she wasn't the only one with attention focused across the room. Women noticed him, many of them too occupied ogling Lord Lindsey to conceal their admiration.

She brought her eyes back to the earl and found them locked with his attention. Caught in the act, she swallowed and jerked her head away.

"Wouldn't you agree, Dearest?" Lady Derby prodded.

Caroline hadn't the slightest idea where the discussion had led, lost in shameless examination of the rogue across the room. "Of course, Mother."

Agreement was always her chosen path when dealing with parental conversation.

"Mind that you endeavor to show admiration for whatever the gentleman offers as conversation and express a mild curiosity in his interests when the subject is suitable. Two questions at the most as it pertains to the topic. Remember to align your habits with his."

Advisement of a romantic nature seemed excruciatingly awkward when offered by one's mother, but if Lady Derby had any idea what her daughter had just witnessed, and with whom, she'd think twice about suggesting an alignment of habits. Not that anyone, her mother, father, or herself, would consider the Earl of Lindsey a potential suitor, never mind husband candidate. Caroline almost laughed outright at the ridiculous notion. Still, her mother continued as she was often apt to do.

"Lord Fellmore is an avid ornithologist and cuts a dashing figure in his formal ensemble this evening. I will pursue an introduction."

Under her mother's direction, Caroline located Lord Fellmore where he stood by the window. His eveningwear was dark blue, his waistcoat embellished with a swirling design of white embroidery. His neck had gone missing, seemingly ambushed by a frothy lace cravat. Had he a plume in his lapel he couldn't look more like the birds he admired. He hadn't asked her to dance and she experienced a brief flutter of relief. Lord Tiller was the one person with whom she'd wished to share a waltz, and he hadn't shown an interest, unfortunately.

"No, thank you, Mother. Don't trouble yourself." Caroline slid a glance over her shoulder on a curious impulse, nothing more. The Earl of Lindsey was gone and all the better for it. She didn't need a distraction. Certainly not one with overwhelming virility and a piercing gaze that sent her pulse into a skitter. Lashes that long were wasted on a man. She quirked a grin borne solely of self-amusement. At least he hadn't bestowed one of his infamous half-smiles upon her. She would have hated to wrinkle her skirts as she'd collapsed, overcome by his startling handsomeness. Stifling another urge to laugh, she spun to face her mother and nearly leapt straight out of her slippers.

"Lady Derby, I am charmed."

The Earl of Lindsey pressed a kiss to the back of her mother's hand while the Dowager Countess Grandville continued their introduction.

"And this is Lady Caroline Nicholson, Lord and Lady Derby's daughter, my lord." The dowager gestured toward the earl. "May I present Lord Cromford, Earl of Lindsey."

Somewhat flabbergasted, Caroline watched, mute and otherwise caught off guard, as she methodically offered her gloved hand.

"Ah, Lady Nicholson, it is my esteemed pleasure to meet you, although I can't help but feel you look familiar."

"Lord and Lady Derby have only just relocated to London from Italy, Lindsey. Naturally, Lady Nicholson was with them," the Dowager Countess interjected. "I suspect you are mistaken, unless you were running about Rome recently."

"Of course." He released her hand and matched her eyes, though she no longer experienced the fleeting shock which preceded their introduction. "Such uncommon and remarkable beauty creates a lasting memory. It's my error, I'm sure."

She should thank him for the compliment albeit she knew he toyed with her, his veiled reference to the scandalous scene in Lord Albertson's study not unnoticed.

And then he smiled, half-smiled actually, and her heart thudded in approval. She waited, and though her knees weakened the slightest, she maintained complete consciousness. Relief swept through her as the foolish suggestion came to mind.

The first notes of an arrangement wafted through the air.

"May I have the next dance of the evening, Lady Nicholson?"

The arrogant gleam in his eyes dared her to refuse. The subtle press of her mother's elbow against her arm insisted she accept. Clearly Mother had no idea of the earl's reputation. Caroline silently thanked her attentiveness to teatime conversation and smiled at his invitation. She truly had no choice.

* * * *

Lindsey tucked Lady Nicholson's hand into the crook of his elbow and guided her to the marble tiles. He'd taken her by surprise, but he held no doubt she wouldn't call him out on it in the same abashed and utterly charming manner she'd adopted in Albertson's study. He would explain about that scene if he could. But honestly, his father's demands had little to do with his desire to dance with the fetching debutante on his arm. He'd allow himself a measure of indulgence even though his complicated world produced a steady schedule of misery.

True, there was that troublesome second condition of his father's will, but Lindsey pushed it from his mind and gathered Lady Nicholson into position for the quadrille. There would be no heir begetting on the dance floor. The lively music began and so did they, at first in complete silence, as if the two of them were held in a strange and mesmerizing stalemate.

He needn't concentrate on the steps. He was accomplished as a dancer, as in most everything. While a neglectful childhood might break those with lesser will, it had instilled in Lindsey a thirst for perfection in every area of his life, if for no other reason than to prove his father's poor opinion false. The late earl might have bemoaned Lindsey's tailoring and expensive taste in horseflesh, but it was by the old man's negligence that the discerning habits had formed.

Now, as he fell in with the melody, he allowed his senses complete control. Lady Nicholson wore a light floral perfume. Something unfamiliar, possibly chosen in Italy for its exotic appeal. Was it orchids? He inhaled deeply, memorizing the fragrance as they glided through the first turn. His hand at her waist held firm, the slight curve beneath his palm enough to send a hum of desire so keen it insisted on his attention. He'd danced with dozens of women. Mayhap hundreds. Yet he'd never had such a definitive reaction to merely guiding one through the steps. The blood in his veins began to take notice too, in a rush to reach other more eager parts of his body.

He entwined his arm with hers as the dance demanded and lifted their clasped hands higher. She was slim in the right places, generous in the areas men preferred most. Her flawless skin held a rosy glow that he'd like to believe he'd provoked but was probably a condition of their activity. She hadn't looked up yet, seemingly focused on the ruby pinned through his cravat, though her chin angled at a taunting slant he found tempting. He'd like to take a bite of that chin. He clamped his teeth together to vanquish the absurd desire.

They lowered their arms and his knuckles brushed against her waist in the process, likened to a caress although it left him curious and wanting, more than satisfied. They moved through the next steps with ease, her hands held tightly in his.

She possessed an uncommon and striking beauty. Her hair, thick and glossy, invited his fingers to thread through the subtle waves and release the pins to fall free while he gathered the lengths in his fists. He shot his eyes above her head to some nondescript corner across the room, aware of a growing problem in his trousers, though he returned to admire her a breath later, as if he didn't dare miss the opportunity, not when there were only so many notes of music contained in one song.

She fit nicely in his grasp as they came together, and that realization caused a twist of lust to stir his pulse harder. Heat slid along his veins as his wicked imagination placed her in his bed dressed in nothing but gemstones, her hair spilled over his pillows, her eyes drowsy from their loveplay.

Aware of his attention, she raised her chin an infinitesimal degree. Would she call him out now? Berate him for his underhanded tactics? He found himself grinning at the prospect, but as they advanced through the third turn she remained quiet, her lashes lowered.

With that he became increasingly aware of her nearness, her presence and body heat. As if they danced alone. As if dozens of guests weren't twirling past them, only inches apart, invading their private moment. Dancing, with the right person, a desirous and intriguing person, could be easily compared to lovemaking. The entangled limbs and exertion, the satisfying completion of each fluid movement. He inhaled again, rewarded with another breath of her fragrance. It was remarkable and delicate. It could only be orchids. How exotic. *How erotic.*

How old could she be anyway? He was thirty and two, with far more years than she. He should have better control over his impulses after three decades. Damn it to hell, lust was a curse, not a pleasure.

At last she looked upward and her gaze collided with his. For a breath, his heart stopped. Just for one beat. He missed a step and recovered without notice. Her eyes searched his, their crystal blue depths a mixture of bewilderment and curiosity. She blinked several times in a row. Could it be she perceived his physical reaction to her? That she too realized this was like no other dance before?

Color bloomed on her cheeks and it affected him in a sensual manner. Which emotion instigated the reaction? Embarrassment? Anger? Forbidden thoughts? His attention settled on her mouth and its bow-shaped curve, the top lip peaked and full over the plump bottom vee, tempting him to nibble and suck, to draw that lower lip into his mouth and taste her from the inside out. Her lips curved with a hesitant smile, as if she knew the path of his thoughts. But then he could be mistaken. For all the women he took to bed, he knew little of gentler considerations and intended to keep it that way.

* * * *

Caroline dared a glance upward and gasped. The Earl of Lindsey studied her and she knew not what to make of it. They moved through the dance in perfect time—or at least she believed they did. She was unsure what her feet were doing down below her skirts, all logic distracted by the effort to calm her pulse. His smile held the power to steal her thoughts.

She'd danced before. Her family attended several social events in Italy, but this unlikely encounter troubled her. It stripped away her usual confident demeanor and left her with a fluttering stomach and absent vocabulary. She had no idea why, unless having witnessed the earl's conquest earlier provoked her awkward discomfort now.

Somehow that didn't ring true.

Awareness sparked between them, not just in a superficial notice, but something deeper, as if their very souls spoke to each other. A heady rush of desire reminded she hardly knew the potent man who held her, and yet that fact proved all the more invigorating, as if there remained endless layers to discover. The world around them faded into insignificance and each breath, turn, and touch provided tinder for her curiosity.

The steps in the dance forced them to drop hands. She took a deep inhale, as if free from his spell for the time being. No matter. How long could a song last anyway? In the absence of pleasant conversation, it seemed an interminable span of time.

Still, she was far too intelligent to stare at his neck through the remainder of the dance. Albeit she could pass considerable time staring at *him*. The shadow of his Adam's apple showed above his startingly white cravat; the crisp neckcloth held in place by a blood-red ruby.

"My lord."

His eyes sparkled, the obsidian depths full of myriad wicked secrets. His dark lashes lowered. Whenever he glanced downward, candlelight dusted the tips and lent him the appearance of being otherworldly. Curse her damnable imagination.

"Yes, my lady."

A hint of cinnamon accompanied his reply. How easily one could be fooled into thinking otherwise, that here stood a respected gentleman who possessed honor and fine reputation. Oh, his handsomeness distracted while his clever smile drew one in.

"Why did you ask me to dance?" They turned in a circle and his fingers tightened around hers in what she could only guess was a purpose to guide her, nothing more.

"Why not?"

"I would think you'd already had your fill of my company after we conversed in Lord Albertson's study."

"Is that what we did?" That charming half-smile made a brief appearance, bringing with it a reminder of exactly where his hands had traveled on Lady Jenkin's person. "You didn't stay long enough to accept my apology."

"I didn't realize one was forthcoming."

"My point exactly."

The music swelled and then subsided gracefully, the dance near its end. She suddenly wished for more time, for no other reason than to tell the Earl of Lindsey every reason why he was insufferable. Her temper simmered just below the surface, but she refused to allow the man the satisfaction of knowing he'd goaded her to anger.

"You look fetching when you berate me mentally." His deep voice brimmed with amusement.

How was it he read her thoughts and divined her emotions? His reputation was well earned.

Incorrigible scoundrel.

Insufferable libertine.

Rogue.

Rakehell.

"Fetching indeed."

Chapter Four

The following night brought with it a diversion that heightened Lindsey's determination by its very nature of appalling necessity. While, much to his surprise, verbally sparring with Lady Caroline during their dance had proven enjoyable, this evening he faced an arranged task with an absence of enthusiasm, his pursuit of future freedom the sole motivation to see it through.

Accepting the situation for what it was, he tossed a coin to the driver and stepped down from the hired hack. A melancholy swirl of fog wrapped around his boots even though the hour was well past eleven. He wore a black greatcoat and beaver hat pulled low over his brow though he saw no one about in this corner of Mayfair. Lady Jenkin waited in the brick-faced town house across the cobbles. His bootheels on the pavement lent a hollow echo to the silence.

Much like the lady herself, the message had been direct with the set hour he should arrive. She assured the staff would be abed, the back door unlatched, and her body his to claim once he climbed the stairs to her bedchamber. Lindsey appreciated her effort, the arrangement convenient. She'd worked quickly since the ball last evening.

No more than a shadow in the darkness, he moved alongside the house and slipped through the French doors precisely as planned. He paused, but nothing more than the faint tick of the clock on the mantel could be heard inside. He crossed the thick-piled carpet and eased into the hall, immediately on alert as an elongated shadow crossed his path. A footman who hadn't retired, or perhaps sought a midnight snack, approached in the darkness. Lindsey receded into the opposite corner beside an ornamental urn filled with peacock feathers. There was no easy escape, but he wouldn't allow the servant to interrupt his evening's plans. At the last moment Lindsey stepped from the wall with isolated intent.

"Sorry, good fellow, but it's past your bedtime." His gloved fist connected with the footman's jaw and snapped the young man's head back at a sharp angle.

Lindsey rolled the unconscious servant to the wall, still rubbing his knuckles as he advanced to the main stairs. It took less time than he'd expected to locate Jenkin's private gallery, but then these Mayfair town houses were basically all the same inside. He nabbed a hand candle off the hallway sideboard, entered the private gallery, and closed the double walnut doors behind him in silence. Jenkin's prized art collection was a sight to behold and had Lindsey more time and better lighting, he might have appreciated the paintings on display. As it was, he had eyes only for the Nona.

And there she was, as if she waited for him in all her naked glory between the double windows and mahogany bookcases.

With eloquence and respect, he unhooked the frame from the wall, reversed the painting, and withdrew his knife in one fluid motion. It took only a minute to pry the tacks from the back of the wooden frame. Then he rolled the cloth and secured it inside his coat beside his knife before moving about the gallery. With deliberate care he disturbed various works upon the walls, upset several paintings, and removed two more canvases to disguise his specific goal. He then folded the additional works and stuffed them deep into his coat's inner pocket.

Satisfied with the scene, he left the doors wide open, replaced the candle, tucked his hat into his waistband, and rushed down the corridor to Lady Jenkin's bedroom.

He didn't knock.

Instead he burst into the room and strode purposefully to her bed where she too waited, reclined against a multitude of satin pillows, her body clad in a wispy scrap of silk similar to the painting in his pocket.

"My lady." He affected a tone of distress. "You need to dress and summon the authorities. I have bad news to share." He regretted the farce he perpetuated and mentally cursed his father for forcing his hand in the matter.

"What?" Startled from expectation of an altogether different greeting, she sat up too quickly, the sheets tangling around her legs as she scrambled to the edge of the mattress. "I've waited for you all night. What's happened?"

"There's been a mishap. It appears the house has suffered an intrusion of some sort. Your footman is knocked unconscious and lying against the wall downstairs, while the doors to the gallery are wide open. From my quick assessment, the room seems in disarray." He took her hand and pulled her to standing.

"I left the back door unlocked for you." She hurried toward the wardrobe and opened a drawer.

"You should summon the authorities and hire a runner. Wake the butler and have a messenger sent. I regret I can't assist you in this." He backed a few steps toward the door.

"No. Of course not. The present predicament is more than enough scandal for the evening." She shook her head vehemently and reached for her wrapper. "You need to go. Hurry." She caught his gloved hand as he retreated. "Our plans are ruined, but only for this evening. You must leave now."

"True enough. My presence only complicates the matter. It benefits no one for me to be found here."

He didn't waste another minute and moved toward the hall, down the stairs, and out into the night.

* * * *

Caroline swirled a spoonful of sugar into her tea and leaned closer to her dearest friend and youngest female cousin, Lady Beatrice Notley. Beatrice had been affectionately called Bunny by her family and friends throughout her childhood, but now, as a young debutante enjoying the season, she insisted the adolescent endearment be forgotten. Caroline found it difficult to retrain her thinking, but she tried to catch herself whenever the name Bunny found its way to the tip of her tongue. Beatrice and her mother came to tea often since Caroline's family relocated to London. Previously she hadn't seen Bea or her three older sisters since they were children, but the two of them took up as if no time had passed from when they'd picked wildflowers and chased newborn lambs in the grassy fields of Lincolnshire. She had always relished the summer days when Beatrice and her sisters had visited.

Despite enjoying her cousin's company today, Caroline had trouble following the conversation with dedication. The persistent memory of her dance with the Earl of Lindsey wouldn't allow a moment's peace, and her inability to identify why she'd become so affected proved a further distraction. It was as if he'd stirred up some wave of curious emotion she didn't know she possessed, and now the disturbing feeling wouldn't subside. But why? It wasn't his handsome good looks or solid physique.

She'd met fine-looking gentlemen before without developing an unhealthy infatuation. Nor was it his dark forbidding gaze or the way his long lashes tipped with the slightest curl upward. She refused to believe it was his infamous half-smile. No matter it promised indecent wickedness, for she'd managed to remain upright when he'd teased her. What good fortune to have been born immune to the earl's charms. She almost giggled at the absurdity of it all.

"What *are* you thinking, dear cousin?" Bea inflected just enough stress on the words to imply she had a very good idea where Caroline's thoughts had wandered. "And why so ever did you entertain a waltz with the Earl of Lindsey when I specifically aimed you in the direction of Lord Tiller?"

"Circumstances changed." She murmured, though a quick glance toward her mother and aunt assured she wouldn't be overheard, their conversation lively and animated. "Lord Tiller seemed less them impressed. He didn't request a dance or prolong our conversation. Instead, without my instigation, the Earl of Lindsey appeared at my mother's side. Before I could disguise my shock, I was dancing a quadrille."

"The earl is handsome, and quite the catch if one is wily enough to win him. Several women have been after him for years now. There's no debate about that. Although, I doubt a lady exists who could win his affection. While he's known as a collector of hearts, most of society would label him irredeemable while simultaneously admitting it detracts nothing from his overall appeal. Those unforgettable eyes make him a favorite with the ladies. Inevitably, I'd hoped for more success with our plan."

"The season's just begun."

"There's never a minute to waste in these matters." Beatrice set her teacup down on the table. "Lord Tiller is just one of many eligible candidates. Granted, his reputation is impeccable and his heritage top-drawer. Still, it will take a bit of work to find you the right match. Your father has provided a generous dowry. Four thousand pounds is no small sum, and we should be wary of gentlemen with pockets to let and a congenial smile to convince us otherwise. Not to imply the earl is of that order. Of course, there's the matter of his age."

"His age?" A vivid image of his dashing appearance clouded her question. He certainly didn't appear advanced in years. "He hardly has one foot in the grave." An irrational desire to defend him forced the words from her mouth.

"Posh. Lindsey must be at least thirty and you a mere two and twenty. While an age difference of that span is not altogether uncommon, I'm certain you'd appreciate a younger, more energetic husband."

He'd certainly appeared *energetic* in Lord Albertson's study. And during their quadrille straight after.

"I wonder why we're even discussing the earl. It's not as if I'd consider him as a suitor. I hardly have an interest." That might not be entirely accurate, considering he'd intruded upon her every waking moment since their dance. Society regarded him as the worst example of gentleman, but to his credit it seemed he didn't give a fig about the ton's perception. Still, it was best she banished any misplaced curiosity when it came to the earl. "I can't imagine Lindsey is seeking a wife or any female's dowry. He must possess considerable wealth. His wardrobe alone would cost a fortune." The memory of the blood red ruby pinned through his cravat punctuated her sentence.

"Oh, his is old money. Properties, gemstones, investments and such. If anything, he's in need of an heir, but likewise the earl is a walking scandal. I'd keep my distance if I were you. Most especially if you wish for a polite, respectable gentleman in earnest."

"Of course I do." Caroline squared her shoulders and met her cousin's eyes to underscore her dedication to the task. "You mustn't believe otherwise."

"You possess all the finest qualities required to have your pick of suitable bachelors." Beatrice smiled. "I'm confident you'll receive several offers before the season's end."

"That would be lovely. I'm eager to embrace marriage." Caroline's gaze strayed to the framed landscapes on the wall of their drawing room. Her father admired art in many forms. It was his love of oils that led them to travel to Italy. Though he hadn't brought home any new selections recently, she suspected the investment in his collection helped fortify their finances and thus her generous dowry. "But let's not forget the most important quality when discussing agreeable husband choices."

Beatrice eyed her expectantly.

"I wish to fall in love, and I'll settle for nothing less." Caroline placed her teacup beside her cousin's. "Without true affection, a marriage is destined to fail."

"Honestly, Caroline, you possess a romantic view of things. Men and women wed for any number of reasons, and I'd wager more than half the ton is married by convenient arrangement and not passionate attraction." Beatrice looked amused.

"No matter how small the percentage, I'm determined to be in the rare group that's given their heart, not just their hand." She nodded her head in the affirmative, adamant in her decision. She wasn't some flighty female enamored with the thought of poetic emotion. She was a sensible, intelligent woman who believed life should be shared with a man who she admired and respected for his faithfulness, trust, and security. She wanted to be held in his arms, cherished and protected, while also having her voice and ideas heard with mutual respect. And naturally she hoped for an enjoyable relationship in the bedroom and a full satisfying life of laughter and deep affection. Her parents had a pleasant marriage, suited to their lifestyle and manner of thinking, but she wished for more, a deeper connection, and she didn't think it was unreasonable in the least.

No doubt, the Earl of Lindsey would have laughed at her purpose. No doubt, a man of his jaded perception knew nothing of true love. Or cared, for that matter. A man who would prop a woman atop a stranger's desk and work his way under her skirts was dangerous indeed.

Still, with a beat of unbidden peculiarity, a shiver of intriguing desire accompanied that conclusion. She shook her head again, this time in the negative and with more rigor. Why did she waste her time with these considerations? She should scrub her brain clean of any thought which included the Earl of Lindsey and forget the pleasing scent of cinnamon she'd detected when they'd danced and the heated strength of his nearness. He was exactly the type of man that invited gossip and scandal. Exactly the type of man she needed to avoid.

Blast her imagination for insisting he occupy even one minute of her attention.

"Tonight, not only will I be in attendance, but Louisa and Dinah as well. We'll see to the most advantageous introductions, sure to have your dance card filled with hardly an effort. Popularity is contagious that way. Once you dance a number or two, more gentlemen take notice and then wish to fill a slot on your card."

"It will be wonderful to see your sisters again." Caroline smiled. "We were quite boisterous in our childhood years. I have many amusing memories of our times together. It's a wonder we didn't give everyone in earshot a megrim with our chatter."

"We probably did," Beatrice continued. "Even with the baby keeping her busy, I know Charlotte will miss seeing you tonight."

Their voices rose and the sudden laughter caught the attention of her mother and aunt.

"How are Charlotte and Viscount Dearing? They must be over the moon at the birth of their son." Caroline's face lit with the mention of her newest relation, wee baby William.

"The three of them compose the loveliest little family." Lady Notley donned an appreciative expression, her smile a tribute to her emotion. "There's a true love match if ever I saw one."

Considering the haste and surprise surrounding her cousin Charlotte's unexpected nuptials, Caroline regretted missing the event. With her family in Italy and Charlotte's wedding arranged and completed in less than a fortnight, there was never a question as to whether or not Caroline's family could attend. Still, to hear her aunt speak with high regard concerning the marital bliss between Charlotte and Dearing fortified Caroline's belief in finding one's perfect match. If her cousin could marry a stranger in less than fourteen days and achieve love, dedication, and now a darling son, then Caroline knew with surety, and a bit of effort on her part, her hopes were not unreasonable.

"Who will be the next to find their way to the altar?" Her aunt beamed with the insinuation it could be either her daughter or niece and she'd be equally pleased.

"My daughter is sensitive by nature, and while she possesses a generous heart and seeks to see the best in everyone, she would do well to be more prudent in her belief all the world is as caring as she. I offer her plentiful advice. At least now that we've come to London there will be several gentlemen of title and personality to spark her interest," her mother added with a note of expectation and glanced at Caroline. Heartfelt emotion softened her eyes.

"It's not that I'm purposely difficult, Mother." Desperately attempting to conceal a defensive tone, Caroline kept her answer short, though she leaned closer to Beatrice to finish in a whisper: "Mother's advice is somewhat unparticular. As long as the man has all his teeth and two good eyes, I believe she'd give her blessing. On second thought, his sight may be negotiable."

Beatrice smothered a fit of giggles as she reached for a small sugary cake from the tea tray. "She's not very different from my mother. They wish for us to be happy but seem to have a different definition of the word."

Bea navigated society like a sea captain, her knowledge of the social register's most notorious rakes, daring debutantes, and handsome bachelors commendable. Still, Caroline preferred to form opinions on her own. A wistful smile curled her lips. Perhaps she needed to examine exactly what she wished for in a marriage beyond love and desire. Those two qualities were most important. But what of his appearance and temperament? Did she wish for a conversationalist? An abstemious, somber partner? Certainly, she had no interest in a man who pulled attention to himself like a magnet. Lindsey's lovely dark eyes and piercing gaze rose to mind with clarity.

No, uncommon handsomeness would not sway her opinion. What would impress her the most and show the gentleman's character in its best light would be an act of selflessness even at a loss to his personal benefit. It seemed society as a whole was more concerned with a person's wealth and material possessions rather than the actual fiber that composed one's personality. As two people came to know each other and understand the workings of the mind and heart they formed a bond, and that aspect of a relationship interested her most.

"I only want what's best for you, Caroline." Her mother's forehead wrinkled, as if it would be preposterous to think otherwise. "At times I believe your spirit too bright for society, that's all. You must maintain a conservative demeanor at all times, even if you yearn for adventure."

Caroline swallowed the reply that sprung to her tongue and brought her teacup up for a sip to ensure no words leaked out.

"We'll have another ideal opportunity to survey the bachelors at this evening's entertainment," Bea continued, undeterred by Caroline's silence. "There will be dancing at the Duke of Warren's social and an exhibit of fine art. His Grace collects sculpture and assorted paintings from around the world."

"Oh, will Father attend then?" Caroline aimed this question at her mother. "He so often declines to accompany us, but he'd enjoy this type of affair more than other invitations for music and dancing."

Lindsey was an accomplished dancer. Would he ask her to partner again were their paths to cross?

"Yes, I believe he plans on it," her mother answered, and for a moment Caroline forgot her own question and considered her mother's words in relation to private thoughts, her heart all too anxious to skip a beat.

The moment didn't last as her mother continued, her attention now turned to Caroline's aunt. "My husband isn't often available to accompany us to these affairs, but the lure of a gallery filled with paintings will snare his interest."

"Then Beatrice and I should take our leave so we can all prepare for the festivities this evening."

Her aunt stood and her cousin followed, while a flurry of excitement hummed its way through Caroline.

Anticipation was a wonderful companion.

Chapter Five

Dishonesty was a fickle bastard. Especially when one was forced to lie and steal. Lindsey cursed and poured two fingers of brandy before he paced across the carpet in his study. Restless and displeased, he swallowed the liquor in one gulp, then paused beside the chair where he'd discarded his coat. With a breath of resignation, he withdrew the Nona from his coat pocket and unrolled the painting with care, staring at it with ambivalence.

It's not stealing when the item already belongs to you.

The mental conclusion lacked conviction and wouldn't take hold. Damn his father to hell for making demands from the grave. For driving him to manipulation and theft.

Lindsey strode to his desk, unlocked the right drawer, and deposited the artwork inside. He would need to collect the other two paintings before he could restore the earldom's financial security. The information his father had provided was unclear but whatever the details, it melted down to the same. The three paintings together were priceless. Their worth composed a large portion of fiscal investment. They were stolen and lost to the dark market, where collectors hoarded and bartered without conscience. And now he was tasked with their recovery.

Previously, he'd assumed the earldom's wealth was secure, but his father's letter intimated finances were not nearly what they needed to be, and these reduced circumstances required his urgent attention. For Lindsey to continue to live without compromise, he was forced to set about the task no matter he was disgusted with the endeavor. At least once the paintings were returned to his possession, he'd have the equity and security the value of their ownership granted. The trouble was found in laying claim to them again, not to mention the amount of secrecy involved.

It proved challenging at first, his father's documents and failed investigations yielding little. Yet now, after years of untraceable existence where his father met with little success, the Nona had resurfaced. Lindsey hadn't hesitated to act, unworried about consequences and pleased with the outcome. He possessed proof of ownership and authenticity in the few papers provided by his father's solicitor in the form of preliminary sketches done by the artist. But what of the complicated process of locating the other two paintings and laying claim to them? Finding the Nona and retrieving it from Lord Jenkin's gallery had been nothing more than an uncomfortable inconvenience. What of the two missing pieces? Who knew how long and involved the pursuit would become? Would his father's solicitor continue to tighten the noose until Lindsey was destitute?

Tired of mental riddles, he snatched his gloves and called Hobbs, his butler, to have a carriage brought up from the mews. A visit to White's was in order. With any luck, a few of his comrades would be about. He needed distraction, and not the female kind.

As was his hope, he entered the club and stepped into the throng, an eclectic mix composed of every rank of nobility, as well as a handful of young come-uppers. He approached his usual chair, a sturdy Bergère with leather cushions, situated near the left corner of the room across from the hearth. The position kept him amid the conversation and yet provided a direct line of sight to the entrance. While the location ensured he was aware of who came and went, he also desired enough detachment to have a private discussion if needed. He matched eyes with the occupant in *his* particular chair and without hesitation the man vacated the seat.

Lindsey nodded as he passed. He wasn't a bully or a tyrant. Depending on whom one asked, he was described as a silver-tongued charmer, randy womanizer, or enigmatic aristocrat. In truth, he was none of these in entirety, a combination of selected traits. Above all, he was never intentionally dishonest or deceitful. *Until now.*

And perhaps that chaffed the most.

That his father could coerce him to be someone he wasn't and never wanted to be. And too, the second condition of the will, a demand that would go unfulfilled, as he had no desire to produce an heir. He'd almost laughed in Barlow's face, and would have if Lindsey didn't burn with rage at the reading of that bloody letter. While he enjoyed a tumble as much as any hotblooded male, he lacked the skills needed for parenting and took great effort to avoid the condition. Besides, what kind of father could he ever be, considering his sire's example?

Experience had taught him love was a lie, at the least an unreliable emotion. He'd seen too much of what love did to the afflicted. He'd seen ugly things, things a child or man should never witness, all in the name of that condition.

Love, marriage, commitment…none of the three were in his life's immediate plans. Perhaps someday. It didn't matter. The women who kept his company were generous with their favors and easily pleased with a sparkling bauble for their enthusiastic attention. He preferred it that way as much as his jeweler did. The brief relationships he'd entertained were more of sexual gratification than deeper emotion. He rarely spoke during the physical act, and if he did spare a word it was curt, no more than a command of necessary movement, not an intimate request between lovers. He was far beyond the age when a gentleman sought a fresh debutante to groom for the role of obedient wife.

This reality brought with it another, and the tempting image of Lady Caroline arose in striking detail. She'd surprised him, and he wasn't a man who was caught unaware often. When they'd danced, it was as if their bodies communicated, *mayhap their souls*, on some unnamed, intangible level. He was certain she'd sensed it too. In those moments she'd offered a calming respite and he'd found a modicum of peace, an unexpected connection, although the shock caused her to examine his cravat for almost the entirety of their dance.

Devil take him. That was rich. Better sense mocked him in a loud voice. A jaded earl beyond thirty years bewitched by a twenty-something debutante purer than the white linen of her maiden's bed.

He stifled a chuckle of self-deprecation. He might lie and steal as forced by his father's plan, but his own moral compass rebelled at dalliance with an innocent ingénue.

An unexpected connection.

What utter tripe and nonsense.

A strong drink was needed to purge these thoughts, and he summoned a footman at the ready with a generous brandy at the same time Lord Conrad took the seat to his right.

"Lindsey." The attentive viscount slanted a glance in his direction. "What has you looking grim this evening?"

"Nothing." He tapped the rim of the glass with his pointer finger. "I haven't a care."

"Rubbish." Conrad signaled a footman in want of a drink. "If that's true, your good moods look exactly like your bad ones these days."

"What does it matter?"

Nothing was said for a minute or two, and the ambient noise around them swelled to remind they sat in a place of amiable consort and not in a church pew.

"Hardly a familiar face about for conversation." Conrad surveyed the room, as if looking for better company. "No doubt they're all crammed into the Duke of Warren's town house clamoring for a glimpse of the recent renovations."

"Home decorating. That's what titillates our crowd of late? The season must be more dismal than usual." Lindsey's droll reply found its mark.

Conrad laughed before he answered. "Only the crème of society was invited, and no one wishes to be the guest who has missed the event." He cleared his throat. "Except you."

"And you," Lindsey offered, only mildly interested in the conversation for the distraction it provided. He'd ignored Warren's invitation, too focused on retrieving paintings and reclaiming his sanity.

"Uh, no." Conrad shook his head vigorously. "I'm for His Grace's door in another thirty minutes. By then the initial hubbub caused by silk-covered walls and ornate wood trim will have subsided and the refreshment table will be refilled. Warren plans to announce the newest addition to his gallery, and that's the most interesting part of the evening as far as I'm concerned."

"Indeed." Lindsey only half-listened to Conrad's chatter, more involved with the removal of a miniscule piece of white lint from the sleeve of his coat. The news might have proven interesting if weeks ago Lindsey hadn't hired men to obtain a detailed inventory of every piece of artwork housed in the city, from personal drawing rooms to the British Museum. It was how he'd known to engage Lady Jenkin at the Albertson's social. Any hope of the remaining paintings showing at His Grace's affair this evening was nonexistent.

Undeterred by Lindsey's silence, Conrad continued. "Warren's collection is worth a veritable fortune, and the newly acquired piece has the ton chomping at the bit to discover what His Grace purchased when he attended an exclusive auction by an Italian nobleman in Rome recently."

This statement, the latter one, snapped Lindsey from his distraction.

Conrad drained his glass and stood, reconciled to a loss in the one-sided conversation. "I'll be off then. Good to see you, Lindsey."

"One minute there, Conrad."

* * * *

Caroline took a sip of arrack punch and listened attentively to her cousins' vociferous discussion.

"Tonight's event has roused a wide assortment of gentlemen from the cardroom. What a refreshing change." Louisa scanned the crowd from behind her fan.

"The selection is as enticing as the dessert trays," Dinah added.

Beatrice stifled a laugh. "Albeit it depends on how one defines tempting."

Caroline found it all a bit overwhelming. She'd never made it a secret she wished to find a suitable match this season. She hoped to begin the next stage of her life. It was the natural course of things. But how her mother and aunt had enlisted Louisa, Dinah, and Beatrice in the bachelor search—*bachelor siege*—unsettled Caroline's usual calm demeanor.

She scanned the room as she'd already done twice, her eyes taking in every corner, skimming along one wall to the next until she forced herself back to the conversation. All too soon she allowed her attention to wander again. Beaus escorted ladies in a kaleidoscope of color and motion on the dance floor and to her cousins' benefit, the ballroom was full of gentlemen of every variety. Viscounts in vivid silk waistcoats and earls in finely tailored eveningwear capered about the room in convivial conversation.

Well, except one earl.

She'd hadn't seen the Earl of Lindsey and berated herself for noticing his absence. She supposed a man of his reputed existence would find most seasonal social events a boring endeavor. Still, she couldn't decipher what held her so restless this evening or why she persisted with demure surveillance until her eyes landed on the man himself at the main entrance across the marble tiles. Then everything seemed to make sense again.

Ridiculous, really.

Why would a notorious scoundrel bring her the smallest measure of peace when he represented the exact opposite of what her heart desired? Security. Loyalty. Love.

She released a long-held breath. The earl looked even more dashing than the first time she'd seen him. Granted, during their quadrille her heart beat too hard for her to do anything other than concentrate on his cravat pin and count the steps in the dance, her senses overwhelmed by the potent pleasure of his nearness.

With a weak reprimand she reminded herself she'd need to get past this unusual interest in Lord Lindsey if she were to seek a husband in earnest.

"There's Lord Granger. Now he composes the perfect match. His hair is as golden as candlelight, and when he smiles..." Dinah's voice faded away, as if she'd become lost in her own description.

"You sound smitten, sister," Beatrice teased. "Are you helping our cousin or considering the male population for your own intent?"

Dinah waved a gloved hand in a dismissive gesture but refrained from answering. For the next few moments they stood in inspection of the surrounding guests and Caroline took advantage of the stall in conversation.

Lindsey had entered with a young man nearly as tall as he but only half as well-dressed. They conversed casually, their expressions proof of their friendship.

"Someone has caught Caroline's eye across the room," Beatrice offered in a sing-song clip, and all three cousins turned in unison to investigate the suggestion.

Caroline hurried to supply an innocuous answer. "Who's the handsome gentleman beside the Earl of Lindsey?" She rather liked saying his name aloud. It made her pulse race.

"That's Lord Conrad." Louisa leaned a little closer, her fan aflutter as she spoke. "Careful. For a moment there, one might have thought you'd lost your head after a single dance. A rake will do that, you know. Enchant you with compliments. Charm you so completely you can't remember your name. He'll leave you breathless and unaware until it's too late to do little more than cry over your poor decision."

Spoken in a hushed whisper, Caroline wondered if Louisa hadn't learned that lesson much to her regret. She immediately glanced at her cousin, but Louisa had already returned her attention to the crowd. Did she avoid eye contact on purpose?

"I'd like to see the Duke of Warren's extensive collection of artwork. My father will too. If you'll excuse me, I'm going to seek him out." Caroline turned, her cousin's words almost lost as she stepped into the crowd.

"We're equally as intrigued and will meet you there shortly," Dinah called after her.

Caroline darted her eyes to the area where she'd seen the Earl of Lindsey, but he was gone. Her unexplainable curiosity was troublesome, and she'd be all the wiser not to pursue the misplaced distraction. Still, a pang of disappointment accompanied the conclusion.

She filed away that emotion for later contemplation and neared her parents where they enjoyed the festivities. Her mother sat at an ornamental table amid a jovial conversation. "Father, would you like to walk through the gallery and view His Grace's fine collection?"

Her father's face lit with a smile. "As soon as your mother finishes, dear. Why don't you find your cousins?" He gestured toward the arched doorway which led to the hall and beyond. "I see they're poised to leave."

One glance confirmed her father spoke truthfully, and with little more than a nod she crossed the tiles and once again joined Beatrice, Dinah, and Louisa. Maneuvering through the crowd in the corridor consumed their attention, so they spoke little, though once they reached the elongated gallery where the Duke of Warren displayed his appreciation for the arts, it proved easier to converse.

They paused in front of a sculpture which depicted a warrior of Greek or Roman mythology. Caroline couldn't be sure.

"Do you suppose without clothing all men look as this one does?"

Beatrice posed this question, and Caroline's eyes widened with the bold query from her youngest and usually most timid cousin. City life had certainly changed certain aspects of the ladies' personalities.

"Hardly." Louisa didn't say more.

Caroline turned her attention to the sculpture. It was large, nearly six feet if not taller. The artist had carved the marble with exacting workmanship, each groove, ripple, and smooth span of muscle realistic in detail. The figure wore a flowing wrap around his lower half and in his hand held a disc of some sort, his pose indicative he played at a sport or participated in a competition. His shoulders were wide, tapered down to a lean waist, where the repetition of carved muscles caused her fingers to twitch. She wished to reach out and coast her fingertips over the marble in order to appreciate their strength. Did the Earl of Lindsey hide an equally magnificent physique beneath his impeccable wardrobe? Did he have finely formed muscles? His shoulders were easily as straight and broad as the sculpture before her. A sudden warmth flooded her skin at the wayward thoughts and her cheeks heated for no reason beyond her overactive imagination.

She forced her eyes away and spun, determined to focus on a more mundane offering, perhaps a still life or pastoral scene that hung on the opposite wall. Several guests crowded the gallery and she blinked hard twice, anxious to engage in a subject far from her current preoccupation.

Instead her eyes locked with the Earl of Lindsey, not two strides behind and apparently fixed on her with the same devout study she'd given the warrior sculpture.

He smiled, or at least half his mouth hitched up in silent greeting.

Her knees went weak, but by only slight degree. It was the heat of the gallery crammed with too many guests. Nothing more.

She held his gaze longer than she should and that proved a mistake. Lord Conrad noticed and immediately stepped forward, Lindsey at his elbow.

"How can a gentleman appreciate the arts when four beautiful women stand before him?"

Lord Conrad's flattery caused her cousins to preen, but Caroline glanced down to her slippers, all at once unsettled. Still, Lindsey approached and it couldn't be ignored; she'd all but invited him with her lingering attention. Now she'd suffer her cousin's speculation because of it.

Chapter Six

Lindsey had one specific purpose. Disinterested in crowded ballrooms, he'd invited himself into Conrad's carriage only to learn more of the artwork promised to be unveiled. At least with the hour near ten, he wouldn't have to suffer fools for overlong.

But then he'd noticed Lady Nicholson.

She'd most certainly noticed too.

Her cheeks bloomed with a soft rose color that somehow caused *him* to feel overheated. She was far too tempting to be flittering about a social event without a gentleman on her arm. Where was her father or brother? Precious treasures need always be protected, or they could be stolen without thought.

He followed as Conrad initiated introductions and conversation, content to remain silent instead of take the initiative. Much like the paintings adorning the walls, Lindsey enjoyed the ability to admire at the moment.

"What do you suppose His Grace has hidden under that cloth?" Conrad slanted his head toward the platform at the top of the room, where a circle of guests gathered in wait of the reveal. "Something sensational enough to bring the ton out with anticipation."

"But you're here, aren't you, Lord Conrad?" Louisa teased. She tapped him on the arm with the tip of her fan. "Curiosity seems to have driven most every lord and lady out this evening."

"And a good dose of fear," Dinah added.

"Fear?" Conrad shook his head, a bemused expression on his face.

"Fear of missing the moment, the pinnacle subject of gossip which will last at least a day or two," Louisa continued.

"Until something or someone else provides the latest *on-dit*," Beatrice agreed.

Lindsey watched as their little group advanced closer to the masterpiece poised for display. The Notley sisters pursued a lively interchange and Conrad enjoyed their attention. Lindsey adjusted his gait until he fell in behind Lady Nicholson.

A gong sounded and a hush fell over the crowd. Behind him, several people rushed to find the ideal vantage point and the swell in the narrow gallery became a nuisance. He stepped forward to distance himself at the same time an unexpected jostle occurred at his back. His sleeve inadvertently rubbed against Lady Nicholson's bare arm and his entire body tensed. She immediately glanced over her shoulder, meeting his eyes with an unreadable emotion. He forced a smile, and after a beat she offered a hesitant grin in return.

"Pardon me, my lady." He leaned in to offer the words near her ear. Orchids. It was definitely orchids. Her hair was drawn away from her face, fastened at the back in an elaborate display of braids and ringlets, and while he thought the light fragrance of her perfume the only temptation to his black soul, he realized he'd enjoy nothing more than fanning his fingers through the silky lengths of her hair as the pins fell helplessly to the floor. He'd list kisses across her delicate jaw and nibble a path down the slope of her neck until her pulse quickened against his mouth in sensual invitation.

The lethal combination of lust and possibility shot fire through his blood as his mind painted the image. Meanwhile, an unnamed emotion rivaled his desire with equaled strength. He wanted her kiss, a taste of her sweet mouth and beyond, to explore every inch of creamy smooth skin covered by finely spun silk. He'd devour her to her delight, a wicked lick at the back of her knees, a teasing bite to her instep, until he feasted on each and every sensitive curve and silky crease—

"It's too crowded in here." She flitted her eyes to his and then away. "I anticipated my father's company for the unveiling but hardly think he'll be able to locate me in this crush."

Her words were a much-needed bucket of cold water, and Lindsey drew a long breath to regain clarity. A head taller than those around him, he surveyed the crowd, though he had no idea for whom he searched. When he returned his attention to Caroline, he found she watched him too.

* * * *

Caroline stared at the Earl of Lindsey, her body and mind calibrated to his nearness. He somehow made her aware of her own femininity, that she was all woman and he, pure masculinity. It was the strangest reaction.

When he'd accidentally brushed against her arm, a prickle of anticipation coursed through her, and she couldn't imagine why she'd respond in such an absurd manner. She'd watched his jaw tense before he smiled. He wasn't unaffected either, the same as she'd noticed during their dance. And when Lord Conrad had approached and initiated conversation, the earl had withdrawn until he'd measured his stride to keep pace with hers, despite she'd intentionally slowed.

Could he wish to know her better, or did she simply present him a convenient alternative to escape the frivolous banter of her cousins? Caroline couldn't know.

She forced her eyes to the platform where the Duke of Warren addressed the crowd. She barely heard His Grace's words, the distance and distraction of Lindsey beside her too powerful to allow for comprehension. It was as if every cell of her being was in tune to him, their existence aligned though not a word was spoken between them.

She attempted a step to the left for no other reason than to achieve distance and dispel the unnerving tension, but the crowd was having nothing of it, and she found herself forced to the right without warning or provocation.

Lindsey caught her bare arm with his gloved hand as she leaned precariously, quick to adjust her footing. His hold didn't linger though his forefinger trailed along her skin in a touch that had nothing to do with keeping her upright. Her skin shimmered with a rush of heat beginning at her breastbone and spreading beneath her corset in a sheen of perspiration. She'd barely managed to reposition herself when his voice was at her ear.

"Accept my apologies again, my lady." His heated breath stoked an unruly fire alive in her veins. "The crowd is eager and impatient. Are you all right?"

"Yes." Her answer was nothing more than a breathy whisper. "Whatever lies beneath that cloth better be worth the inconvenience of these conditions." The humor of her reply caused her to bite her lower lip. The cloth of the warrior sculpture? Lindsey's elegant dress gloves? Or the drape which hid the painting on the easel?

Her attempt at indignation likely failed. When he'd leaned down to speak, his straight nose and strong chin created a handsome profile beside her. She noticed the dark shadow of tomorrow's whiskers along his jaw and detected the masculine scent of his shaving soap, something spicy with a hint of cloves. *Utterly male.* She stole another subtle sniff. How incredibly proper and yet recklessly tempting, to be so close to this powerful gentleman and at the same time amidst the entire ton with nothing to hide.

"The evening has already proven its worth to me."

He straightened before she could respond.

"Caroline, come to the front so you'll have a better view." Beatrice turned halfway and with a wave of her hand coaxed Caroline forward.

"I'm fine. It's too tight to move." She returned her cousin's gesture in reverse, as if to dismiss her of responsibility.

"When His Grace has completed his announcement, would you gift me with a waltz, Lady Nicholson?" Lindsey murmured for her ears only.

Wasn't that a dangerous question? She hadn't yet recovered from their first dance, the memory hypnotic enough to keep her dizzy. Her cousins had warned that further association with the Earl of Lindsey would deter potential suitors and discourage other, more modest gentlemen. The wisest answer was to decline. She could easily report that her card was already filled.

"I would enjoy that, my lord." She didn't look at him fully, afraid of what she would read in his expression or, worse, reveal in her own.

Further discussion was obliterated as the Duke of Warren's voice boomed above the crowd. Warren stood before the easel, the corner of the cloth clenched in hand. Caroline had missed most of what was spoken earlier, though she knew His Grace intended to show a newly acquired collectible purchased during a recent trip to Italy. She caught the end of his sentence as it trailed out over the assembled guests.

"...and so, it is my honor to share with you a work of distinguished historic acclaim and a masterpiece for its workmanship and irreplaceable value."

A hush fell over the crowd, so awestruck and eager, and Caroline could hear the smooth slide of the satin drape as it revealed the gilded frame for all to see.

"I give you the Nona."

A swift gasp of appreciation passed with lightning finesse through the crowd in sharp contrast to the black curse that sliced the air beside her. She raised her eyes to Lindsey, his expression thunderous and eyes narrowed in anger.

At that same moment, her father succeeded in his effort to find her, pushing through the crush at her back and gently touching her arm to draw her attention. In the span of a smile and nod, she lost sight of the Earl of Lindsey. One moment he stood at her side, until she'd glanced away to acknowledge her father, and then he'd disappeared. How the man managed to part the crowd mystified her, though the scowl she'd witnessed might have warned those who crossed his path to move quickly. His presence intimidated.

Her father pulled her attention from the crowd. "Would you like to admire the painting at a closer advantage?"

"Yes, although I suppose we'll have to wait our turn. It appears everyone is a sudden admirer of Italian culture this evening. You respect the arts in earnest, Father."

"I'm hardly the most discerning in the crowd, and as you know my interest lies more in studying the workmanship than the actual piece as an investment or adornment."

"The fine paintings you've collected are outstanding examples," she replied as they maneuvered a step closer to the platform, though her mind remained on the Earl of Lindsey's unexpected reaction.

"Someday, when you've married and have established your own home, perhaps you'll add a few of my collection to your walls." He chuckled at her side. "A selfish fatherly wish, I suppose."

"I would enjoy that very much."

Throughout their discussion, they'd managed to gain ground and now stood before the platform. The Nona was a simplistic painting in many ways, displaying a single partially nude form of a woman in a garden, but to a collector the piece was invaluable. Whether one admired the layering of color and texture or appreciated the symbolism of the composition, like her father, she understood the painting's appeal.

If her tutor of Italian history was worth his reputation and her memory served correctly, the painting was one of a collection depicting the three personifications of destiny. In Roman history, the Nona was the goddess who spun the thread of humanity from her spindle, and therefore represented fertility and continued life.

She assumed the Duke of Warren desired the painting for its prestige and monetary worth, as would any nobleman with interest in cultural arts. She flicked her eyes around the room again, but Lindsey was nowhere to be seen.

In consolation, she watched her father's intense study of the painting. He likely noted the masterful brushstrokes and texture, but for her the picture struck a chord of vulnerability. She longed to carry a child and have a family one day. A sharp pang of sadness abbreviated the thought. The future was uncertain, or at least some aspects were, and she'd rather not fall into melancholy here, where she couldn't find a moment's reprieve from the jovial celebration. Perhaps she'd sneak away to the lady's retiring room and reorder her unruly emotions.

"Uncle, we are here to collect you." Beatrice, followed by Dinah, joined them before the platform. Louisa was not at their side. "Aunt Julie would like to move into the dining room and has sent us to find you."

"All this commotion over such a little painting." Dinah donned a sassy smirk.

"It's quite valuable." Lord Derby straightened and began to lead the ladies from the gallery. "Especially if a collector is fortunate enough to have purchased the other two pieces."

"I'd much rather spend my time dancing," Beatrice added. "Besides, we have plans of our own, don't we, Caroline?"

They hurried along the hall and returned to the ballroom. Her father quickly crossed to escort her mother into dinner, the first course ready to be served. Caroline lingered with her two cousins and watched the guests who danced across the floor in the first of the last two waltzes of the evening.

Caroline considered her next course of action. No matter she told herself to forget about the Earl of Lindsey's request for a dance; his sudden disappearance in the gallery was curious and almost guaranteed he had no intention of claiming her before the final arrangement was played. And yet, some reckless part of her heart wished he would materialize beside her as he'd managed the other evening and clasp her glove in his to escort her to the marble tiles.

Such fanciful romantic tendencies were unlike her sensible nature, and without a way to explain them she blinked the ideas away in hope it would ward off disappointment.

* * * *

Lindsey watched the Duke of Warren where he stood beside the refreshment table in conversation with another guest. Upon Lindsey's approach, the young lord noted his expression and made a hasty retreat. Warren turned and the two began speaking, a formal greeting unnecessary.

"Still driving people off with no more than a glare?"

"At times the skill proves convenient," Lindsey answered.

"For a man reputed to charm every female with nothing more than a turn of the lips, I'm not surprised the opposite holds true." Warren indicated a passing tray of brandy and Lindsey nabbed a glass.

"The unveiling made for quite a show. You kept every guest breathless. Well done, Your Grace."

Warren chuckled softly, though he knew exactly what he'd achieved. "It's a valuable acquisition."

"An admirable one too." Lindsey needed to proceed with care. The last thing he wished to incite was competition. Besides, the irking debate of whether Lord Jenkin's painting was authentic or indeed the Duke of Warren possessed the true work of art needed to be handled gingerly. The artist was deceased. It would take a proper inspection to determine which painting was genuine, and that presented a difficult task. Neither he nor the Duke of Warren would accept the reality of being duped with any welcome. Yet they both couldn't come out on the right side of things, especially when the painting rightfully belonged to his father.

"You must have a reliable source to unearth a painting thought lost to history for too many years to count," he prodded, his eyes matched to Warren's to detect how the words would be received. A weighty pause ensued.

"If you're after an investment, you won't find me of any help." Again His Grace chuckled. "I'll not reveal my business associate and have you purchase all the best pieces before I consider them."

"A shrewd approach." Lindsey beat back his impatient temper.

"I believe it so."

"With your permission, I'd like to examine the Nona privately." He took a chance on the duke's hospitality, though no one could suspect Lindsey's true motives.

"Feel free to inspect it at your leisure. I've had the painting placed in my study." Warren angled his head toward a pair of mahogany doors at the back of the room. "Why not take advantage of the dinner hour? The last waltz is at its end and I'm needed in the dining room. Proceed out the doors and down the hall on the left."

Warren didn't say more and left before Lindsey could thank him. He coasted his eyes across the ballroom, settling on the few couples who lingered even though the gong chimed to call guests into the meal.

He regretted not claiming the last dance from Lady Nicholson, but in this he couldn't be deterred. Was the Nona he possessed a counterfeit? Could Lord Jenkin have been fooled into purchasing a fraud? And what was the likelihood that after so many years of disappearance, two versions of a missing painting would surface within days of each other?

He shook his head to clear it. Damn his father and the games he'd intertwined with the future solvency of the earldom. While Lindsey had sufficient savings, there was no getting away from the truth. He'd had two solicitors examine the financial stability of his father's claims and found himself trapped, his father's proposition a sinking reality.

Still, the second condition of the will's terms, that he beget an heir as quickly as possible, was so preposterous Lindsey wondered why he made any effort to fulfill the first half.

At least one thing proved true. He needed another brandy. Mayhap two.

Chapter Seven

This wasn't becoming a habit. At least that's what Caroline told herself as she stole inside the Duke of Warren's private study. When had she become such a delicate flower? She wasn't, nor would she pretend to be. The only child of practical parents, she'd been raised an intelligent equal, who received tutoring and education befitting any woman her age. But while her cousins had come to maturity amid the capricious social arena, Caroline had traveled, learned to appreciate the world through the arts, and relied on her own intuition for guidance more often than not.

So then why now did she find a need to pull inward and away? She refused to believe her unhealthy interest in the Earl of Lindsey could be the cause. She didn't know the man and shouldn't have a desire to do so. An unfulfilled dance request was nothing to incite a forlorn reaction. It seemed too often she reminded herself of that fact.

Closing her eyes in another long blink, she rebelled against her true fears, that she'd never find who she needed, a husband who would accept and love her unconditionally. Her cousins had no idea of the bleak sadness that dwelled deep in her soul. She suspected she couldn't even voice the words. The gentlemen she met, any candidate for future husband, would wish for a family, and Caroline knew her greatest doubt existed in that her body would not cooperate.

Moving farther into the well-lit study, she remembered the shocking scene played out by Lindsey earlier in the week. The earl was an unrepentant scoundrel. No doubt his kisses melted a woman's bones. Could she truly blame the lady for her avaricious begging? Caroline had spent the last two evenings torn between wondering what it would be like to be adored so intimately and admonishing herself for entertaining the question.

She forced a laugh to relieve a beat of nervous tension and the sound echoed in the empty room. Why were her emotions so scattered?

Across the carpet, the easel that held the coveted painting was left obscured beneath a large drape, as if the Duke of Warren wanted it kept hidden. Perhaps in wait of his private appreciation after all guests had departed. Caroline moved in front of it and drew the cloth to the side before she leaned close to examine the woman in detail. The figure was mostly nude, her skin done in a rosy hue, her face colored with what could only be industrious joy as she extended her arm and unraveled the thread of life from her distaff and spindle. Caroline knew the myth associated with the subject. This piece depicted the first stage in the three incarnations of destiny. It showed the giver of life symbolized by the thread at the start of the spindle. She recalled, in the myth, the second goddess cut the length of string to measure someone's life, and the third, sadly, represented death.

How ironic to find herself here before a painting epitomizing everything she might never have, a child, family, and fulfilling future. Panic and an irrational sense of loss rose up inside her, bitter and sharp, but she hammered it down and away.

The door latch rattled and she spun, caught where she should not be, this time with no dark corner as refuge.

Her heart beat triple time as Lindsey slipped inside, closed the doors, and secured the lock. He was alone. She took a deep breath. He looked magnificent. "My lord."

My lord.

He smiled. That same half effort that sent women into vapors. She withstood the impact but appreciated the rumor more thoroughly by the experience. Perhaps there was something to it.

"And we meet again, my lady." His strides ate up the distance between them until he too stood poised before the easel. "I wonder if Fate isn't playing a wicked game at our expense."

"Fate?" It took a moment for her to recover her good senses. His nearness set her equilibrium awhirl. "Coincidence perhaps. It seems we both prefer quiet, or at the least, to inspect the private study of whomever has invited our ungracious attendance to their affair. I find after an hour or two, many of these societal events become predictable." She'd spoken her mind, and her mother would suffer a case of the vapors if she were to discover Caroline's boldness.

"Your honesty is refreshing. A lady should always speak her mind. Any man worth having for husband or companion shouldn't feel lessened by your thoughts and opinions."

She was at a loss for words after hearing the earl's unexpected remark, though her mother's advice slithered through her brain to remind of conventional etiquette.

You must maintain a conservative demeanor at all times, even if you yearn for adventure.

Luckily, Lindsey didn't wait for her reply and continued in a silky voice she was anxious to hear again.

"I have no doubt after your travels these evening affairs run toward the mundane. Everyone yearns for adventure now and again, and women are no exception."

She returned his smile, feeling much more like herself considering he loomed next to her, tall and virile. The man had a potency about him that urged every part of her femininity to alertness. Her regard for his point of view rose a notch. What would he say next? Anticipation caused her pulse to thrum, and inside her stomach a dozen butterflies took wing.

"And what is your opinion of this piece?" He angled his head to inspect the artwork closely, pushing the cloth up and over so it hooked onto a corner of the wooden frame.

He wished to hear her viewpoint? How enlightened. And unexpected. "You'd likely be surprised." She dropped her voice to a murmur, hoping he wouldn't pursue the subject further.

"Is that so?" He resettled his gaze on her. "Because you abhor the subject matter or find the workmanship inferior?" He stepped back and shifted his position to inspect *her* more closely.

His eyes roamed over her face and then lower, where they took on a carnal gleam. Heat raced across her skin. She'd worn one of her most flattering gowns this evening, for a bit of variety, not because she'd hoped to see the earl again. The gown was a new design of imported silk the color of ripe peaches. The bodice was flattering yet not over-revealing, though the way his gaze devoured her she wondered what he found so interesting. She forced herself to supply an adequate answer to his question.

"The artist is accomplished no doubt," she replied, emboldened by his persistence. "But I'm left at crosses with the subject matter." That wasn't a complete truth. At least not in a manner she would reveal to him. Tremulous feelings of inadequacy, unfulfillment, and failure threatened to shatter her calm disposition. She wouldn't cry, nor would she confess the despair of her heart. If she accomplished her goal and found an ideal gentleman to wed, one who could love her in return with understanding of her complicated condition, gratitude would replace the emptiness eventually.

"You're a lovely little liar, aren't you?" His eyes pierced her with their acute interest. "Not captivated by Roman mythology though you lived in Italy for a time?" He seemed unaffected by her reluctance to reveal more.

"I believe artwork should evoke emotion, touch the heart, and cause one to have distinct feelings." Oh, and this painting did all those things. If he ever knew, she'd be exposed as the worst hypocrite.

"And the Nona causes you little reaction?" He tensed, and she wondered if he knew she spoke false.

"Oh, I wouldn't say that. Mayhap too many." She stepped closer to the painting and pretended to peruse the goddess intently. "And you? When you see this beautiful piece of art, what do you feel?"

* * * *

Lindsey might have laughed if her question didn't force him to confront unpleasant realities. When he'd discovered her poised in front of the easel, her bottom outlined by the smooth silk of her evening gown, his mind conjured images having little to do with art appreciation. Their conversation pleased him, her beauty uncommon in its purity, and he found in regard to their age difference and worldliness, he was intrigued. More than he'd care to admit.

But finding the Nona here, when he'd only secured the same painting from Lord Jenkin's private collection, proved disturbing. The fact he may have stolen a replica evoked rage, mistrust, and resentment. Damn his father in hell.

"It's nothing more to me than oil and pigment on canvas."

"It must cause some reaction," she insisted.

"Then I feel curiosity." He tamped down his anger before she called *him* a liar. Because he was. Without a doubt.

"Curiosity? I wasn't expecting that."

This seemed to effectively cut off her questioning. Now it was his turn.

"Do you believe the scene depicted by the artist? Do you accept we are no more in control of our lives than an ancient myth suggests?"

"I'm not sure how to answer that." Her voice quieted, as if she spoke to herself more than to him.

"You must believe in something."

"I do. Love."

Her expression revealed she'd blurted out her answer before she thought better of it, and now perhaps regretted it. He'd hoped for a genuine conversation. Too often women were instructed to keep their thoughts to themselves and defer to a male point of view. He'd always found that belief lacking.

"You possess a romantic nature then." He accredited her answer to youth, his world-weary soul too immune to consider the notion. Opportunity seemed more likely. Besides, love was for fools wishing to invite pain with nothing more than a grand illusion. Love was a thorn, unforeseen while one admired beauty, and discovered when one held on tight. A change of subject was in order. "How is it we find ourselves alone in another man's study for the second time in three days?"

"I sought respite from an unwelcomed situation the first time." Her lovely mouth flattened into a line of disappointment.

"This time too, I suppose. I missed our dance this evening." He closed the space between them to less than a stride. Silence stretched. He watched her eyes change with the mood, and a twinkle replaced an earlier skepticism. Her irises were an unfamiliar shade of blue. One only an artist would be able to label. "How can I make amends for my irresponsibility?"

She didn't respond, though he noticed the fluttering beat of her pulse at the base of her slim neck, and the earlier lust-filled images he'd entertained rose with vivid clarity. Would her skin hold the same fragrance as her hair? A light, ethereal scent that reminded him of the extensive floral gardens at Kingswood, his country home, the same which dared him to believe in fanciful nonsense instead of hard, unrelenting consequences.

He waited, determined not to hurry the moment though he knew exactly what would occur and believed she did too. As before, she'd lowered her eyes to his cravat, which offered him an invitation to admire her in closer proximity than the painting earlier. Her lashes against her alabaster skin composed a delicate portrait in shyness, but her gasp of surprise as he touched her, and the flush of her rosy warm cheeks, declared other emotions battled for attention.

He tipped her chin upward with his fingertip, cursing his gloves and the formality that prevented him from knowing the heat in her skin.

"Would a kiss suffice as reparation, my lady?"

Blame it on some misplaced irrational urge, but once he tilted his head with his eyes matched to hers, his jaw at the perfect angle, there was no denying it would happen. The persistent prick of conscience which reminded she was a young innocent, and he an older disillusioned rake, lost out to raw want.

And he hadn't wanted anything by his own choice in so long, whether manipulated by his dead father or commanded by a lifestyle perpetuated by meaningless distraction. Somehow this kiss meant much more than he cared to examine.

She granted consent as her lids fell closed, a soft sigh on her rosebud lips instead of an objection. He wanted to capture that breath, to inhale it, if only to possess something of hers, the freshness, the hope in their fleeting moment that would happen and then never happen again.

Impatient and restless, he wanted her kiss and he would have it. As soon as he lowered his mouth and settled his lips over hers, a visceral shock arrowed through him so intensely he almost withdrew.

Almost.

But to stop would be the death of him, and right now he had no reason to hurry along the journey.

She tensed, a slight pause to indicate she'd experienced it too, then she melted into him and any flimsy shred of conscience he might have possessed evaporated. He slanted his chin and captured her mouth more fully, deepening the kiss, his heart in a race against time as if inside, in the dark corners of his soul where the truth lived, he knew the moment was too pure to last.

Were she to pull away now he'd suffer on a level he'd never known, and that one startling thought proved so odd and unexpected he discarded it as soon as it formed, grasping on to desire to allow the more familiar, safer emotion to take hold.

He ran the tip of his tongue along the seam of her lips, licking the corners with an eager bid to entry. She reacted, half gasp, half moan, and he wasted not a moment, the lush invitation of her mouth far too tempting to deny.

* * * *

Caroline had been kissed before. She'd allowed a few gentlemen suitors the advantage of an embrace while in Italy. Those kisses had been wet mostly, and overpowering. They'd caused her to panic slightly, to experience fear instead of pleasure. On each of those occasions she'd withdrawn promptly, ended the exchange, and refused to allow it again. She'd soon discovered, after three encounters, she either chose the wrong men or knew nothing about kissing.

But now, wrapped in the circle of Lindsey's strong arms, his warm chest against her heart, his decadent mouth tasting hers, she realized the truth. She'd truly known nothing about kissing. Because anything she'd experienced before hadn't been *kissing.*

Good lord, the pressure of his mouth on hers would be her undoing. She melted into his hold and shuddered with desire. He ran his tongue in a smooth line across her lips, and much to her mortification she moaned as sensation racked through her. When he slid his tongue inside to rub against hers, she lost sensible thought altogether.

This was no forceful demand, the kiss precious and intimate, as if they spoke without words, communicated with nothing more than emotion. She wanted it to last forever, the shimmering vibration of pleasure and excitement that flooded her senses and extended outward from the fluttering inside her stomach to each fingertip. Her knees refused to cooperate but the wall of his chest, all warm wool and masculine scent, supported her in their mutiny.

He deepened the kiss and she allowed it, each stroke of his cinnamon tongue against hers divine, a new experience like nothing she'd ever encountered. Heat licked through her skin to ignite her veins. As if bewitched, he pulled her further into a sensual dream as seamlessly as the nude in the painting unraveled the thread from her spool. Somehow, by the mere act of kissing, he successfully undid her steadfast proper beliefs, her body all too ready to leap at the tempting freedom he offered.

Desire washed over her in waves of heady awareness, and she recalled a time when she was younger and her family had visited Brighton. Giddy with excitement, she'd waded out too far, the ocean alluring and beautiful. Before she could think better of it, the tide took control, tumbled her under, head over heels, to wrap around her with intense demand, winding so tightly that her delight soon turned to peril. It was that singular thought which caused her to pull away from Lindsey's embrace.

As enticing and pleasurable as it was, it held dark dangerous power she wasn't ready yet to explore.

At first, they stood motionless, their eyes matched. His brow lowered for the briefest moment, but whether he was surprised or confused she couldn't decipher. He stepped back a stride, and the space proved helpful in restoring her breathing rhythm. She surmised he needed the additional air as much as she, though when he turned to look at her again he appeared as unaffected and polished as earlier.

Pity her heart thrummed in her chest like it wished to break free.

"Are you angry?"

His murmured question, peculiar if examined closely, forced her to focus on the present moment. "Not at all."

"I've wanted to do that since the moment I saw you hiding beside Lord Albertson's bookcases."

"I wasn't hiding."

"Whatever you were doing..." A sly smile played at the corner of his mouth, and she found herself fascinated all over again. "You didn't object, or make yourself known."

"I'd hoped you would be quick about your business, do whatever you needed to do without additional conversation, and be off to rejoin the festivities."

"I see." This apparently brought him amusement. His eyes twinkled as he stared at her directly.

"Do you?" She smiled now too. "I've found often enough that actions speak louder than words."

"Some believe that." His expression changed, though he still held her with his eyes. "My father usually expressed his answer to my questions with his hands."

"That's not what I meant." Her heart twisted with a mixture of shock and sympathy, all former emotion vanquished.

"I know." He didn't say more, and the silence built between them.

"I can't be found here with you. I'll be ruined." Her voice came out husky and uncertain, and she swallowed in an attempt to regain equilibrium. Lindsey might appear the unrepentant rogue, but there were layers upon layers to this intriguing man.

"As would I," he agreed too quickly.

"You?" She didn't mean to sound peevish, her scoff unladylike. Her emotions were running all over the place. "Gentlemen have all the advantage, the rules unjust."

"Your view is too simplistic, darling."

"Don't call me that." A swift memory of that same endearment muttered to Lady Jenkin sprawled atop a desktop ruined the effect quite neatly. "Is it what you call every female who spares you attention?"

Her question hit the mark, though his expression revealed he was more impressed by her perception than repentant at having been accused.

"Fair enough, the word means little to me." He didn't say anything further, but then his eyes once again found hers, the intensity there similar to the fraught moment before he swept her into his arms. "Lovely is a more appropriate descriptor."

She dismissed his compliment without thought, though her heart thudded with pleasure. "Regardless, were I discovered here alone with you, I would be the one ruined."

"And I contend, I would be also. I'd be forced to marry, and that's a disastrous condition I intend to avoid at all cost."

"Oh." His reply proved too difficult to unriddle at the moment. "I see."

"You shouldn't waste your curiosity on it." He smiled fully, and she was doubly charmed, by his handsome features and, too, that he could easily discern her introspection.

"Isn't it the course of things that you wed and produce an heir? That you continue the line and honor the title?"

"Of course." He chuckled, seemingly with amusement. "Though I've never been known to do what's expected."

"So you'd rather pursue shallow distractions and release yourself from the true obligation to your heritage?"

"I wouldn't put it in those words, though I can't expect you to understand when I don't myself." He inhaled deeply. "Besides, you're trouble, my lady. More to my surprise, the kind of trouble I apparently can't resist."

"What is that supposed to mean?" She wheedled, calmer now, thinking clearly and at the ready to leave before their bandied topic of conversation turned into a shocking reality.

"Nothing more than you're as curious as I." He reached out and stroked a fingertip across her lips, his gloves no barrier to the heat of his touch. "Now, to avoid further complication..."

She wondered to what he implied. Her curiosity had never led her to feel as confused as she did now.

"I'll leave immediately, and you'll stay a beat longer. Thereby anyone who happens to be in the hall, which I doubt is anyone at all, will never know we've spent this time together."

But I will.

A lingering and pleasurable tension hummed through her veins still.

He left straightaway, and she could only stare after him, the click of the door an end to their interlude.

Barlow would decrease the allotments with each passing fortnight. He didn't have time for indulgence.

* * * *

The following evening, Lindsey continued to deliberate the frustrating predicament of Lady Caroline Nicholson as he waited for Mills on a dank street corner near the edge of Seven Dials. Any respectable gentleman wouldn't be seen in an area that tempted the worst sort of danger, but the assistance his friend could provide in verifying the authenticity of the Nona was invaluable and worth the risk. While this part of London might be home to the worst breed, it also guaranteed anonymity, something that couldn't be found on Bond Street or any other locale frequented by the ton, no matter the fat purse or social influence.

Lindsey patted his coat to confirm the Nona remained in his possession. One could never be sure a sly pick-purse or thief wouldn't somehow distract long enough to lighten his pocket. He held no doubt he could hold his own if it came to fisticuffs, but if the would-be attacker had a pistol, he'd be forced to surrender his valuables without a fight. While he carried a knife in his boot, he had no desire to be left bloody in a dark alley in Seven Dials. Thieves and their kind were a dishonest and unfaithful lot who found the utmost loyalty when they banded together to take down an upper.

His gaze fell to a nearby trio of steps which led to the closest tenement. The stones were crumbled beyond repair. Below the hollowed-out recess, two rats fought over an indistinguishable morsel. He hoped it wasn't an indication of what was to come. He had no desire to confront the Duke of Warren or, worse, continue his search for a painting that seemed to have multiplied overnight.

On the verge of impatience, Lindsey spotted Mills as he crossed the street. The viscount claimed he had an acquaintance who could discern whether or not the painting in his possession was indeed the original. How this process would happen, Lindsey had no idea or interest. His father's receipt of purchase wasn't evidence enough. A reference to preliminary sketches done by the artist fortified his father's claim, but Lindsey knew the appearance of the second Nona made it clear things were not as they seemed. And so he found himself here, relying on his friend who insisted this chap in Seven Dials could authenticate artwork.

The sooner Lindsey locked the Nona away, the sooner he could move on to the next search and locate the second painting. Dependable knowledge

Chapter Eight

Lindsey couldn't think straight. Oh, he'd managed intelligent conversation and mingled sufficiently with the Duke of Warren's guests, but he was for the door and out into the bracing night air as quickly as the evening allowed.

How could it be? A slip of a girl, *a debutante no less*, had rocked him to the core with a single kiss. He was a fool. A fool mesmerized by the past and all the opportunities missed, no doubt.

He signaled for his carriage and stood at the foot of the limestone steps in wait, his mind too anxious to relive the encounter, his body mercilessly strung tight.

It began innocently enough. A gentle kiss, almost chaste, meant to soften the fact he hadn't shown for their dance. A selfish act to satisfy his curiosity, nothing more. It wasn't meant to awaken lustful desire so intense he'd barely managed to keep a leash on his control.

And when she'd whimpered, that faint lovely sound from the back of her throat right before she'd withdrawn, as if it pained her to do the right thing, her needs and yearnings on the verge of compromise as much as his own. In that single moment, he would have taken her down to the carpeting and stripped her bare, her body to his, each delectable inch to be savored. Oh, the pleasure they'd find in each other.

He drew another cleansing breath and blinked hard as his carriage pulled to the gravel drive. He had important matters to attend, and his thinking couldn't be clouded with allusive fantasies. His father's solicitor had spoken truthfully. While there were sufficient funds in the coffers at present, the financial stability of the earldom demanded he reclaim the paintings, as they constituted the bulk of collateral and fiscal holdings.

of the sister works and their whereabouts had been difficult to obtain, but with the ton suddenly interested in the Duke of Warren's collection and Lord Jenkin no doubt on the verge of suspicion with his misplaced conclusion, timing was on Lindsey's side. Inquiring about the paintings and prodding for information would appear nothing more than speculation about the topic of the moment. It could stimulate reliable clues in regard to the other two works, and hopefully he'd reclaim them and be done with the matter entirely.

In that, at least the solvency of the earldom would be secure. He dismissed the other contingency of his father's will without consideration.

"Mills." Lindsey acknowledged his friend with a curt nod and low greeting. "I appreciate your help with this cursed situation."

"My man is reliable, and as quiet as a vacant tomb. He knows art. He also knows when to talk and when to be quiet, and that more than anything has kept him in business for over a decade."

"Business." The word came out with a cynicism Lindsey hadn't intended.

"Buying, selling, reselling, storing..." Mills indicated which way to go with a wag of his chin. "Keeping secrets, spreading rumors. He's a hand in all of it, and as for artwork, he can tell a forgery from an original with nothing more than an examination of the piece."

"How is that possible?" Granted, Lindsey wasn't keen to understand all the intricacies, but when he'd viewed the painting in the Duke of Warren's study it appeared identical to the one he'd taken from Lord Jenkin's gallery.

"A proclivity acquired by a need for survival, I suppose." Again Mills indicated a right turn with a quick gesture of his hand. "And too, there's all those coins just waiting in your purse."

True enough Lindsey brought along the sum Mills had mentioned, happy to pay for the information he needed.

They paused as an old man, hunched at the shoulders and dressed in drab, torn clothing, crossed their path with a mangy dog at his heels. Then they continued farther into the plaid of cross streets, the eerie tap of their bootheels on the cobbles the only sound that met his ears.

"Why couldn't we have taken a hack right to your man's door?" Lindsey didn't mind walking, though he realized the farther he advanced into this web of alleys the more difficult it would be to extricate himself if the need arose. Perhaps he should have put a knife in *each* boot.

"It's just one more block or so." Mills turned a sharp left. "Another reason my man has been in business so long is that no one knows where to find him on any given evening, and venturing into his territory is a risk not all uppers are willing to take. Though by no mistake, he completes a fair amount of transactions."

Another stranger, this one a gentleman easily distinguished as a respectable sort by his posture and clothing, hurried from a dingy doorway across the street. He kept his head down and advanced on long strides, as if he couldn't flee fast enough.

"See there." Mills slanted his head in the departing man's direction. "Were we in a ballroom we might very well know that person. But he certainly doesn't want to be recognized here, whether he's selling the family's silver to pay his gambling debts or pawning his wife's jewelry to afford a gift for his mistress."

"Understood."

At last they slowed at the mouth of a long alley. It was incredibly dark; the street lamps that had marked their passage at the beginning of their travels had long ago vanished. He realized now Mills must have counted the blocks, leading him like a mouse through a maze to find the correct location. They advanced down the narrow alley and before a wooden door, where the viscount knocked three times in succession and then waited a beat before knocking twice more.

Lindsey didn't know what to make of the scene, seemingly misplaced from a child's ghost tale. But he needed Mills' help; he couldn't very well bring the Nona to the British Museum to be examined by their expert curator. Still, he rued the fact he stood in his best leather boots in a murky puddled alley at a ridiculous hour waiting for some nefarious fence to confirm his stolen merchandise. The irony rankled. Time stretched, and he began to believe no one would answer the door. He forced his thoughts somewhere pleasant.

What was Lady Caroline doing at this hour? Was she already asleep? Somehow, he didn't believe that true. Did she read in bed, her hair unbound and silky, strewn across the pillows? If she did, it was some romantic tome of poetry, no doubt. The contrast between that enticing, pristine image and his current surroundings evoked a muffled chuckle, but all amusement evaporated when he considered she many very well be out at a social event on the arm of some swain—

The panel opened and a stringy lad waved them inside.

Good thing he had cause to refocus. He didn't like the jab of displeasure that accompanied his last thought.

Again he followed Mills, who trailed the young boy into the bowels of the tenement, the candles every twenty feet or so hardly adequate to light their path. He heard the squeak of vermin across the floorboards more than saw it and preferred it that way.

When they reached the rear of the residence, the boy simply disappeared into the darkness. Lindsey and Mills stepped into a well-lit room and the sudden change in lighting caused a moment's pause while his eyes acclimated.

A squat man who possessed at least fifty years stood at a large rectangular table. Various pieces of artwork and collectibles littered the room, some covered by burlap and tied tightly with string. The man eyed them as they came forward, his attention on Lindsey, as he could only assume the chap already knew the reason Mills had brought him along.

"Let me have her."

Introductions and the like were unnecessary. The least familiar the better, although Lindsey wouldn't instigate questions until he knew more about the man before him and not the other way around. He slid a hand into his coat pocket and produced the Nona. Then he placed it on the table and carefully unrolled the canvas.

For a moment the three men peered down at the painting in silence, but then the fencer, with a spry grace Lindsey would have thought impossible, slid the Nona forward and produced a long, thick piece of glass. He moved the curved lens over the painting while not a sound could be heard. He repeated the process on the back of the canvas, which baffled Lindsey further.

Lindsey eyed Mills, who merely crimped his lips in affirmation to wait. The minutes ticked by until at last it appeared the examination was over.

Pushing the Nona across the tabletop, the fencer met his inquisitive stare. "She's the real thing."

"Are you sure?"

The man's greying brows raised to his hairline. "If I said it, I'm sure."

Apparently, Lindsey was to accept his word as the definitive answer. He looked toward Mills, who gave a confident nod. When nothing else was said Lindsey went back into his pocket and produced a purse for payment, tossing it to the table, where the coins inside clinked against each other upon landing. "Thank you."

The fencer did little more than grunt his reply.

"Have you had many forgeries coming in? Or heard of anyone earning their keep by producing reproductions so well done, even an art conscious Duke would be fooled?" Mills asked.

The older man narrowed his eyes. "I'm not in the habit of sharing what's meant to be private, or the other way around." He reached across the tabletop and collected the coins. "My boy will show you out."

With their meeting at an end, Lindsey rerolled the Nona, wrapping it in the same cloth he'd used as protection, and returned it to his pocket for safety. Then, following the lad who made a timely reappearance, they left the tenement directly.

* * * *

"Mother, the weather looks fine. Perhaps we should have our tea in the garden." Caroline glanced in her mother's direction as she turned from the window. The sky was cloudless, a vivid blue that seemed a rarity here in London in comparison to the Mediterranean climes she'd grown accustomed to in Italy.

"That would be pleasant, although you must wear your bonnet. You wouldn't want to mar your complexion. The Seton social is this evening. I should imagine your cousins will wish to continue your introductions. There's so many young handsome gentlemen in London, you will have many choices."

"Perhaps." Caroline wrinkled her nose at her mother's favorite topic of conversation. True, Caroline wished to find a suitor with the goal of marriage, but all this plotting and planning dampened her spirits and ruined any idea of romance to be found in the situation. "One can't very well predict with whom one will fall in love."

The disappointing reality of Lord Tiller's lack of interest was soon replaced by the charming image of the Earl of Lindsey. How did he spend his days? Did he favor horses at Tattersall's or gambling at White's? Was he active in Parliament? There seemed a great many things she wished to know about him, and yet he was a rake of the first order and no one she should lend a second thought.

Despite knowing this, she found herself preoccupied with images of him when she knew it was nothing more than a waste of time. Yet that conclusion did little to discourage her. She briefly touched her fingertips to her lips and then dropped them away. She returned her gaze to the outdoors beyond the window and recalled the heat of his hand at her back when they'd danced, how he'd held her fingers tightly and offered her that charming smile, which at times had indeed weakened her knees.

"My lady, a delivery has arrived."

Croft, the house butler, came to the door and startled her from her forbidden thoughts. She glanced over her shoulder, surprised to see an elaborate display of lilies in shades of pink and white held high in the servant's arms, the delicately cut-crystal vase quick to refract sunlight from the windows. The bouquet was enormous. It obliterated half of Croft's body with its width.

"How lovely." Lady Derby rose from the chaise in a rush to inspect the delivery. "Place it here, please." She indicated the mahogany side table between the wing chairs near the hearth.

"I suspect they are for you, Caroline. Oh, do come and read the card." Her mother sounded especially thrilled. "Lilies are hothouse flowers, which could only mean the gentleman who sent these is sincere in his intentions."

"I'm not sure I agree with your theory." She plucked the card from the stems and opened it promptly. The preposterous idea that it would be from Lindsey flittered through her mind, but she refused to consider it. Logic was one of her most dependable qualities, though of late it had all but abandoned her. She opened the note and read the words aloud. "With fond memories of our dance. Lord Hutton."

"Lord Hutton." Mother came to stand beside her, her finger tapping against her chin in a pose of thoughtful consideration. "I don't recall him, though he definitely remembers you." She reached forward and stroked a fingertip over one of the blooms. "Do you remember the dance you shared?"

"No, unfortunately I don't." Too much time and brain power spent reliving her quadrille with Lindsey was to blame, as it had wiped every other dance away. Once he'd kissed her, she was quite certain she couldn't remember her birthdate if she didn't make an effort to concentrate.

"Perhaps tonight he'll attend the Seton's event and you'll have the opportunity to thank him in person," Mother suggested.

"Yes, I hope so." *And Lindsey, of course.* She stared at the flowers. They were beautiful and costly, but she couldn't recall Lord Hutton, and the lack of connection left her unaffected. She should like to remember the gentleman with fondness if he went to the trouble of sending such an elaborate gesture. It served as yet another example of why her mother, aunt, and cousins were approaching marriage in a disapproving method, one that generally ignored the romance found within a courtship, the interplay of desire and attraction, and the undefinable pull that brought two people together.

She wished for love and understanding. She hoped for a long loyal union filled with common interests and enjoyable conversation with her husband. They would have one another for several decades to come, so the natural inclination that she wished to fall deeply into love and passion with the man she intended to marry was the one irrevocable aspect she held dear. Something about the way her cousins and mother regarded courtship, like it was a business negotiation to be sought and contracted, unsettled Caroline.

Besides, she had only just arrived in London. True, she pursued marriage, but the systematic methods of those who worked on her behalf left her feeling cheated of the most important aspects of the courting process. Romance, attraction, desire…she wasn't sure when these qualities became a priority, but they were high on her list now. Naturally, she needed to attend events and experience introductions, but that didn't erase her misgivings. Her mother and aunt approached the subject of marriage with the same demeanor one would possess when overseeing the household budget. Caroline yearned for the rare anticipation that accompanied true attraction. A secret smile curled her lips.

"My lady." Croft reappeared at the door. "A gentleman caller for Lady Caroline is at the door."

Her heart hiccupped with a repeat of her first ridiculous conclusion, and she forced herself to calm.

"Show him in, please." Her mother's smile widened further, if that was possible.

A few minutes later Croft returned with Lord Egerton stepping on his shadow.

Caroline smiled then too. She remembered the amiable gentleman from the Duke of Warren's social and his kind attention to their conversation. He'd appeared genuinely interested in what she had to say and possessed a congenial nature.

"What a pleasant surprise." Lady Derby sent Croft for refreshments, and after initial introductions and niceties concluded they sat on opposite sides of Lord Hutton's bouquet while Mother hovered at a respectable distance near the mullioned windows.

"It's a lovely day." Caroline didn't know what else to say. She hadn't expected him to call, and therefore hadn't given conversation much thought.

"A fine day for a phaeton ride through Hyde Park, if I may be so bold."

Apparently, Lord Egerton had a specific goal in mind.

"What a splendid idea." Her mother joined the conversation, her face a beacon of enthusiasm. "Caroline, why don't you fetch your bonnet. You don't wish to keep Lord Egerton waiting."

Chapter Nine

"I owe you my gratitude." Lindsey nudged his Arabian onto a more discreet bridle path in Hyde Park, far and away from Rotten Row and its congested parade of dandies. "I hadn't the slightest idea how to authenticate my investment and will continue to rely on your associate in the future if needed."

"It was no trouble." Mills wrapped the reins around his fist and aimed his horse to fall in with Lindsey's. "Actually, I've given your predicament considerable thought, most especially in regard to the remaining paintings."

"Have you? Well, if you know of their whereabouts or how I can take possession of them, I'd appreciate the information with haste." The sooner he could fulfill his obligation and lay to rest his father's ridiculous demands, the better. It didn't matter he planned to ignore the second contingency. He might not have worked out the particulars, but he doubted Barlow would stand firm on such an outlandish demand, especially if the earldom's solvency was at stake.

"You may not like what I suggest."

They galloped a length, slowing the horses as they neared a more populated bend in the path.

"Fair enough, though I'm open to suggestions, as I readily have none." Lindsey knew Mills to be straightforward, so his friend's hesitation proclaimed more than his words likely would.

"It's only an idea, mind you, and it may very well be out of bounds, but…"

This time his prevarication had everything to do with maneuvering their horses through a throng of young bucks racing across the green. As soon as they regained privacy Mills picked up the thread of conversation.

"You mentioned yourself that there was no way for you to discern whether or not the Nona was authentic. I trust my man's assessment, and I'm pleased you wound up on the right side of our recent inquiry, but the Duke of Warren has been fooled and he's none the wiser for it."

"And?" Lindsey reached forward and rubbed his horse's neck. Infinity was a rare Sabino Arabian stallion, chestnut in color except for high white markings on his knees and hocks. Lindsey had his pick of several immaculate purebreds in his extensive stables, but Infinity was more than a dependable mount or smart investment in horseflesh. The stallion was his family. Lindsey usually kept his prized mount at Kingswood Manor, his country estate, but this season he'd decided otherwise.

"All I'm suggesting is that if there's a forger out there who possesses talent so fine his work is near indistinguishable from the authentic, it would save you time and frustration by hiring the man to produce the remaining two pieces in the collection." Mills relayed all this without taking a breath, apparently anxious to rid the suggestion from his head.

Lindsey allowed him to stew longer than necessary, simply because they'd been friends for so many years it was impossible to resist the opportunity. "An interesting proposition."

"That's it?"

"What did you expect? That I slap you on the back and congratulate you for suggesting I commission counterfeit artwork so when discovered—"

"*If* discovered—"

"*When* discovered, would leave me destitute and label me either a fool or a fraud? Worse, it would perpetuate a diabolical incentive for blackmail were the forger to decide he no longer wished to keep my secret quiet." Lindsey held Infinity at a canter, though the horse was eager to go.

"At what risk to himself?"

Mills' incredulous expression brought Lindsey to laughter. "You're a good friend to suggest it, but I'd rather find the originals and be done with it."

"As you say." Mills paused in thought. "What will you do about the duplicate Nona?"

"Nothing at the moment." Lindsey brought Infinity to the starting line of the racing green. "As long as I have the original, I'll not concern myself with another's gullibility or mistaken purchases."

"And so, the search for the Decima begins."

"So it does."

The two men kicked their horses into a run, and Lindsey relished the race. He was anxious to expend the perpetual tension that arose upon the reading of his father's will and hadn't subsided since, always at the ready under his skin to incite anger. But that wasn't entirely true. He amended the latter after a beat of contemplation. There was a chance meeting or two when he'd experienced blessed relief. The fleeting interludes with Caroline. Their dance. That one unforgettable kiss.

He shook away an immediate spike of lust and the inviting encouragement to relive their embrace. Instead he focused on more logical pursuits as his horse accomplished the lawn, the animal's hooves in sync with the tempo of Lindsey's determination. He loved the reckless speed of a good ride, and with Mills left to a cloud of dust, Lindsey also welcomed the pride of winning.

Still, he couldn't dismiss Caroline from his mind so easily. Did she prefer the outdoors to society's functions? He'd always found a certain peace in nature. As a child he'd often run off behind the estate house to lose himself in greenery and escape his father's temper. Did Caroline ride? Sidesaddles were cumbersome, but he'd like to think she enjoyed a good trot. He housed thoroughbreds of every variety. No doubt the perfect mare waited for her in his stable.

With the path at a swift end, he reined in Infinity as neatly as he rearranged his thoughts.

"We should change our course or we'll proceed straight into the daily promenade."

Mills' voice reached him from behind and Lindsey jerked his head up, his focus cleared, any earlier unexpected musings dismissed by his friend's clever timing. All the better for it. He had no room in his life for a debutante, never mind a young miss interested in pursuing some idealist version of wedded bliss.

Love.

Wasn't that her answer when he'd questioned her two nights past? She wanted love. So many people did, and yet the result delivered overwhelming disappointment more often than not. He'd never experienced so strong a bond that he'd ever label it love, not from his parents or any woman who fell into bed with him. Perhaps because he never spoke of the emotion, willing to give his body but not his voice. Words were powerful. Actions more inconsequential. If by chance he ever found himself lost to emotion, he knew he'd offer not just his vow or his physical self, but his very soul, his heart hers to break. That level of vulnerability secured he'd never take the risk in a wager he'd never accept.

He might have left it at that and changed the subject to White's or Tattersall's, but he had the unfortunate luck of glancing to his right, where the end of South Carriage Drive forced the peacocks and flirts to congregate as the ton's finest turned their gigs and open-air carriages. This too was of no consequence to him and should have been forgotten without consideration, except atop a bright navy-blue phaeton, with her face alight with pleasure, sat Lady Caroline and some nondescript gentleman he didn't recognize.

She looked quite fetching, her hair caught up in a flattering twist, the dark strands that had escaped her coif at play along her slender neck. She wore a pale pink pelisse that made the color in her cheeks as inviting as her soft petal lips, and he found his body reacting with a pulse of untenable yearning, his seat in the saddle increasingly more uncomfortable with each exhale. There was no way to explain the unbridled lust that surged through him, and yet he couldn't ignore it either.

"Who do we have here?"

It was the exact question he'd formed mentally as he considered Caroline's escort, but he quickly discovered Mills wasn't of like mind. "I don't know the gentleman."

"Gentleman? I'm speaking of Lady Caroline," Mills replied, his tone a bit too wolfish for Lindsey's liking.

"I thought you considered her ordinary."

"Did I say that? Perhaps you misheard and I said extraordinary."

A spike of misplaced possessiveness tightened Lindsey's jaw, and he forced himself to a more casual expression. "Perusing the debutantes? I wouldn't have guessed you'd invite the misery of an innocent's fanciful company."

"I'm not getting any younger. Neither are you, for that matter," Mills goaded. "I've recently realigned my priorities, and it's time for me to beget an heir and a spare. After you pointed her out the other evening, I took an interest. Lady Caroline is the most delectable morsel to grace a ballroom in the past five seasons."

"She's not a morsel." *She's a decadent feast.* He measured his tone, though even to his own ears the words came out on a growl.

"She is to me, and unless her father has asked you to act the guardian, I'd appreciate if you'd not adopt the role."

"You're not right for her," Lindsey persisted. "She's young."

"Again with the age?" Mills' chuckle transformed into a smirk. "I'm not dead."

"What could an ingénue offer that you haven't already experienced? Boredom, no doubt." *Everything refreshing and new.* He was a lying bastard.

"I won't know until I keep her company," Mills answered too quickly.

"And you'd wish for a wife with maidenly sensibilities?"

"That can be easily remedied."

Lindsey curled his fingers into a fist, his grip on the reins almost painful. Mills nudged his horse forward. "Besides, you've put me at the altar before I've even gained an introduction. The lady may possess an annoying twitter or garish laugh."

Her voice is lovely and lilting.

Mills continued his verbal meanderings as he steered across the lawn. "She might kiss like a cold fish."

More like an angel.

"Not that either would deter me if I found her pleasing. I'm an able educator atop the bedsheets if the situation warrants attention."

Mills slanted a glance over his shoulder and Lindsey aligned Infinity, though he didn't reply. His jaw ached from clenching his teeth, and at the same time better sense rebelled at his unwarranted rage. He'd no right to feel anger when the lady was free to do as she pleased. Perhaps that was rub. Some misplaced sense of protectiveness evoked by their coincidental meetings. But he'd be damned before he remained immobile. With a click of his tongue that sounded too much like a black curse, Lindsey urged Infinity forward.

* * * *

Caroline smiled at Lord Egerton, the morning air the perfect antidote to her preoccupation with the Earl of Lindsey. Conversation flowed easily; the gentleman was a gregarious sort who seemed confident and kind.

She suspected why he would be popular with the ladies, his hair a tawny color that glinted in the sunlight, his eyes a warm brown, though she couldn't help but contrast his appearance with the thunderous dark visage which composed the Earl of Lindsey.

Something in Lindsey's forbidding glare spoke to her. Was he hiding a secret or inviting her to sin? His kiss certainly spoke to the latter. And while his reputation warned her away and proclaimed him the worst kind of unrepentant libertine, through their scant conversation she believed he was likely misunderstood, and that singular aspect called to her heart.

She shook away these misplaced opinions and watched as Lord Egerton managed the phaeton, accomplishing the sloping curve of the drive to aim the carriage toward the return path. So fixed on reorganizing her focus, she startled when a male voice addressed her escort and the phaeton slowed for conversation. A sudden prickling of awareness teased the hairs on the back of her neck to alert a change. She moved her eyes upward.

"Mills, good to see you." Lord Egerton addressed the stranger who'd brought his horse beside the phaeton. "Is that Lindsey behind you?"

"Good morning. Capital day for a drive."

The earl's deep tenor rippled through her, quick to stir up every emotion and question she'd worked so hard to put to bed last night.

"Have you had the esteemed honor of being introduced to Lady Nicholson?" Egerton slanted his shoulders so she could see beyond his person. "Lords Mills lives at the Albany on Piccadilly, as do I. Behind him is the Earl of Lindsey, a friend of Mills."

And mine.

Or at least she hoped.

A grin teased the corners of her mouth as she looked from one gentleman to the other. Lord Mills seemed good-natured. His hair was windblown, and he had creases about his eyes from smiling. In contrast, Lindsey looked as if he might ignite at any moment. The intensity of his stare was definitely heating her from the inside out.

"My lady, it is my honor."

Lord Mills clasped her glove and bowed his head to place a kiss to her palm. It all seemed rather formal for a roadside morning meeting in the park.

"Lady Nicholson, we meet again. Is it possible you've become even lovelier than last evening?" Lindsey bowed his head politely, though he didn't reach for her hand.

She'd have liked if he would have done so.

Mills jerked his attention to the right and speared Lindsey with a look that said he expected answers later. She wondered at their conversation before they'd approached, especially when she caught a fleeting look of satisfied bedevilment in Lindsey's eyes. His magnificent horse snorted, as if in agreement.

"Gentlemen." She nodded in greeting. "This fine morning has brought all of London to the park." She turned toward the congested fairway and back again.

"High season is always like this," Mills added. "Have you never experienced it before?"

She didn't have time to answer before Lord Egerton interceded. "Lady Nicholson has recently relocated to our fine city from Italy." He puffed out his chest, as if by sharing that bit of news he'd won a prize of some sort.

"Then she must be anxious to see the most popular venues," Mills angled.

Caroline noticed Lindsey's contrary expression, his mouth in a grimace suggesting he struggled to keep choice words locked tight. Meanwhile, the other two men continued on as if she wasn't even present, their strategic squabbling over which locales she deserved to see and who would escort her there monopolizing their conversation.

Lindsey clicked his tongue and realigned his horse until he'd moved to the other side of Egerton's phaeton, evenly positioned next to her. She looked into his dark eyes, gleaming with devil-knows-what, and caught her bottom lip beneath her teeth to suppress an unwarranted sense of elation.

"So here we are again."

"Yes." Her voice sounded breathy. She needed to speak of mundane things, or her mind and heart would lead her astray. "Your horse is quite handsome."

His eyes fell to the animal and he stroked the stallion's neck in a show of affection. "Infinity is an Arabian, and a loyal friend."

She extended her hand and flit her eyes from the horse to Lindsey to ask permission.

"Of course." Half his mouth tilted up in a smile that reached for her heart. "Infinity is the epitome of urbane good breeding. He would never harm you."

She matched his grin, and her heart thudded a heavy beat. Something about Lindsey set her senses awhirl, and she all at once remembered the heat of his nearness during their dance, the strength of his fingers wrapped around hers and the mesmerizing scent of his cinnamon kiss.

"I'm attending the Seton's Assembly this evening." She withdrew from stroking the stallion's glossy coat and straightened in her seat. "You still owe me that dance, my lord."

It was terribly forward. Her mother would have suffered an apoplexy, but the thought of a gathering without the chance of spending time with Lindsey caused the invitation to pale.

"I always pay my debts, my lady."

He didn't say more. He maneuvered Infinity to the other side of the phaeton smoothly, as if nothing had transpired between them though her pulse raced faster than the wind as proof of the contrary.

Chapter Ten

"I'd say our work here is done." Beatrice touched the dance card dangling from Caroline's wrist and nodded at her two sisters. "All but one slot is filled, including a waltz with the estimable Lord Tiller."

"Your mother's report of this morning's achievements, a bouquet and a ride in Hyde, is further proof of our successful efforts," Dinah added. "You'll receive a dozen proposals this season. I'm sure of it."

"Which means you'll have the power to choose for yourself, dear cousin, and not have the decision forced upon you or demanded by a cruel twist of fate. That alone is a rare and wondrous predicament. All you need decide is whether he'll be fair-haired or not, tall or stout, conventional or daring, wealth is a requirement regardless…" Louisa's conversation fluttered away as she turned to accept another glass of Negus.

"It truly isn't as easy as you suggest." She wouldn't argue the point, though not one of her cousins seemed to have an interest in the most important quality to be found in a husband: the desire for abiding affection. So many gentlemen amid the ballroom were handsome, well-dressed, and deep in the pocket, but she required a quality not easily distinguished by an introduction or dance. Was it wrong to want love and not convenience? To hope for mental and physical compatibility? She'd heard enough tales of husbands who kept mistresses to satisfy their sexual proclivities or spent evening after evening at the club to stimulate intelligent conversation. She refused to accept a marriage which perpetuated either avocation. Still, a sharp voice reminded she had no right to be particular, considering her own situation.

"I see you have an admirer across the floor."

Dinah startled her from the emotional argument, and with a somewhat subtle inclination of her fan indicated Lord Mills on the other side of the ballroom.

"Wonderful." Her pleasure was genuine. Perhaps Lindsey had accompanied him. They'd appeared familiar friends in the park this morning. Not that it guaranteed the earl had decided to attend. Peculiar how her immediate thoughts pertained to Lindsey. He did say he always paid his debts though. Didn't that imply he would show at this evening's affair?

She must have dallied too long with hopeful considerations, because Lord Mills crossed the tiles and bowed elegantly to their grouping, all the while his eyes matched to hers.

"May I claim a dance, Lady Nicholson?"

"How perfectly divine. You have but one opening left," Dinah murmured behind her.

Caroline's smile faltered. She'd purposely reserved the second waltz for Lindsey, hopeful he would appear at her elbow and sweep her onto the dance floor. Their quadrille was thrilling, but a waltz where he held her elegantly in her arms—

"Lady Nicholson?" Lord Mills' voice held a dubious tone.

"Of course." She offered her card and retrieved the pencil she'd stored in her reticule, believing it no longer needed. "I look forward to it."

With a nod of acknowledgement, Lord Mills wrote his name in the only empty space and returned the card at the exact moment Lindsey joined their grouping.

"Lady Nicholson."

He bowed his head in greeting, though he didn't make a show of kissing her hand. Did he not wish to? That was twice now he hadn't done so. She was beginning to feel more the fool for anticipating his touch, only to be left disappointed.

"Lord Lindsey, good evening." Her cousins twittered in conversation behind her, though she noted Lord Mills remained attentive to her alone. She took a small step backward to block the tiny occasional table where she'd left her punch and then angled toward Lord Mills. "Does anyone else feel parched?"

"Allow me to bring you a glass of refreshment."

Mills didn't wait for another word, and when Caroline turned her attention to Lindsey, a twinkle of merriment danced in his heated gaze.

"You sent the man on a fool's errand, didn't you?"

"Why so ever would you think that?"

"Your answer is no answer at all, minx."

One half of his mouth curled upward, and she found the effect no less impactful for having experienced it multiple times. He looked absolutely dashing this evening, though she couldn't readily decipher what it was about him that ignited her pulse. Was it the way his dark hair caught a gloss from the candlelight? The sensual gleam in his eyes? Or the striking image of enigmatic confidence and restrained power he presented, perfectly tailored in fine evening clothes, from the pristine cravat at his chin to the tips of his shiny Hessians? He leaned forward slightly and his voice, rich and smooth, rumbled low and mischievous beside her ear to obliterate her mental musings.

"Should I expect to find you in Lord Seton's study at midnight?"

A laugh escaped before she could catch it. "Not this evening, no. Although you're too late for dancing. Every line on my card is filled." She wiggled her wrist, and the paper dangling there swayed with emphasis.

"I will step aside then, not to discourage your bevy of attentive beaus."

She opened her mouth to object, but Lord Mills returned to effectively put an end to their teasing banter. The musicians struck their instruments and without warning her first dance was claimed, though while she moved gracefully to the floor her heart tumbled over itself, anxious to continue her flirtation with Lord Lindsey instead.

* * * *

"What was that all about?" Lindsey leveled a stare at Mills which conveyed the emotion behind the question.

"The refreshment or the waltz?" Mills moved toward the terrace doors. "I've not done anything out of the ordinary, and as I told you earlier, I've begun to think of my future."

Lindsey didn't reply and stepped out onto the marble slab, the night air quick to cool a portion of his anger. "You have your pick of the season."

"Perhaps." Mills joined him, and as was their habit they strode far from the festivities to escape being overheard. "Be kind, or I'll withhold the information I've learned concerning the Decima."

Lindsey dismissed his curious preoccupation with Lady Caroline, better explored later this evening. In his bedchamber. *Alone.*

Instead he sharpened his focus, prepared for whatever information Mills possessed. "What has your contact discovered?"

"The last receipt of purchase for the painting was indeed made by your father, though the canvas surfaced soon after the theft as collateral made in an outlandish wager between Lords Riley and Olmon just two months ago. Riley is prone to foolish gambling. I'm told he once wagered his wife's heirloom jewelry without her knowledge. Needless to say, there's little peace in their home since he lost that bet."

Lindsey listened attentively though he could do with less detail, anxious to get at the information he needed.

"So does Riley have the Decima? Or Olmon?"

"Neither, unfortunately. Olmon won it from Riley and sold it discreetly to Viscount Jamison, who lost it when his estate went out on the rocks. The bank claimed his land and all his assets, but before they could determine the worth of the painting, or even its rightful owner, *you*, the Decima disappeared again."

"Bloody hell, I feel like you're reading a chapter of a gothic novel." For the hundredth time in the last month, Lindsey cursed his father. "So where does this leave me?"

"On your way to Bedfordshire, I'm afraid."

"Bedfordshire? What the hell for?" One disadvantage of secluding oneself on the terrace was the absence of brandy, the perfect antidote to the low simmering rage that took hold. Why did everything begin and end with his father's malice and manipulation? His childhood home was in Bedfordshire. Did Mills' comments have something to do with a return to Kingswood Manor, his country estate? He hadn't returned since the reading of his father's will, the house too full of ugly memories.

"For a fox hunt and country party thrown by Lord and Lady Henley." Mills glanced toward the ballroom, where the festivities remained visible through the French doors.

Was he anticipating his waltz with Caroline? Lindsey waited for him to continue, though now he was equally as anxious to return inside. That in itself proved troublesome. Why was he so drawn to her? Was it her untouched beauty of mind and body? Her optimistic outlook? And if he persisted, would he ruin that quality? Spoil it as he sought to know her better?

Mills cut in and forced him from his mental debate. "According to my associate, Henley recently inquired of the painting's worth. All done discreetly, in low tones, so no one would suspect he'd taken possession."

"Inquiring about the Decima's resale value doesn't necessarily guarantee he has the painting in hand."

"I never mentioned guarantees, and besides, it's all the news I have. Considering you've nothing else to go on, it's at least worth your time."

"I suppose beggars can't be choosers."

Mills started toward the terrace doors. "You're hardly a beggar, although from what you've told me the earldom is headed in that direction. One country party is not a high price to pay. Under other conditions you'd enjoy the festivities."

"I received an invitation to the hunt a few days ago and discarded it neatly. I'm uninterested in attending the barbaric ritual this year. As you know, I'm unavoidably busy but I'll remedy my acceptance in the morning."

"See. Fate has already arranged the specifics."

"Perhaps." Lindsey didn't say more, a large share of his attention busy examining his unhealthy attraction to one of the ton's sparkling debutantes. Beneath those realizations lay a deeper truth, hidden in the darkness of emotion and vulnerability. Despite generous company and ample popularity, loneliness often crept in. He was a man surrounded by people and all the more alone for it. True, it could be he searched for something, but he'd be damned if he knew what it was. It definitely wouldn't be found in a trio of priceless paintings. *Or a beautiful young ingénue.*

They'd reached the doors to the ballroom and Lindsey watched the couples circling the gleaming tiles. A week in the country would keep him away from Caroline, and while he wasn't pleased by that circumstance, much less the idea Mills would be sniffing around her slippers in his absence, the separation would do well to incapacitate his fixation. She'd become a distraction, occupying his thoughts too often.

Caroline deserved someone hopeful and idealistic. A gentleman with a loving family and pristine reputation, not a man who'd lost all optimism years ago due to the cruel realities his life had to offer. True, he was a titled man of advantage, but for all his potential wealth he had little love in his life aside from the camaraderie of a handful of friends.

There was the matter of Mills though.

"Care to come along to Bedfordshire? My country seat is there, and if need be we can leave Henley's and drink better brandy within Kingswood Manor. There's nothing like clean air after the smoke and smog of London. And besides, you have a way in the cardroom equal to mine. You could aid me with information recognizance." Having supplied a multitude of valid reasons, Lindsey waited on his friend's reply.

Mills looked toward the dance floor, and with a stroke of ironic happenstance Lady Caroline twirled by on the arm of some tall dandy.

"I'm not sure." Mills hardly glanced over his shoulder as he moved toward the doors to rejoin the festivities. "I'll let you know on the morrow."

* * * *

Caroline was barely replaced at her cousins' sides before their anxious inquisition began.

"You must tell us every detail," Louisa insisted as she grasped Caroline's elbow and steered her through the crowd. "Let's move to the retiring room so we can hear you properly."

The four of them advanced as one toward the hall, the crowd parting smoothly, as if aware there was no stopping their collective effort.

"He was kind in every way." Caroline searched for words to describe her recent waltz with Lord Tiller. She didn't wish to disappoint Louisa, Dinah, or Beatrice, most especially when they prided themselves on successfully filling her card with the most impeccable husband candidates, yet she couldn't confess she'd experienced none of the thrilling breathless excitement her dance with Lindsey incited. Even now, as she relayed her feelings, she felt no spark, her nerves calm and intact, her heart in its usual predictable rhythm.

"Is he as smooth a dancer as he appears?"

"Yes. He has fine form." She smiled in Beatrice's direction and maneuvered around a large ornamental fern in a brass pot near the threshold to the hallway.

"And did you converse while in his arms? Is he as witty as we're made to believe?"

"He is exceedingly polite."

Dinah's expression begged her to elaborate and Caroline quickly continued, aware her answer didn't suffice. "He's every example of gentlemanly aplomb." *And in that way, quite ordinary.*

"That's all?" Louisa prodded.

"I haven't socialized in London long enough to make a fair comparison." She hoped this explanation satisfied her cousins, because in her heart she knew the truth. By no means did Lord Tiller offer the clever repartee she'd enjoyed with Lord Lindsey, never mind the searing pleasure of his touch. The memory of the earl's kiss still caused her heart to pound in reckless havoc.

Good heavens, she was taken with him. Would everyone become a comparison measured by her interactions with Lindsey? How would she ever find a husband if she clung so tightly to this delusional fancy?

They'd reached the hall and beyond to the ladies' retiring room, where they settled on two cushioned benches near the corner, separated partially by a screen used to discreetly repair wardrobe issues.

"He's remarkably handsome and strong," Caroline mused, the earl still alive in her thoughts though she knew well enough her cousins would misinterpret her comment.

"He is, isn't he?" Beatrice sighed and matched eyes with Louisa, who subtly bit into her lower lip.

"You were lucky to dance with Lord Tiller this evening, as he's for Bedfordshire on the morrow." Dinah's announcement shook everyone from their daydreams. "Hopefully you've left a lasting impression."

"Really? Why?" Caroline asked. "The season's only just begun."

"Lord Henley is running the hounds early," Dinah quickly supplied. "His wife is due with their second child come the change of season, and he doesn't wish to cancel the annual event. In the past there have been lawn games and evening festivities, but the fox hunt is the pinnacle of the gathering. The excitement brought on by the competition and its champion are too much to sacrifice. Henley has merely moved the date forward."

Caroline looked from one cousin to the next. She had no idea how she'd ever manage the ton if it wasn't for their knowledgeable support. Would Lindsey also leave London? Females weren't normally included in country fetes unless the lady of the house planned activities. Being in the family way, Lady Henley might forego the work and responsibility.

"Father said we're not to go, no matter we're being included. Mother has never gotten along well with Lady Henley, and he warned we're not to invite disharmony for the sake of a single gathering."

"For the sake of reputation," Dinah demurred in an irritable tone.

"I see." Caroline sat quietly a moment though all around her organized chaos ensued. Ladies rearranged their hairpins, unwrinkled their flounces, and pinched their cheeks vigorously in preparation of returning to the ballroom. Her own thoughts scattered and reorganized with the same pace. Would Lindsey attend Lord Henley's hunt, or would he remain in London where she'd have the chance to dance with him again? A nervous flutter accompanied the suggestion. Mayhap she should sneak off to the study at midnight. Was there an unspoken invitation in his tease, or did she search for any reason to believe he was interested in her otherwise?

"Lord Tiller is a crack shot and excellent horseman," Louisa mentioned in a singsong voice that had everyone twisted in her direction. "Last year, he caught the fox and won its tail, although it should be noted he wouldn't have met with success had Lindsey participated properly."

Caroline waited for her cousin to continue, at war with her desire to know and a reluctance to appear over-interested.

"Lindsey's animal is superior horseflesh and easily makes everyone else's mount appear as if it runs on three legs. He leads the pack every year, and yet I have it on good authority he intentionally moves aside and allows others to corner the fox and win. It's a wily maneuver if ever I heard. He leads the race and then allows another to gain the glory." Louisa took a well-needed pause. "Oh, Caroline, I cannot wait for you to see Lord Tiller atop his stallion. He cuts a handsome figure."

"So the Earl of Lindsey does attend." She drew a breath to solidify her disappointment.

"He's not one who should occupy your concern."

"Oh, no. Of course. It's just he's compelling in a maddening way." She strove for a casual tone.

"I do understand, although by compelling I'm apt to think you mean irresistibly handsome, which is a dangerous thought indeed." Louisa's slender brows dipped slightly, as if she drew on past experience.

A short silence followed as the ladies continued to survey the room.

"How long does the Henley party last?" Caroline bit her lower lip, hoping her continued interest wouldn't instigate unwanted questions.

"At least a week. At times two," Dinah supplied. "It all depends on how well the men get on with each other."

"I suppose we should return to the floor." Beatrice stood first. "I'm promised for the quadrille and it's already past eleven."

Louisa and Dinah joined their sister and together they began for the door.

"Are you coming, Caroline?" Beatrice glanced over her shoulder with the question.

"I need another minute," Caroline answered with a nod. "Go ahead and I'll see you shortly."

Chapter Eleven

It was ridiculous to loiter in the hallway near Lord Seton's study, and more foolish madness to hope Lady Caroline would find her way across the estate merely by his veiled suggestion earlier. For all he knew she danced the night away in some lucky gentleman's arms and hadn't given him a second thought since he'd stepped away earlier.

He had no explanation for his desire to spend more time with her. Perhaps it was the knowledge nothing would amount of their association. The lady was far too clever to become besotted by his attention and furthermore had proven the name on everyone's lips, her instant popularity and likeability sure to find her a match before season's end. It was what she desired, wasn't it?

This thought, more so than any other, drove him inside Seton's study and straight to the brandy decanter. He'd taken a taste only when he heard the door open and close, the lightest step an instigation to his change in mood.

"It would appear we are of like mind this evening." Caroline's voice reached for him across the dim room. "A role reversal of sorts, where I find you hidden away from the festivities instead of the other way around."

"Indeed." He replaced his glass on the sideboard. She looked hesitant, or did he read something in her expression that wasn't there? "The hour is late. Have you missed the evening's last dance?"

"I was promised a waltz, but my partner didn't show." She moved toward him with grace and elegance, though his thoughts shifted to a more sensual path. When she finally turned toward him fully, her delicious lips poised in a flirtatious smile, it was a swift punch to the gut. She embodied uncompromised beauty and at the same time possessed a regal elegance as fresh as the morning's first rays. He'd enjoyed dozens of females, more than that, if he spoke honestly, and yet for some unnamed and mysterious reason the woman before him evoked a sense of longing and desire so strong, it shook him to his soul.

That, in itself, was dangerous indeed.

"Had we music, I'd waltz with you here, no one the wiser." His eyes darted over her figure, swathed in silk to tease and tempt, hiding all her precious smooth skin and luscious curves.

"Silence is its own music, isn't it?"

Her astute intellect enchanted him as much as her heart-shaped face and perfectly formed lips. He stood before her now and bowed, extending his bare hand in her direction. Whatever game she played, he wished to participate.

"My lady, may I have this waltz?"

"I'd be delighted."

They said nothing at first. The impact of holding her in his embrace rendered him speechless for several exhales in succession. Her fragrance tempted him to lean in close and taste, feel, explore her silky skin. Orchids. Mayhap it wasn't a perfume at all, and her skin naturally carried the lovely scent.

Was this a seductive manipulation not unlike the ploys of rapacious mamas seeking to snare the biggest prize for their marriage-minded daughter? He didn't believe her so coy or devious. Without doubt, he would be fine at the outcome, his life already splintered into multiple directions, but would she think something of their association that would never come to pass?

She wanted a future he could not give.

Still, Mills was wrong for her. Mills was an unrepentant rakehell who'd made use of too many women to list. No sooner had the thought formed than Lindsey realized he spoke more of himself than his friend.

"Why are you here?" His voice was nothing more than a rasp in their silence.

Her brow winged up with the question. "Why are you?"

He almost laughed at her audacious parry.

Her cheeks flushed a becoming shade, and he moved closer still.

"I've tired of the crowds and conversation. I'm not usually in attendance at society's more formal gatherings." His voice softened, though he was reminded of why he was suddenly forced to skulk around old estates and barter for information. He wouldn't allow his father to intrude on this moment. "And what is your reason?"

* * * *

Caroline begged her heart to calm. She'd foolishly wished Lindsey would find her in the study, and while that wish may have turned itself inside out, they were still here together, and that was all that mattered. "I hoped you would be here."

A sensual gleam lit his dark eyes before it extinguished just as quickly. "You're far too honest for your own good. Other gentlemen will take advantage of that fine quality."

Now a hard glint entered his stare, as if the suggestion alone spurred him to anger.

"Advice from a renowned rakehell and scoundrel?" she teased.

He chuckled, caught in his own game, and the sinfully rich sound echoed through her though their bodies barely touched. They stood motionless within the dance frame, but she wouldn't complain. The pressure of his hand at her waist moved her closer the smallest degree. The warmth that seeped through his palm caused her to wish they touched skin to skin, without barriers between them.

"One with a bit of sense."

"I will take your warning under advisement then. You know more of London society than I."

"Ah, that is true. You're newly arrived but fast becoming acquainted."

"My father wished to leave Italy with haste. It suited my mother and I'm of an age..."

He didn't press her to finish. "A measure of years instead of depth of experience is a careless way to view life."

She considered his comment. It was peculiar and quite telling, if nothing else. "But optimism is the greatest strength." She continued with her raillery.

He seemed to ponder his answer thoughtfully. "Every strength can be a weakness, given the right conditions. When you discover this to be true, you turn that weakness into a strength so it doesn't destroy you, scar you indelibly, or cause you regret."

She accepted his shrewd answer as the confession it was, a brief peek into his soul. And then she continued, anxious to keep their conversation light. "I suspect you possess a wealth of insight," Caroline countered. "Won't you share a little?"

"It's true I've lingered near the edge of the ballroom floor, an observer by choice, out of range of motivated mothers and their flighty giggling daughters."

"Might I remind you I witnessed the scene in Lord Albertson's study. I have an idea where you *linger* and what range you occupy."

"Saucy minx." He looked at her directly. "You're far too clever for your own good."

She was unsure if his remark was complimentary. "You believed I'd take one glance at your infamous smile and melt into a puddle at your feet?" She held his stare without blinking. "You're too arrogant by half."

"You like me anyway."

She had no idea how to answer that.

"I could offer you a few scraps of information, if you desire. If nothing else, I could advise you on which gentlemen to avoid."

Her mother's frequent advice was an irritant, most especially as it consistently contradicted Caroline's thoughts and feelings. It would be curious to hear what Lindsey added to the subject.

"An expert on eligible bachelors then, are you?" she added, enjoying the moment.

"Not at all." He chuckled and the vibration of his rich voice echoed through her. "Though I'm most knowledgeable in the functioning of the male mind."

"I see." She ventured a smile. "You would tell me with whom to converse and what to say?"

"I wouldn't dare." He shook his head slightly. "You need no assistance in that area. You're more eloquent than you believe."

"Thank you." It wasn't just the compliment he offered, but his kind regard for her thoughts and judgment, so unlike her mother's reminders to remain quiet and agreeable, to mute her own ideas. "My mother believes I should suppress any wayward feminine longings, take a long walk or concentrate on improving my embroidery to diffuse the carnal needs that often plague men but have no place in the embodiment of a refined lady."

"I disagree, though no insult is intended to your mother." His gaze held her entranced. "Allow your inner desires freedom, Caroline. Women are no different from men when it comes to pleasure. They're only more delicate and graceful in the manner in which they express it."

Their discussion paused, and as they stood in each other's arms all levity evaporated, the air between them fraught with suggestion and tension. Neither of them spoke again, and the silence slowly transformed to intimacy, as if their souls had waited patiently through the conversation and now demanded attention.

She hoped he would kiss her again, wanted it more than her next breath. Some invisible force bound them together. Some unexplainable yearning from her heart called to his. Was she fooling herself? Lost to a romantic daydream? Or did he feel it too?

Her body was quick to recall the stroke of his tongue against hers. She'd never been kissed that way before, and it caused too many feelings inside her to sort and label. It was forbidden, and yet breathtakingly intimate, to be joined so closely, tasting each other.

Her pulse leapt faster with the lingering remembrance, and when he canted his head slightly she allowed her eyes to fall closed, already lost to the memory of his kiss and all too anxious to experience it again.

Every muscle within her seemed poised. A tight coil of anticipation began in her stomach, lower, in her sex, where she shamelessly grew wet and anxious. She slid into his embrace, their waltz abandoned, their kiss begun.

The first press of his mouth sent through her a heated jolt of sensitivity so strong she gasped from the shock. He grinned against her lips, that famous half-smile that was alleged to cause women to swoon. The rumor proved true after all.

He ran his fingers across her cheek, angled her face to hold her firm, possessing her with the slightest touch. She tensed, too caught up in the heat that flooded her veins, the swirl of sensation and anticipation that urged her to return his passionate entreaty and encourage his attention.

He wrapped his arm around her back and brought her flush against him while he deepened their kiss, his tongue at play along her lips. She opened to him with no hesitation.

He tasted like cinnamon and brandy, addictive and forbidden, but oh so alluring one couldn't help but chase the heady temptation despite knowing it would certainly lead to danger. Each stroke of his tongue, wet hot velvet, sent sensation spiking through her to settle deep in her core. Her breasts tingled, the tips sensitive and aching where they were flattened against his hard chest. She clenched her thighs beneath layers and layers of silk, yet no matter how tightly she tensed, her body disobeyed. She became impatient with yearning. Yet it was only a kiss. One kiss. His kiss.

As if he sensed her struggle or experienced the same, he broke his hold, whispering kisses and featherlight touches across her cheek and against her ear.

"Caroline." He spoke her name, his voice brimmed with wickedness, nothing more than a growl against her ear.

She committed the sound to memory. With no time to answer and no mind to do so, she swallowed, her throat dry and body throbbing while he continued his exploration. She was lost to the exquisite pleasure he offered.

He kissed beneath her ear where the skin was tender and sensitive, the hot tip of his tongue quick to lave over each inch afterward. The shadow of whiskers she'd admired on his jaw now rubbed against her neck with intimate sensuality, her breathing stilted as she gripped his shoulders, unsure she could withstand another moment of his wicked assault. Her body pulsed in response to his attention, her every muscle held tight. What was this uncontrollable lust he evoked in her with nothing more than a kiss? Heat streaked through her as he nipped her collarbone, his breath hot against the same path.

Was she a fool, her body's reaction the sign of an unexperienced and sheltered lady? Or was this moment unique? Did he experience the same intense bond? He returned to their kiss, a lock of his hair brushed against her cheek as he straightened, and the look she saw in his eyes ignited a riot of desire within her. All intelligence abandoned her.

* * * *

More.

It was a litany in his brain demanding attention, but Lindsey forced himself to ignore it, the lady in his arms too innocent, far too precious. Unfortunately, it was replaced by a word much more lethal.

Mine.

Harnessing every ounce of resolve, he broke away, so shaken he swore his hands trembled. He drew a sharp inhale and worked to regain composure. How one of the season's delicate ingénues could disturb him to this level wasn't something he could begin to understand at the moment.

He slowly stepped away, somewhat assured when he recognized she appeared equally as disoriented as he.

"That shouldn't have happened." He cleared his throat, the words raspy at first. "Forgive me."

Her brilliant blue eyes searched his face. And then she licked her lips and he all but pulled her back into his arms.

"You have no need to apologize." Her brows dipped with the reassurance. "I came willingly into your embrace."

The basest part of him reacted to every word from her mouth, every syllable she spoke, anxious to distort and twist into clever innuendo. What would he have done had he not rallied the tiniest shred of conscience? His body still hummed with tension, every muscle strained, his breeches tight. He longed to draw her down to the chaise across the room and discover all the beauty she kept hidden under silk and lace. He hungered to taste her skin in one long caress that began at her mouth and finished at her ankles.

"God help me."

"Lindsey?"

He jerked his head up and found concern in her eyes. She'd never addressed him so informally.

"You shouldn't be here." He put another stride between them for no other reason than to keep his hands from reaching for her again. "I'm not good for you." This statement came easier for the truth found in it.

An unladylike snicker conveyed what she thought of his opinion, though only a moment ago he swore she was as shaken as he. How had she recovered so quickly?

"I can hardly agree with that, but surely I'm missed, most especially at this late hour." She moved toward the door and glanced partially over her shoulder only as she bid him good night.

Chapter Twelve

Caroline watched the landscape pass in a blur outside the carriage window as she traveled with her mother toward Bedfordshire. Her father had refused to join them. As it was, it proved no simple feat to accomplish the trip to the Henley country party. Caroline's family hadn't been invited, and once her mother learned her aunt had declined, the event was dismissed without discussion. After Caroline returned from Lord Seton's ball with Lindsey's kiss alive on her lips, she wished to attend for no other reason than to see the earl ride in the hunt, the tales of his masterful skill almost legendary and too, the temptation of another intimate interlude made her heart quiver.

With few resources at her disposal she'd written a note to her cousin Louisa, who had somehow managed to have an invitation delivered to Caroline's address. At least that's what Caroline assumed, considering the formal request arrived only two hours later. Still, her mother saw little sense in displacing the family for a week to journey to Bedfordshire, where they knew few guests. Caroline posed a firm argument that attending the exclusive affair would grant her a rare opportunity to converse with the choicest gentlemen in a more relaxed setting, without the avaricious competition found within a ballroom. Her mother was not convinced.

Adding to that difficulty, her father was adamant he had no wish to accept the invitation. He stated important matters needed his attention during the week, and therefore they'd all stay put in London. A heated discussion ensued. For the first time since she was a child, Caroline refused to capitulate and challenged her parents' decision. They were not swayed.

Worsening the situation, her father seemed especially rigid in his refusal. She had no idea why, as he wouldn't elaborate, but with no recourse she could hardly argue the point, when traveling to Bedfordshire and attending a country party for a week was asking more than it appeared.

Of late she'd noticed a recurring strain between her parents. She couldn't be certain and was never privy to their shared conversations, but she suspected the problem stemmed from financial concerns. Traveling abroad, maintaining an admirable lifestyle, and keeping everyone in silk stockings was an expensive endeavor. Not to mention the necessary bills from the modiste for her ballgowns and fripperies all accompanied by the promise of her generous dowry, were she fortunate enough to make a match this season.

Caroline never questioned the family income, but with a few overheard words and mild observation she'd begun to suspect her parents worried over their fiscal stability, and that in turn weighed heavily on her heart. Nevertheless, she yearned to see Lindsey again and reminded her parents Bedfordshire was less than a day's travel and wouldn't require the inconvenience or expense of a coaching inn.

The situation took an odd turn when an elaborate bouquet arrived from Lord Mills. His card expressed hope in crossing Caroline's path at the Henleys' country party. It was a stroke of luck her parents looked favorably upon the viscount's interest, and the matter was finally decided. In the end it was Lord Mills who granted her the chance to see Lindsey again, even though she hadn't encouraged Mills during their shared dance and knew him only as a friend of the earl's.

Now, having nearly reached their destination, the carriage slowed to a crawl. Beyond the window, Caroline noted the long line of traffic as it approached the Henleys' impressive property. Lush rolling lawns led to a wide gravel drive lined with ornamental boxwood hedges cut in graduating heights, as if to lure visitors to the front door. An elaborate arched entryway sprawled at the center, where two branches of limestone stairs extended in opposite directions, forcing approaching guests to choose sides.

Caroline imagined the grandeur to be discovered within the main house, as the exterior exceeded any expectation she'd formed during the ride. A bevy of servants met each equipage as it rolled to a stop, footmen at the ready to collect reins, lead carriages, or direct in the distribution of luggage, while housemaids of every level kept to the marble stairs, anxious to provide service once the need was required.

Glancing to the opposite bench, she noticed her mother appeared equally entranced, though their progress had slowed to a stop. How she wished her father had accompanied them for no other reason than to ensure her mother's enjoyment. Would her mother wish to accompany her everywhere throughout the day? A beat of guilt rose up in silent admonishment. Since when did she behave so selfishly? *Never.* Yet she couldn't stop thinking about Lindsey and the thrill of watching him command his magnificent horse in the fox hunt.

"I've never seen Father so adamant about refusing a social event." She hoped her mother didn't think the worst for her insistence.

"Nor I." Her mother glanced across the interior with a slight smile. "But you shouldn't let it bother you now that we're here. The estate looks lovely, and how splendid it will be for you to enjoy the festivities, most especially if it allows you the chance to meet interesting gentlemen."

A jolt of anticipation shot through her at the thought of seeing Lindsey again.

"I'm excited." Her tone gave away everything her words did not.

"As you should be." Her mother's expression showed understanding, though a hint of sadness clouded her eyes. "Just promise me you won't do anything foolish. You won't ride—"

"I'm here to watch the hunt, not participate." A swift objection escaped before she shook her head to emphasize her mother shouldn't worry. The carriage grew quiet again, and she envisioned Lindsey atop his magnificent stallion, impeccably dressed in his perfectly tailored coat, as handsome as the devil himself.

She loved horses. Adored them, actually. They were such majestic animals with noble bearings. They reminded her of fairy tales. But she hadn't ridden since the accident, and she missed it terribly. Naturally she understood her mother's concern, and respected her parents' wishes, but deep down she didn't want to be coddled. If her parents knew she'd often shunned convention, hiked up her skirts, and secretly ridden astride when she was alone in Lincolnshire, they'd both be disappointed.

"Genteel ladies don't participate in sport," her mother continued, her tone pensive. "And while you're grown now, as your mother I still worry. We almost lost you, our only child, and I couldn't survive if another accident occurred."

"There'll be no accidents." Caroline adopted a tone of calm reassurance and reached for her mother's hand to nestle between her own. "I know we never speak of it, but it doesn't mean I don't remember the fright or the pain. I would never do anything to relive that experience, no matter it was an incident no one could predict or prevent."

"You can prevent it by never riding a horse again," her mother chided, her tone filled with telling emotion.

"That's ridiculous. Men and women ride without difficulty every day." Caroline withdrew, relinquishing the hold on her mother's hand. "I'm not scared of horses or riding, and neither should you be."

An uncomfortable silence stretched between them, perhaps each of them lost in their own considerations. Caroline closed her eyes with a hard blink to ward off the sorrow that took residence in the depths of her heart. Even though years had passed, she carried the result of her riding accident with her always.

Being thrown from the saddle when her horse startled might have caused death, broken bones, or permanent disability. Instead she'd suffered internal damage that caused her to bleed to such extent her mother had fainted at the scene. Thank heavens the two grooms who'd accompanied them had the good sense to summon help and have Caroline returned to the house as quickly as possible. Dr. Fuller, the family physician, had examined her within an hour, and while she was lightheaded from blood loss and a bruising contusion he labeled a concussion, she suffered no other pain.

That was, until the irregular bleeding began. After the accident she'd had her flux for almost a month without stop. Her mother worried and hovered at Caroline's bedside, anxious for her daughter to return to normal. The physician supplied few answers, at times assuring she would reclaim a regular cycle, and at others expressing concern that the absence of a monthly term would prove the accident had rendered her barren. With each day that passed, deeper concerns etched into her mother's face, while the unasked questions on her lips proved unbearable.

At last, when the bleeding stopped, Caroline was relieved to unburden her mother and begin to live life again as normally as possible. Except she never experienced her monthly courses from that day forward. No one, not even her maid, knew of this. Ashamed, nervous, and petrified she would never be able to bear children, Caroline told not a soul. Her maid believed Caroline kept these matters private since the accident, and therefore never asked questions. Caroline allowed her maid to believe that lie, unwilling to subject herself to the chance her mother discovered the truth. Surely her mother suspected Caroline suffered damage, but to what extent remained unknown, and Caroline preferred it that way, too horrified to discuss it. Yet at times, Caroline swore she could see the knowledge in her mother's eyes.

Like at this moment, when the reality she needed to find a husband who would overlook her defect crowded into the interior of the carriage and took a seat on the bench beside her.

She clenched her eyes closed and reopened them, forcing the memories back down into the dark recesses of her soul, unwilling to allow remembrance to dampen her enjoyment of the Henley party. Then she brought a smile to her lips, knowing she'd need to find a gentleman who would consider marriage to a woman who could never grow a family.

In an unfortunate habit that grated but could hardly be dismissed, her mother initiated conversation again and proved she'd considered similar possibilities as she offered unsolicited advice.

"You shouldn't rule out an older gentleman for your choice of husband, Caroline. Someone who isn't interested in physical relations. A man who perhaps already has a family and only wishes for companionship in his later years. You needn't be called upon to produce an heir—"

"Mother!" Caroline's outburst sounded harsh in the quiet of their carriage. "Just because my future may be uncertain doesn't mean I don't wish for compatibility and enjoyment in the bedroom."

Her mother's expression reflected a mixture of disapproval and surprise. "Hush. If anyone heard you mention enjoying personal marital duties you'd be ruined. Young ladies don't speak of such things."

Apparently older women don't either.

Still, nothing, not her mother's modest thinking and overprotectiveness, society's pressure, or Lindsey's scandalous reputation, would change her mind. Whenever she was in the earl's company, she experienced an undeniable and intense connection, as if he called to every level of her being. She turned her secretive smile toward the window. If nothing else, she would enjoy his attention before settling on an uncertain future.

* * * *

"I'm not sure how you've managed to drag me out here when I originally had no intention of attending." Mills applied chalk to the tip of his wooden cue at the billiards table in Henley's study.

"I sought your advisement." Lindsey stared at the green felt, unwilling to allow his friend to detect the dual purpose in his eyes. "Isn't my company worth the day's travel?"

"Are you in search of honesty with that question?" Mills placed his cue against the cushion and measured his shot. With a jerk of his arm he slid the stick forward and sent the white ball gliding across the table to connect with the red one where it waited. "In truth, I had a greater interest that conveniently aligned with your travel, so why not accomplish both objectives simultaneously? It took little doing for me to send a bouquet."

Lindsey watched his friend closely, unclear to what Mills referred. Mills had resisted at first, and then agreed to Henley's invitation, so something important must have prompted his change of decision. "Thinking to best Infinity in the hunt? I'm open to a wager. I'm not paupered yet." He murmured the last bit to ward off a discussion of his finances, then gauged his next shot and successfully connected.

"I'm not foolish enough to race against your horse. I admire his bloodstock and wish you would consider my generous offer to have him stud within my stables. Nevertheless, when it comes to the hunt, you valiantly allow another to the spoils every year." Mills laid down his cue and made for the sideboard, where an assortment of liquor waited patiently.

"I see no honor in killing something vulnerable. You dislike my horse because he can run forever?"

"He may go on as his name states, but he's prime horseflesh, with a master who has never known limits."

Lindsey chuckled. "I thought this trip contained a singular purpose, *my* purpose." He couldn't ignore he'd left Caroline in London so he could search for a bloody painting. While he needed to find the Decima, he'd somehow cast himself in the role of her protector, and he disliked the idea of the lady milling about society beyond his watchful vigilance. He'd noticed how the young bucks eyed her with interest. Any unattached gentleman with an ounce worth of sense would pay call and further his suit, and that didn't sit well. Worse, a cad with empty pockets might somehow convince Caroline he was worthy when all the bastard sought was her handsome dowry. He'd hate for her to have regrets. To that end, she needed him to advise her if the situation warranted intervention, and how could he do that if he was rusticating in Bedfordshire, a full day's ride away?

At least, this was the lie he used to mollify his impatience.

"Brandy or port?"

The clink of crystal brought his attention to the present. "Brandy." If the Decima matter wasn't resolved by the week's end, he'd need the entire decanter.

"I laid the bait. I've only to wait now and see if my efforts are fruitful." Mills continued his explanation as he came forward with their drinks.

Lindsey didn't dig deeper. He had no desire to involve himself in his friend's matters unless called upon, his mind occupied with his search and expedient return to London. "What about determining the location of the painting?"

"Dependable information has proven elusive." Mills took a swallow from his glass. "Though I've learned there's a Mr. Powell who has a special interest in the Fates. He's nosed about the shadows left in the wake of my inquiries. I don't know the man, nor have I had the opportunity to meet him, but it's said he enjoys vingt-et-un as much as his liquor. If we don't find him this afternoon, I have no doubt he'll show in the cardroom later this evening." Mills dropped into a worn leather chair with careless ease.

"Then so shall we."

"There was a time when I knew every face at White's, but those days are long past."

"Rubbish." Lindsey huffed a breath of annoyance. "I'm not so old, and you're half a year younger."

"More the reason for me to settle my future."

Lindsey wasn't accustomed to Mills having such intentional goals, and he found the conversation unsettling. And too he remembered the attention his friend had paid Caroline when introduced in London, the sod's desire to dance with her and the not-so-subtle way Mills had watched Caroline at Hyde Park. A lick of temper caused Lindsey to clench his teeth, lest he say something that revealed too much.

Mills continued, as if Lindsey's silence signified little. "There's no denying you have excellent taste."

"Have we returned to discussing my stallion?"

"Actually, no."

Replacing his cue against the table, Lindsey abandoned the game and moved to stand near the hearth. "Then the painting?" It was common knowledge the collection of oils was worth a fortune. The fact his father had kept ownership silent for over a decade was impressive, though it didn't matter who claimed them if Lindsey couldn't locate the remaining two pieces and once again secure fiscal stability. If a private collector managed to obtain the paintings, both would become impossible to find, lost to him forever.

"Wrong again." Mills chuckled. "If I'm forced to be here with you instead of at some Mayfair gathering flirting with a fetching female, I thought to combine my interests."

"So you're actively seeking a wife? You weren't jesting earlier?" It was the Devil's good fortune Caroline was left behind in London.

"I'm curious as to why you aren't more about heir getting."

Lindsey muttered a foul curse. Would his father's reprehensible interference give him no peace? "The plague of any aristocratic rakehell."

"It doesn't signify you're opposed to the idea. Why not marry a nondescript willing female who will melt at the sight of your dashing smile—"

"You think my smile dashing?"

"Get the task done, produce an heir, and deposit your wife in the countryside with a large allowance. It's a perfectly acceptable practice, and you would be returned to your philandering ways within a year. Less, if you abandon your morals."

"Tempting offer." *Despicable, really.* Shameless. One he would never consider even though he had a reputation to uphold. Mills didn't need to know the truth of it, though. That his father held him by the throat. That recently he'd come to wonder if he wouldn't mind going to bed each night with a loving woman beside him. If nothing, Lindsey was wickedly loyal. At the moment his loyalty was reserved for himself, but if he ever took a wife, he would honor and cherish her until his last breath. "I have no interest in being tied down."

"That's not what I heard from Widow Gillet last season."

"Well, there was that." Lindsey wrestled with his laughter before he refilled their glasses and settled on a seat. "I have broken countless hearts, most times with the worst form. I can't imagine a female who would have me and volunteer for the inevitable disappointment she would discover in my character. Notwithstanding her father would have to approve of the match in the first place."

"You exaggerate to serve your purpose. Many a reputed rakehell has come to heel and reform."

"Perhaps." Though Lindsey had no desire to change his habits. Instead of voicing this, he smiled, a roguish grin that contained anything but sincerity. Still, conversation of no consequence would serve his purpose, their discussion better focused on the most important subject. If Powell sought the Decima, there was information to be had, and at the moment, any lead had potential, as he had no other course. He needed to find the man as soon as possible, learn what he was about, and return to London. He wouldn't label the cause of his burning desire, but the sooner the task was completed and he was on the road, the easier he could breathe.

Chapter Thirteen

Caroline and her mother followed two young maids wearing lace caps into a grand foyer graced by slender chinoiserie vases brimming with elegant hothouse flowers. An expansive circular staircase wound toward the ceiling, and when they reached the top the maids led them down the corridor to the left. Dark mahogany doors marked the hall at measured intervals, the many rooms made ready for the influx of travel-weary guests in need of respite.

Caroline was shown to a bedchamber three doors away from her mother's. She discovered the interior to be spacious and welcoming, decorated in delicate yellows and mossy greens that conjured a peaceful feeling of being outdoors. The light scent of lemon and beeswax strengthened the illusion. A bank of diamond paned windows on the far wall offered a view of the elaborate estate gardens below, their abundant colors at full blossom. Through the glass she noted a wide stone wall jutted forward in perpendicular position to the house, its eastern side covered with ambitious flowering vines, their blooms upturned in thirst of the sun.

When her eyes met the horizon, her brows rose in surprise. In the far field, several gentlemen were atop their mounts while ladies stood in pockets of conversation and meandered the walkways in pairs, the scene a blur of color and activity. It was close to impossible to discern anyone's identity from this distance, but she tried nonetheless. Her mother didn't expect her company until the evening meal. Perhaps a walk in the garden would prove refreshing after the confining travel of the carriage. She went to the bellpull and rang for a maid. She needed a bath and change of clothes before she ventured out. She only hoped she could hurry fast enough not to miss the opportunity Fate placed in her path.

Little more than an hour later Caroline emerged from her rooms, her hair in a damp coronet, the best her maid could arrange considering the imposing duress of Caroline's impatience. When she'd glanced out the window before leaving her rooms, the congregation of guests on the back lawn had thinned considerably. She told herself this would make locating Lindsey all the easier, as their bodies communicated on some unspoken level the same way his presence called to her in a crowded ballroom.

She'd decided on one of her new day gowns, a flattering design in butter-yellow silk that complemented the color of her eyes. Hope inched higher. Too high for her own good. The young maid who'd arranged her hair had chattered out a long list of activities planned by Lady Henley, but Caroline couldn't remember a scrap of the schedule now.

She followed the staircase to the ground floor and farther toward the rear of the estate. Every room, corridor, and corner hummed with activity. Servants went about their tasks and guests greeted each other with jovial camaraderie.

Caroline had nearly reached the French doors leading to the gardens when her path was intersected by a tall woman who exited a nearby room.

"Oh, I beg your pardon." Caroline caught herself just short of a collision, doubly pleased she'd been able to stop. The lady glowed with happiness, her condition hardly disguised by her flowing gown. Caroline's suspicion the ebullient lady was Lady Henley, the hostess, was confirmed not a heartbeat later.

"Oh, dear, excuse me." No matter the near mishap, the smile never left the lady's face. "I am Lady Henley, and you are?"

"Very sorry. Excuse me. I almost bumped into you in my hurry." After a quick breath, Caroline continued. "Thank you for your gracious invitation. My mother and I are thrilled to be here at your gathering."

At Lady Henley's blank stare Caroline realized among the throng of beaus and beauties, her hostess had no idea who she was. "I'm Lady Caroline Nicholson. I arrived earlier this afternoon, and my mother, Lady Derby, accompanied me."

"Yes, of course." Lady Henley nodded happily. "A relation to the Notley family's fine collection of females. Someday I will convince your aunt to attend my husband's annual event. Mayhap when the baby arrives." She placed her hand over her stomach in a protective gesture, and Caroline's heart squeezed for all the wrong reasons.

Refusing to acknowledge the unpleasant reaction, Caroline forced a pleasant expression and indicated the forward hall which led toward the rear of the house. "I was about to take some air and walk in the gardens. Would you like to join me?"

"No, thank you. I find I tire easily these days." Lady Henley turned as if to leave immediately. "I think I'll nap before dinner, but do enjoy yourself. If you follow the path to the east along the stone wall, you'll discover the Canna lilies have reached full bloom. They're a sight that shouldn't be missed. And, Caroline, I'll arrange for you to sit beside me tonight at dinner. That way we can become better acquainted and share the conversation I'm to miss right now."

"I'd like that. Thank you." Caroline nodded before she slipped down the hall and out the back doors onto the slated path. The scuff of her slippers was soon lost to the ambient noise of conversation and jocularity. Eager in her pursuit, she followed the oval-shaped stepping-stones atop the gravel path toward the gardens and beyond. It was shameless, really, to purposefully place herself in a position where she might meet the Earl of Lindsey. But no matter the sound admonishment her conscience waged, her heart and curiosity won out. She didn't pause.

Rushing now, she hardly glanced at the glorious blooms Lady Henley had suggested she admire, passing them in a blur of orange and green fueled by irrational, misplaced hope. Lindsey would be surprised to see her. But would he be pleased? She hoped so.

She walked farther down the path, parallel with the waist-high wall that curved to the left and beyond her line of sight, keeping on until the rumble of argumentative voices slowed her progress. Rounding the corner, she saw three gentlemen cast in shadow at the path's end adjacent to a long hedgerow of Guelder-rose. She immediately identified Lindsey. The late afternoon light limned his profile in gold against the dark green leaves.

Lord, he was a striking man.

Lord, he was angry.

Her breath caught as he wrapped his fist in another man's cravat, and with a fast reversal hauled him backward to the stone wall. What could this be about? Alerted by her approach, Lord Mills stepped from the shadows and strode to stand beside her, several yards from Lindsey's confrontation.

"Is something amiss?" She kept her voice low and her eyes fixed on the unfolding scene before her.

"Nothing of which you should have a care." Mills bowed slightly in greeting, a sly smile on his lips. "Men and their arguments, too often made a fool over proprietary feelings brought on by a fetching female."

"Over a woman?" She hardly kept the surprise from her voice.

"I don't mean to sound indelicate," Mills continued, undeterred by her dubious tone. "Suffice to say the gentleman with the wrinkled cravat is interested in a woman Lindsey wants for his own."

"I see."

This news unsettled her. Was Lindsey warning the other gentleman away from a lady of whom he held in esteem? Or was the man a jealous husband who sought to caution Lindsey his current dalliance needed to come to an end? No matter the choice, an ugly emotion churned in her stomach and she forced her eyes away, only to bring them back again as she sought to make sense of the scene. Lord Mills' expression offered nothing in way of understanding, no more than a mixture of satisfaction and concern.

"How well do you know the earl?" she pressed, though she really shouldn't, her mother's redundant advice ringing in her ears.

"Being new to the set, I assume you've learned he's an unrepentant scoundrel."

"Is that why you're such good friends?" She strove to lighten the mood and was rewarded with Mills' laughter. "Truly, I only ask out of curiosity."

"I understand." He nodded his agreement. "But he'll never offer what you want."

"What I want?" She could feel her brows rise high in reaction. Lord Mills' exacting reply went straight to the point.

"What any genteel lady wishes for her future. A home, stability. Children."

Each word struck a different chord in her heart. She wanted a home of her own and the domestic predictability it promised, but of children, she could only wish and dream. Most certainly, any titled gentleman would intend for his wife to bear an heir, perhaps several to secure the lineage. This latter consideration caused her spirits to plummet further.

* * * *

"Tell me what you know about the Decima and we can cease this unpleasant discussion." Lindsey twisted Quinn Powell's neckcloth tighter, but the man's expression remained indifferent.

He'd only just met Mr. Powell through Mills' instigation and the man's nonchalant attitude irritated, never mind there was something unsettling in his demeanor. Powell's appearance held striking similarities to someone Lindsey would rather not consider at the moment, the man at the core of his unrest.

"I have nothing to share, but if I did I would reserve that knowledge for my benefit only." Powell's tone went unchanged, though his complexion reddened.

"I can beat information out of you here or later, in the cardroom. At least if I gamble, I wouldn't have to work as hard." Lindsey thrust Powell away and turned, belatedly aware Caroline stood across the way. He almost doubted his vision. What was she doing here? He'd inquired if she'd accepted the Henley invitation and learned her family had declined.

In that moment's hesitation Powell slunk away as quietly as a snake sheds its skin, dismissed to the periphery. Lindsey would find the man later and extract the information he desired. Now his attention divided, and his curiosity won out. How much had Caroline witnessed, and what the devil was Mills sharing with her? The viscount appeared far too comfortable at her elbow.

"Lady Nicholson." Lindsey nodded his head in greeting. He reached where they stood in three strides. "I wasn't aware you'd accepted Lord and Lady Henley's invitation. Nevertheless, it is a pleasure. Have you traveled with your family?" He struggled to regain a modicum of decorum, his earlier mood, one of distraction and restlessness, dismissed.

"Mother only, and of course our maids." Caroline offered him a strained smile. "Father refused to leave the city."

He didn't know what to make of that.

"Have I interrupted?" Her eyes flashed with intelligence.

The little busybody.

"Nothing of which you should waste a moment's concern," Mills interjected. The tone of his voice caused Lindsey to take notice.

"Are you out here alone?" Lindsey disliked how often he'd discovered Lady Caroline unchaperoned, and yet he'd taken advantage of that very predicament and enjoyed her sole attention whenever they'd spoken directly without the nuisance of another's company. "Does your maid follow?"

"I left her abovestairs. No doubt she's fatigued from the day's travel," Caroline supplied quickly.

Lindsey tamped down his urge to smile. She'd purposely eluded her maid and come out to the gardens alone. Why?

"Would you like to walk? I'd wager all those hours confined to the carriage have caused you a share of restlessness. I've heard the variety of flora maintained here is extraordinary." Mills crooked his elbow in Caroline's direction and Lindsey's irritation grew.

He noted how her consideration darted from him to Mills and back again. Was she asking his permission or wondering if he would accompany them? Were all these questions that swamped his brain a result of a foolish infatuation? This was unknown territory. He was too accustomed to getting what he wanted without effort. He needed a drink and a thorough night of debauchery to cleanse his attitude.

"There's nothing proper about an unchaperoned lady traipsing along the garden path with the likes of you, Mills." He hadn't meant for the words to sound so gruff.

"As if you're the better choice. That would be asking the fox to protect the lamb, wouldn't you agree?" Mills let out a brief chuckle. "We'll join Lord Frampton and the ladies up ahead." He indicated a gathering of six people several strides from where they conversed. "If we stay near the rear of their group, we'll still have the luxury of conversation without appearing unseemly."

"That would be a perfect compromise."

Lindsey slid his eyes to Caroline, her use of the latter word curious. What had she hoped to accomplish when she'd rounded the bend? Did she look for him specifically?

He moved his gaze to where they intended to venture and then back again to watch Caroline loop her arm through Mills' extended elbow. He didn't like it.

They advanced down the gravel pathway to join the others, though they lingered behind Frampton's congregation, sufficiently near enough to be considered above reproach but likewise out of earshot.

Being three persons on a two-person path, he lagged a stride behind. Better to take a moment to reconsider his immediate reply to anything Mills uttered and too, he didn't mind the view of Caroline's tempting bottom outlined by the gentle slope of her skirts. Today she wore his favorite color, which happened to be whatever color she chose to wear.

Mills' voice interrupted his musing.

"The country air has brought a pink hue to your skin, Lady Nicholson. It becomes you."

Lindsey kicked a rock with the toe of his boot. It was an innocuous compliment, and he wouldn't bother remarking on it.

"Thank you, Lord Mills. For the kind words and lovely flowers as well." She dashed a half glance over her shoulder.

He met her eyes with intent. She did have remarkable eyes, their depths full of wondrous mischief. Late afternoon sunlight illuminated her face and he detected a spark of invitation in her expression. Or was that wishful thinking on his part?

"Have you attended a hunt of this grand nature before?" Mills canted his head, as if genuinely interested in the lady's reply. Perhaps he was. Perhaps this was a perfunctory conversation before Mills began his wooing in earnest. Lindsey kicked another rock. A larger one. It skittered forward and just missed the heel of Mills' left boot.

"I understand it to be a spectacular event, although I consider it brutal in nature." She stopped walking, her body turned so she could include both men in her reply, though it was clearly meant for Lindsey. "My cousins have remarked upon your masterful horsemanship and how the quality of your stallion prevents anyone else from having a fair go-around at the race. Is that true, my lord?"

Lindsey had stopped walking when she'd paused on the path, so he took an extra stride to close the space between them. There was a subtle bite in the air that indeed tinged her cheeks to a soft rose, and he wondered at the softness of her skin. He wasn't looking for a May-December arrangement. He wasn't in the market for a wife. And yet whenever he so much as looked at Caroline, his carefully constructed plans for the future may as well have never existed.

* * * *

Caroline kept her eyes on Lord Mills, as he'd turned to begin yet another conversation, but her body was most aware of Lindsey, a scant stride away and looking more handsome than the last time she'd seen him. Perhaps she'd never become accustomed to the manner in which he affected her. A tangle of anticipation and expectation wove tight between her ribs, down lower to swirl in her belly.

Why must he appear so charming? He was a man at ease in his own bearings, able to adapt to any situation, whether high society function or rustic pastoral gathering. Clearly, he didn't give a fig about the ton's perception, and in that earned their enchanted regard. There was no way for her to ignore his handsomeness, the straight strong angle of his jaw, or his penetrating stare made all the more remarkable by a long sweep of lashes, black as soot, or mayhap his soul. She couldn't ignore a distinct antagonistic undercurrent existed when she'd watched him question the stranger. And it remained while he stood with Mills.

"I confess my opinion of the hunt is aligned with yours. In my mind, it seems a grisly sport where the fox is at the greatest disadvantage. Where's the glory in an achievement such as that? To that end, I would never go so far as to sabotage the competition; I merely allow my horse the run and then capitulate. There's no joy in killing such a clever animal."

Lindsey's reply was aimed directly at Mills, though he'd answered her question. Mills seemed unbothered by the remark.

"I've learned you're contemplating marriage this season, Lady Nicholson."

She inhaled deeply to restore her equilibrium and force her thoughts toward Mills' question. "Have you now?" She glanced at Lindsey, and he met her gaze with promptitude. Did he await her answer in kind? "Is this what gentlemen discuss when away from the city? I assumed your conversation would focus on finances or livestock."

"It is only because I believe we share this in common." Mills canted his head. "I've also begun to think of the future with serious intent."

"It's no secret I've marriage on my mind."

Behind her, Lindsey grunted. Or was it a growl? The sound didn't matter, the tone conveyed his opinion effectively. But then he spoke up with deviltry in his eyes.

"Don't settle for Mills. You have a wide selection of prime aristocracy on display this week."

The three of them stopped walking as Lindsey continued, and she dropped her hand from her escort. Mills seemed anxious to speak, though he didn't interrupt despite being insulted.

"*Pro et contra.*" Lindsey's mouth twisted into that smile famed to knock women out of their slippers...even if he spoke Latin. "Consider the pros and cons. Debate which candidate has the most to offer you."

"That sounds rather calculated." And not unlike her mother's relentless plotting for her to find a suitable match. Her mother's advice forever suffocated Caroline's spirit, and seemed to imply a woman's most important goal should be to make her husband feel exalted and superior. She frowned, her brow pleated with dissatisfaction. "I'd rather choose my husband by the bidding of my heart." She moved her attention from one man to the other. Mills appeared nonplussed, but Lindsey's eyes widened the slightest before his lids lowered in lazy approval.

The silence stretched.

"Let us continue after the others." Mills extended his arm again.

"Indeed." Lindsey murmured from behind. "Let us continue."

Chapter Fourteen

Dinner proved interesting. Caroline was genuinely surprised and pleased to discover Lady Henley had altered the arrangement so she and Caroline sat beside each other. It was a gesture of acceptance and honor. Caroline felt better for it, her equilibrium still off kilter after the odd collection of events in the garden. There was the scene between Lindsey and the dark stranger, Mills' intimation the confrontation centered around the earl desiring a particular female, the honest bid by Lord Mills to court her, and Lindsey's strange, sometimes surly, participation in their conversation. It was a blessing she'd only just arrived and had at least a week to sort out these incongruent occurrences.

The Henleys' dining room was nothing short of palatial. An enormous table of black walnut monopolized the center with its generous width. Atop the damask linen, fine white plates gleamed, their reflective nature announcing they were likely the new and exceedingly expensive bone china from Staffordshire, an uncommon sight here in the countryside. A cacophony of lively chatter intermingled with the chime of silver. Perhaps she'd misjudged the degree of formality with this gathering.

Mother was seated mid-table, with a collection of other women nearer her age. Caroline appreciated the separation, as it would offer her more freedom in conversation. At the moment, she hadn't sighted Lindsey but hardly half the seats were filled, as the dinner bell had only just rung.

"Lady Caroline."

Lady Henley greeted her with a wide smile, and Caroline immediately relaxed. "Lady Henley, you look lovely."

And her hostess truly did. While earlier in the day Lady Henley appeared fatigued, this evening she glowed in a gown of auburn silk with delicate floral adornments. Her hair was arranged away from her face, and anyone could see the lady was overjoyed with anticipation for the upcoming birth of her child.

Caroline drew a long inhale, at odds with sincere happiness for her new friend and an unresolved longing that twisted her heart into knots. It was everything she could do not to lay a hand over her own abdomen.

"Thank you." Lady Henley indicated their places, and they waited while a footman rushed to pull each chair from the table. "I've found a late afternoon nap does wonders to restore my energy levels." She plucked a piece of crusty bread from a nearby silver tray at the center of the arrangement. "That, and a fair bit of indulgence."

Dinner commenced with less fanfare than the atmosphere demanded, and Caroline found quick conversation with Lady Henley beside her.

"Please, call me Teresa." Lady Henley touched a hand to Caroline's sleeve. "I believe we were meant to become friends."

"Thank you." Caroline returned a smile. "In London my three cousins have made a concerted effort to include me in all societal affairs and current events, but aside from a few brief associations, I haven't had the opportunity to cultivate a friendship beyond familial bonds."

"Then let me be the first of many ladies who will share the pleasure of your lovely company."

Their conversation paused as they accepted the first course, a steaming bowl of White soup, the aroma of ground almond, veal stock, and cream a delight to her appetite.

"I assume you have marriage on your mind."

Lady Teresa's next words were more statement than question, and Caroline met her gaze with a nod.

"Matchmaking has never been a preoccupation of mine, but I do wish you the best. Be careful in your choices and you'll have happiness beyond your most far-reaching dreams. Lord Henley and I were an unlikely match. Several of my closest friends believed me a fool to set my eye on him, but once we danced and spent time in each other's company, it was as if Fate had already decided for us." Teresa lifted a steaming spoonful of soup. "It seemed like we were bound by a force beyond our own making. I thought of him day and night, counting the minutes until the next chance we might spend time together, and he confessed to having suffered the same delightful affliction." She sighed.

"And now you'll have a babe to add to your loving home." Caroline dropped her eyes to Teresa's rounded waist and then back again, unwilling to introduce her own discomfort by staring.

"Yes." A bright smile bloomed across Teresa's face as she turned to peer at her husband seated at the head of the table. "I do hope we have a son first. William places great importance on an heir straightaway."

"So you intend to have more children then?" Caroline hoped her question wasn't too personal in nature. She couldn't keep from noting the radiant glow of Teresa's skin and how every so often she rested her palm atop her stomach in a sentimental maternal gesture.

"Oh, yes." Teresa brought her attention around. "An heir and several spares, if my husband has his say, although I'd never complain. I've always dreamed of a large family and, well, I haven't found the process unpleasant in the least." A blush crept into her cheeks and she waved her hand in front of her face as if she wished it away.

Caroline wasn't certain if the cloaked insinuation referred to the process beforehand or condition afterward, and she could never ask, appalled she'd already pried beyond the boundaries of their fledgling friendship.

"Now, enough about me. I'd like to know more of you, Caroline. I'm so pleased circumstances presented themselves to enable us to have this time together. Has any gentleman in particular caught your eye?"

Unprepared for an answer, Caroline glanced down the table, beyond her mother, who was in jovial conversation with the other ladies seated nearby, and farther to the opposite end, where she noted several seats remained empty. And then, as if she had no power over her own mind, she shifted her eyes toward the doorframe at the exact moment Lindsey entered. The flickering lamps from the hallway alcove served as the perfect backlighting, his entire dinner ensemble in black and the expression on his face as wicked and handsome as ever, the unyielding lines of his profile made all the more alluring by the acute intelligence in his eyes.

"Oh, dear." Teresa exhaled a sigh of disapproval beside her. "Don't be misled by Lord Lindsey." No one could mistake the gentle reproach in her tone. "You'll never catch him. He's a blackguard, or so my husband has told me repeatedly."

"Your husband knows Lord Lindsey well then?" Dragging her attention from the door, she forced herself to look at Teresa, though she could sense Lindsey's presence as he moved forward, almost as accurately as if he'd taken her hand to lead him. Her heartbeat tripped and she itched to glance in his direction again.

"I'm embarrassed to admit before I married, I too became entranced by Lindsey's enigmatic appeal and mentioned it to a friend, who repeated the same to my husband. I only knew Lord Henley in a casual sense, but he did everything in his power to dissuade me from considering Lindsey in a serious manner."

"Perhaps your husband acted in his own interest, besotted with you himself and unwilling to allow competition."

"True." Lady Henley laughed softly. "It does sound like something my husband might instigate, although his worry would have been for naught. My heart was given to him without contest. Even a man as intriguing as Lindsey couldn't sway my devotion once I became acquainted with my husband."

"Yours is a love match." Caroline nodded with surety, bringing her attention back again. She mentally chastised herself. "I desire the same."

"Good luck to you then." Teresa leaned to the opposite side as a footman reached over her shoulder to collect their soup bowls and replace a serving of neat's tongue as the next course. The dish was completed with black currant custard in short glasses with sippets on top, the bread toasted golden brown.

"Lord Lindsey has never behaved untowardly, at least not that I've witnessed in our short acquaintance." Except with Lady Jenkin in Lord Albertson's study, and that matter in the garden earlier. What woman did he warn the other gentleman away from? Perhaps she'd embellished her answer. Still, aside from his heated kiss, he'd never taken advantage. She'd allowed him. *And good lord, that kiss...*

Teresa nodded her head back and forth, as if she couldn't decide on a reply. "I doubt I've ever heard Lindsey described as a perfect gentleman, although he is a prime catch. All the gentlemen here are friendly, and I'm sure they enjoy this annual event or they wouldn't return each year. It provides a handsome opportunity for the ladies to gather and mix with the gentlemen outside the usual ballroom affair. It's peculiar how fickle and yet determined the heart is, able to reject some gentlemen at first glance and yearn for others no matter how detrimental the association. And of course, there's the matter of your age."

"My age?" Caroline straightened in her seat. Surely, she misunderstood. "I'm only two and twenty."

"To my point exactly." Teresa smiled to soften her words. "You're five years younger than me, and that means a decade younger than Lindsey. You've the luxury of time where, clearly, he doesn't. That's not to say he's looking for a wife. I haven't heard one word to prove that true. The only thing he's looking for is some old painting. He questioned my husband concerning the subject."

Caroline considered her words carefully. "And do you socialize with the earl often?" Her new friend possessed a vociferous nature, and dare Caroline label it considerate to indulge Lady Henley's penchant for conversation.

Besides, if Lindsey was interested in artwork, her father could be of help. He collected many fine pieces and enjoyed viewing the galleries. They'd toured too many to count when they'd resided in Italy. With her most recent concerns, she'd specifically taken the liberty to investigate her family's financial stability. Something unnamed nagged at her perception, but she hadn't the time to consider it at the moment. Regardless, mayhap the earl could advise her father of an investment to be made.

"Often enough, I suppose. Lord Lindsey owns the property adjacent to ours to the east. Kingswood Manor, his country estate, is a sight to behold. I could easily lose myself in the luxuriant gardens. My Canna lilies are but a trifle compared to the manicured exotic flowers the gardeners tend there."

Justifying her curiosity with the turn in conversation, Caroline shifted in her seat and eyed Lindsey at the opposite end of the table. With uncanny coincidence he stared back at her. Was it a trick of timing, or had he watched her all along? She could never know. Still, the emotion in his eyes and intensity of his gaze seemed to override the jubilant conversation and congenial atmospheric noise, so that in the span of a few heartbeats the two of them spoke an entire conversation, wordless and meaningful.

"Oh, dear." Teresa leaned closer and murmured near Caroline's ear. "It's almost as if he knows we're discussing him. But heavens, that's impossible." She ended with a bemused twitter of laughter. "Let's change the subject just to be sure."

Caroline crumpled the napkin in her lap to squelch unanswerable questions and then picked up her utensils with determined focus. Staring at Lindsey overlong proved dangerous. Her pulse began a hectic sprint and she released a long-held breath. Still, there was a tempting message in his dark gaze, made all the more appealing by the shadow of his lashes. They must speak soon.

* * * *

Bloody propriety and rules of etiquette. Caroline was seated at least fifteen places from him. Probably twenty. He was too distracted to count. All he wanted was to hear her voice and cause her to smile, but her witty conversation was lost at the other end of the table.

Realizing his mental musings were the complaint of a besotted cad, he took a hearty swallow of wine before he glanced in her direction again. He'd done his best to allow Mills the lead in the garden. With his temper ignited from the confrontation with Powell and the surprise of discovering

Caroline, he'd needed a few minutes to regain his detached demeanor. So he'd remained a step behind the two of them, even though viewing Caroline's hand linked through Mills' arm was only soothed when he averted his gaze to her retreating form, the silk of her skirts little disguise for the lovely curves beneath. An unfamiliar feeling blanketed his heart, both then and now at the remembrance, and while he refused to label it jealousy, no other moniker seemed adequate.

In the garden he'd distracted himself with mental aversions concerning Powell's distinct coloring and the irritating suspicion he looked familiar, although they'd never met before.

But now, Lady Henley's table arrangement kept him from Caroline and he'd rather it not. She was dressed magnificently in an uncommon shade of silk, not blue nor violet, but some shade of loveliness in between. The color made her eyes even more remarkable in contrast to her fair skin. Her hair was arranged in an attractive style, the sides held back by gemstone combs just high enough to reveal the graceful column of her neck. She pushed her food around on her plate, in search of the perfect morsel or otherwise distracted, he did not know.

She remained in amiable discussion with Lady Henley, and he watched Caroline's attention drop to view the lady's condition more than once. Perhaps Caroline desired children. He couldn't tell if it was longing in her expression, his view partially obstructed at times. Yet something was amiss. He'd memorized the nuances of her expressions and noted shadows of other emotions clouded her eyes. A sudden ache in his chest prompted he should have spared her that unhappiness, and the ludicrous, irrational reaction almost brought him to laughter.

Most likely the lady wished for a collection of children. With regret he acknowledged they didn't hold this in common. His father's decree be damned, a family was something Lindsey did not want and would never have. He valued his careless freedom and would not invite commitment and ultimately grief into his otherwise suitable existence.

Caroline, like most women, yearned for the complete opposite. Or so he assumed. No doubt, she would enjoy a daughter. A precious girl with glossy black curls and brilliant blue eyes. Had he a daughter he would indulge her every whim and spend exorbitant sums on imported gowns and satin slippers, never mind the jewelry and fripperies that completed a resplendent wardrobe.

He gave his head a vigorous shake, as if to dismiss the thought, and returned his focus to the other end of the table.

Lady Henley said something that caused Caroline to nod in the negative, and he became transfixed by the inviting blush that stole up her cheeks. Did she blush everywhere? She would if she could read his mind. A fervent urge to touch, taste, explore overtook him and he allowed his imagination free rein. He'd lick across her nipples first, smooth his fingers over her ribcage as he worked his mouth downward to dip his tongue into her navel, lower still to taste her sweet sex.

A burst of laughter from two guests at his right shook him into awareness, and a good thing too, or he'd develop a condition in his trousers that would not easily be explained to the gentlemen on either side of him.

What was wrong with him anyway? He knew better. Innocence was forbidden for someone of his years. He was a disciplined man with a strict code of conduct when it came to proper ladies. He needed a willing mistress and convenient noncommittal arrangement. Instead he sat at this damnable affair, hard and restless.

Best Caroline found a respectable gentleman for a husband. He could aid in her search. A few well-placed words would invigorate interest with the right sort. She might not welcome his advice, but if she never knew of his interference...

Not Mills.

Someone deserving of her rare beauty and intelligence. That's exactly what Caroline needed.

Liar. You don't want her to favor anyone.

She turned her eyes in his direction and the impact of their matched gaze rocked him to his soul.

He was a fool. A man in want of what he could not have. Twice the fool moreover.

Chapter Fifteen

Lindsey strode toward the east wing and aimed for the cardroom, where he intended to win all of Quinn Powell's money and extract information concerning the Decima, or at the least determine why the man was seeking the same painting as he. His father hadn't set a time limit on Lindsey's completion of the will's conditions, but he wasn't fool enough to believe he would ever find peace until the matter was resolved. Barlow, the damnable solicitor, had expressed Lindsey's access to accounts would narrow as weeks turned into months and too, a recent letter from his own man of accounts confirmed a fortification of funds was needed. Time to make haste.

He rounded the rear corner and nearly collided with a gaggle of ladies as they exited a nearby chamber. After dinner, the women had retired to the drawing room for music and conversation while the men had dispersed in a variety of directions, some at billiards or cards, others off to more clandestine pursuits. Lindsey released a sigh as the chattering group advanced. He couldn't be distracted by Caroline at the moment, and conveniently she wasn't among the throng. He'd already spent too much time conjuring wicked fantasies and ignoring his singular goal for this country party, lest he forget his main purpose.

The last of the ladies passed, and he hesitated only when two elongated shadows arrowed across the threshold. Perhaps other lingering guests still needed to move along.

Indeed.

Caroline and her mother came into view several paces behind the former group, who'd already progressed down the corridor in conversation. Drawn by a force he still hadn't mastered, his eyes sought hers. Her face displayed surprise upon seeing him and a becoming warmth crept into her cheeks, quick to color them a fetching shade of rose. She smiled, as if that same flower came to bloom, and his heart thrummed harder.

"Ladies, I beg your pardon." He rocked back and noted the delight on Caroline's face. There was no way for her to have known he would be out in the hall at this moment, but if he read her expression correctly, the incident pleased her immensely.

"Lord Lindsey, how good to see you again." Lady Derby greeted him cordially.

Clearly the woman hadn't heard the worst of his character, or else she'd dismissed it as unsubstantiated gossip, though he doubted the latter. Most especially as he knew the familial relation to the Notley gells and their penchant to stay abreast of societal minutiae.

"My lord." Caroline's voice drew his attention, and the two syllables stroked over him like a velvet caress.

"Lady Nicholson." His voice matched hers with adoration, though he didn't make a show of kissing her palm. He couldn't touch her and then release her. He knew his boundaries. Knew how far he could test his desire. "I was after the gaming room." He glanced toward the left. "I don't suppose you've just finished a scandalous round of whist or cutthroat wager on a toss of dice?"

"Such a charmer." Lady Derby laughed and eyed her daughter knowingly. "Beware his silver tongue, Caroline." She motioned backward toward the doorway they'd just crossed. "I've forgotten my fan in the drawing room and shall be less than a minute. Lord Lindsey, may I be so bold as to impose on your good manners and ask you engage my daughter in conversation until I return?"

"It is my honor and pleasure." He smiled as Lady Derby stepped away and then dropped his voice low. "Your mother is far too trusting. Pray tell me she doesn't appeal to other gentlemen with the same unquestioning sincerity."

"Is it an imposition then?"

Minx. How artfully she'd avoided an answer. He stepped closer, just near enough to inhale her delicate perfume. "Have you explored Lord and Lady Henley's study as of yet? I haven't the opportunity, but know for a fact I'll be in search of a good novel come later tonight."

Her brows dipped in confusion and then buoyed up again.

"Is that an in—"

"There now. It was just where I thought it would be, right as rain." Lady Derby rejoined them, and the mood shifted along with the avenue of conversation.

Had Caroline understood his message?

"Thank you, Lord Lindsey." Caroline lowered into a curtsy, the gesture unnecessary considering their association and the searing hot kiss he had yet to scrub from his brain. Though it did offer a fine view of her enticing décolletage.

He stared after her but she didn't look back, and he wondered if she'd riddled out his obvious insinuation she should appear in Lord Henley's study later this evening. It had become their habit. He knew the paltry excuse for what it was, yet it hadn't kept him from voicing the invitation. He needed to caution her, and that conversation would be best broached in private.

Snapping his head around, he strode toward the rear of the estate and soon located the cardroom, filled with male conversation and the pervasive odor of tobacco and old leather. He checked the room, corner to corner, table by table, until his eyes settled on Powell seated near a shadowy corner.

Something about the man warned him away, but he was determined to recover the lost painting and be closer to ridding himself of his father's interference in his life. Powell remained an anomaly. How would an untitled man, one who appeared more street brawler than dasher, acquire a priceless work of art, or even rub elbows with those who collected fine masterpieces? How had he managed an invitation to this affair? With little effort, Lindsey sensed distrustful qualities in Powell that bespoke of a need for caution. Perhaps he'd already located the thief and not the other way around.

He approached, and Powell's profile, sharp nose and angular chin, issued another series of warning bells to resound in his soul. Goddammit, Powell reminded him of his father. No wonder Lindsey had acquired an instant dislike toward the man. It was inevitable.

"Either join the game or move along. I have no desire to be gawked at all evening."

Powell's rude remark left the other player at the table quiet, their game stalled.

Not one to ignore a challenge, Lindsey strode toward the table and took the only open chair. "Have room for a third?"

"That depends." Powell eyed the player across the felt. "Shall we take his money, Sheffield?"

"Not excepting you always make wagering an interesting affair, Lindsey, I think I shall refrain this evening." Sheffield gave a cut nod and rose from his seat. "I sense a private conversation is imminent." He gathered his coins from the area before him and slid them into his pocket. "We'll continue at a later date, Powell. This interruption is only a delay, not a pardon." And with nothing further to say, the elder gentleman turned and left.

"It would appear I'm not the only one here this week who takes umbrage with your presence. Why not just tell me what I need to know, and then I can forget you just as easily." Lindsey took the deck of cards up and gathered those still strewn across the tabletop. He waited in silence, the snap and clip of shuffling the only intrusive sound. Best to keep his hands busy so they didn't find a way into Powell's cravat again.

"It's always about you, isn't it?" Powell leaned back, his arms dropped casually to his sides. "I suppose a pretentious attitude is expected when one bears a lofty title."

"Is that it? You begrudge me my heritage? Or is it every member of the aristocracy? You've come to the wrong house party then. Though not so much that you wouldn't fill your pockets with our coins."

"Only you, Lindsey." Powell shot forward to lean across the table as his voice sank low and lethal in direct contrast to his actions. "You're a thief in kind to the late earl."

Had Lindsey harbored any fondness for his father he might have taken offense at Powell's insult to the deceased, but it was more the animosity with which he'd spoken the words than the meaning to be found within them. What caused the man to hold such anger? Had his father double-crossed and trapped Powell too? Perhaps they were alike in extraordinary circumstance.

"Have you an issue with my father?"

"Your father." Powell reclined against the seatback, his breath released in a long solemn exhale. "Your father?"

Lindsey replaced the cards on the table and waited. It would be no use seeking information concerning the Decima if he couldn't have a civilized conversation with Powell first.

"Yes." Lindsey didn't bother to suppress a wry quirk of his lips. "Believe me, Powell, if you despise the man, we have more in common than might suit your pleasure." He cut the deck in half and then stacked it again. A familiar feeling of restlessness rolled through him, his nerves on edge. Silence stretched and along with it, tension grew. "My father and I are completely different men." He wouldn't offer more. Instead he picked up the cards and dealt their first hand.

"I doubt that." Powell hesitated, but then a sharpness entered his eyes and he swiped the cards aside. "*Your* father ruined my life."

Lindsey forced an attitude of indifference, though his mind spun with curiosity. "My father was ruthless and unkind. I hadn't spoken to him in years, and upon his death he has continued to complicate my life. I may be more sympathetic to your cause then you realize."

"Unlikely, that." Powell exhaled and collected the cards with reluctance.

"Why don't you enlighten me." Lindsey threw away a five of spades and chose the top card from the deck. All this conversation wasn't getting him any closer to locating the Decima, and while learning of his father's involvements might enrich his heritage, Lindsey preferred a more economic path to the matter at hand.

"You made it clear in the garden that you're searching for a specific painting."

"I am."

"The Decima." Powell tossed his cards to the table and leaned back in his chair, seemingly done with the pretense of amiable wagering. "I may know of its whereabouts."

"You have it?" Lindsey tamped down a lick of temper. "You stole it. You stole it from my father."

"Whose father? *My* father." Powell chuckled, but the sound held no humor. "My father showed me the painting years ago, when I had no idea the knowledge would someday benefit me. But I remembered. Like I remembered everything. All the times I wished to see him and he wasn't there. All the arguments he had with my mother. Or the convenient notion that I could be easily appeased with coin instead of a relationship."

Lindsey waited, though the disturbing list of facts Powell uttered were beginning to assemble into a disappointing conclusion.

"I, too, fell out of favor with my father. Like you, I hadn't spoken to him in many years. But when I reached adulthood, I realized I wanted more from life. I wanted what should be rightly mine, and I recently learned he wanted that too."

"You're talking in riddles, Powell. That painting rightfully belongs to me. I'm the heir. I'm the Earl of Lindsey now, and your father took something that rightfully belongs to my heritage." Frustration and anger made his words come out in a harsh whisper.

Powell laughed. Loud deep guffaws that held sharp humor when they'd only discussed hardship and disappointment. It took a minute for him to recompose his staid demeanor, the angry glint of determination clearly visible in his eyes.

"Yes, you're Lindsey now." Powell shook his head slowly, as if disbelieving his own words. "But your father stole from me."

Lindsey eyed him, his mind at work on a puzzle that still missed important facts.

"Your father stole my childhood. He robbed my mother of happiness as she pined away in wait for the sound of carriage wheels on the gravel drive, her prospects and future fading more each day. He showed us no kindness and neglected his bastard son in deference to his rightful heir. You. You with every advantage at your fingertips."

"You are my brother." Lindsey said the words slowly, allowing every last piece to click into place.

"Half brother. Bastard brother," Powell scoffed. "I was a constant reminder of his secret and thereby best left to the darkness, but the old man is dead now and I have my own business to conduct."

"I need that painting."

Powell eyed him. "Why don't you ask our father where it is?"

"I've no patience for games."

"Just because he's dead doesn't mean he can't give you answers." Powell held his stare without blinking.

His comment brought with it a long pause until Lindsey pushed on. "You said yourself you've never received your rightful due. You want wealth. Name your price and I'll compensate you handsomely for the Decima."

"It's just one piece, when our father possessed so much more. What difference does it make? I have my own interests to tend to."

"I need that painting." Lindsey stood, his restlessness getting the best of him. "You took what doesn't belong to you, Powell."

"I don't have your precious painting. I whispered in the right ears so word would get back to you. This is what I wanted." Powell splayed his fingers and gestured in a sweep of his arm. "For you to realize you have a bastard brother. One who isn't very good at staying quiet or following rules. One who is now in your life."

"My patience is wearing thin. Either you have the Decima or you don't, and if you do, Powell, you took what's not yours. It belongs to me."

"Our father took what didn't belong to him. Have a care, Lindsey. You wouldn't want your father's indiscretions whispered to those who enjoy sharing tawdry gossip. You've only just assumed the title. Pity it would become tarnished so quickly. A bastard is supposed to hide his shame and stay quietly hidden in the shadows, but you won't find I'm apt to do that."

"This isn't a game." A muscle ticked in his jaw as he clenched his teeth. "You're behaving like a spiteful child. We have more in common than you can possibly imagine."

"And to whom should I assign the blame?" Powell shoved from the table and stood, a malevolent glint in his eyes. "I never had a proper father figure to teach me any manners, did I?"

Refusing to dignify Powell's display and too aware they'd drawn the attention of guests around the periphery, Lindsey strode from the room without another word.

* * * *

Caroline paced at the foot of the bed, her heart and head in argument. With a shuddered sigh, she returned her eyes to the mahogany bracket clock on the mantelpiece. Had Lindsey insinuated she should meet him in Lord Henley's study at midnight? She wanted to believe it true even though it was unthinkable. An unchaperoned lady couldn't go anywhere with a bachelor or *a scandalously handsome and reputed rakehell,* much less to an illicit assignation in the middle of the night.

But what if he did intend for her to sneak downstairs to meet him? What if he was pacing the rug, just as she, only she would never appear because she was paralyzed with indecision? She stalled midstride. She wasn't a rude person. No matter she scoured her brain, she couldn't think of one instance when she'd purposely behaved in a rude manner. It would be a social sin to be labeled with the descriptor when she sought a husband this season. She needed to be noticed in the very best light.

True, no one would know she'd behaved rudely if she didn't sneak down to the library. Well, no one but Lindsey. Her stomach plummeted with that realization. She certainly didn't want the earl to think poorly of her. For no intelligent reason she could ascertain, she wished for Lindsey to hold her in high esteem. It didn't matter that a future could never exist between them.

Besides, it was just a kiss—or two—that they'd shared. Not that she planned to repeat that behavior.

She blew out a breath of exasperation and grabbed her silk wrapper. She would never settle her nerves enough to find sleep if she didn't put these unanswered questions to bed. A good book would serve her purpose. And the library was far from the study, away from the temptation that threatened to lead her astray.

Caroline slipped into the hallway, careful to check for servants or guests who might still be awake, and saw no one. Hemming her bottom lip, she moved down the corridor to the backstairs, emboldened by the thought she was safer away from the main entry. If she did encounter a maid or footman, she could easily explain her presence with a request for warm milk or tea and a reluctance to bother the staff, anything to extricate herself from idle gossip. Luckily the need never materialized and the stairs were silent. She eased the door wider and followed the shallow light supplied by the brass sconces mounted on the walls.

Halfway down the treads she heard a footfall, the echo of boots on an upward climb enough to send her pulse into a chaotic rhythm. She readied for the awkward confrontation. Surely any chambermaid or servant could still be at work during this late hour. Especially in a house full of guests. The staff had been more than gracious, so there really was nothing to worry about.

Confident she had no reason to fret, she drew up her shoulders and peered straight into Lindsey's eyes.

"Caroline."

She gasped, and a quivery excitement rippled through her. It was the first time he'd said her Christian name. Her heart thudded at the intimacy, no matter it was scandalous indeed. To be ensconced in a dimly lit corridor far and away from the rest of the house was provocative by itself. Still, she cherished her name spoken in his deep tenor, the single word low and velvety in the shadowy darkness.

"Did I startle you?" He canted his head in concern.

"No." She blinked twice in an effort to regain composure and focused more closely on his expression. He remained a few stairs below her, and yet they could easily look into each other's eyes. She leaned closer and whispered. "Are you alright?" He appeared angry, or at the least troubled for some unknown reason. The mischievous devil-may-care attitude was lost to a solemn weariness in his eyes.

He didn't answer immediately. Instead, he glanced over his shoulder and beyond hers to confirm they stood alone. Then he reclined against the bannister near the adjacent wall as if settling in for a long conversation. The candle lantern on the hook above him left him partially concealed in shadow, but she could see he was in shirtsleeves, his coat caught tight in his left hand.

"Why are you sneaking about this house alone in the middle of the night?"

Apparently he was as adept at avoiding questions as she.

"I was after a book. I couldn't sleep."

"Uncomfortable mattress? Lumpy pillows? A chilly draft in the room?"

Her eyes flared, but she managed to swallow her objection. "Nothing of the kind, my lord."

"And still you choose to slink down the backstairs like a curious kitten. I continue to be concerned about your safety."

"Fancy meeting you here then."

His mouth hitched in a half-smile that caused her heart to flutter. His amusement at her cheeky response added to the pleasure.

"As for me, I'd hoped to return to my rooms unnoticed. I've had enough enlightening conversation for one evening. More than enough, in fact." His jaw tightened, a reaction he corrected belatedly.

"I'm sorry."

"No, you misunderstand." He pushed from the wall and climbed a stair higher. "Meeting you here in this dimly lit corridor before I find my bed is a gift, a much needed pleasant distraction."

"Lindsey…"

"I'd prefer if you'd call me Jonathan. No one does, so thereby you must."

"That wouldn't be proper."

"Because this is?" He chuckled, the sound smoothing over her skin. "Lately, I'm not sure I even know myself. This evening especially. To hell with my title and circumstance. I'd like to be Jonathan with you. Just a man without the constraint of a title and noose of responsibility." He exhaled, and the heat of his breath skimmed her forehead. "A man who finds you extraordinarily tempting."

"Jonathan." Forgetting caution, she tested the feel of it on her tongue.

He approved. At least she thought he did, the sound he made somewhere between a growl and a confirmation.

The air seemed warmer than only a moment before, the quiet staircase suddenly alive with a vibrancy she had no way to explain. Her heart pounded in her ears, ensuring she didn't dream. Still, here she stood in the dusky light of the stairwell, risking the danger of being caught and having to stop or, worse, not being caught and relishing the promised pleasure of what would occur thereafter.

Mayhap she'd fallen under a spell and become enchanted, drawn to him, like one of the characters in those hopeful gothic novels she enjoyed far too much. She reminded herself to breathe. The intensity of his obsidian eyes sent a pang of nervousness arrowing through her. Too often she became blinded by emotion and neglected more prudent considerations. Her mother admonished her, labeled her impetuous, but Caroline simply wished to enjoy life. Still, in the end, caution won out.

"I should go." She placed her hand upon his chest to stay him from leaning forward because she knew she'd never be able to resist his kiss, and yet here they stood in secretive privacy as if in wait. The steady beat of his heart beneath her palm startled her for its strength in echo of her mutual drumming pulse. "Nothing good can come of this."

"You have that little confidence in me?"

"You purposely misconstrue my words." She breathed deep in search of resolute determination and was rewarded with the decadent scent of his shaving soap. "We should leave well enough alone."

"Is that what you want?"

A long beat of silence interrupted their conversation until she finally settled on her thoughts. "I want to marry. And kissing you here in the stairwell will not accomplish that goal."

"So you *have* been thinking about kissing too?"

The man was the devil himself.

He spared no time for her to recover her composure. "I wasn't aware you were included on Lord Henley's guest list, or that you'd accepted the invitation."

"Lord Mills changed that circumstance dramatically."

"Mills?" Lindsey paused, as if cataloging the bit of information. "Mills' life is an unmade bed. You'd never be happy—"

"What?" She drew back to examine his expression more carefully.

"Never mind." He exhaled. "How has your husband hunt progressed so far? Are there gentlemen you wish to know about?"

"Lord Byrnes shared several poems he'd written while the ladies gathered in the salon."

"Byrnes is drowning in debt. He's after a fat purse more than a loving wife."

"Oh." She blinked several times at his blunt opinion. "Lord Himple seems an amiable gentleman."

"The man can't hold his liquor and is as dependable as a cork afloat in the ocean."

"Viscount Menner—"

"Has been left at the altar three times. Makes one wonder, wouldn't you agree?"

A smile curled her mouth upward, no matter he behaved abominably. "Lord Gullet appeared pleasant."

"Lives with his mother and likes it."

"Jonathan." She kept her tone even, though she truly wished to show her amusement. Her mother would be furious if she did so.

"Go ahead and laugh," Lindsey taunted. "You know you wish to. I'd rather like to hear your laughter. Besides, I do wonder if your approach to this is all wrong. While qualities like handsomeness, wealth, and charm are admirable, surely you wish for your husband to have a flaw or two. However else would you endure the mundane?"

He stepped down and recovered his former position against the bannister, and she couldn't keep her eyes from him. He moved with a sensual grace that belied his strong shoulders and tall frame, and yet here in the confines of the stairwell she wanted nothing more than to find her way into his embrace, though better sense warned it a grave mistake.

"In truth, there is only one gentleman who has captured my interest." An exhale of relief chased her confession once the words left her tongue.

"Elaborate on this fellow, this rogue who has you at sixes and sevens."

"He's quite handsome, and I suspect he knows the same." She paused, but only for the slightest beat. "What he doesn't realize is that beneath his polished veneer is a considerate and caring gentleman. A sensitive man. One with a passionate soul."

She looked across the dimly lit stairwell and waited, but he said nothing. A muscle ticked on the side of his jaw.

"On occasion he's left me waiting and, worse still, wanting. He hasn't always kept his word." She watched him closely.

"The cad." He seemed to reconcile his emotions, whatever they might have been. "A foolish fellow if ever I heard of one. I'm certain I could never recommend him to you and maintain a clear conscience."

"I see." Her fingers itched, caught in the silk of her wrapper. How she wished she could reach out and smooth her touch across his cheek. "And yet he causes my heart to beat so fast, I fear no one else will ever affect me in the same manner."

"Is that so?" His voice was no more than a murmur, his expression too complex to decipher. Time stretched with inconceivable impatience, until at last he finished what he meant to say. "Be assured the gentleman wants only what's best for you, Caroline."

Chapter Sixteen

Would his night be composed of nothing but unexpected surprises? Albeit discovering Caroline sneaking down the backstairs in her night clothes was a revelation more than an imposition.

At first glance he'd assumed an overindulgence in brandy had taken hold of his brain. But no, she appeared before him like the best part of a dream, the part when one wishes never to wake.

Hadn't he avowed earlier to find a willing female and lose himself in meaningless release to escape his desire for the lady? His mind struggled for clarity. He couldn't very well run toward the same woman he wished to escape. One didn't slack untamed longing for a forbidden debutante with another taste of her lips. Lust was a bloody inconvenience.

Still, he hadn't planned to seek her out, but then there she was and suddenly everything became much more interesting. And why did he discourage the gentlemen she named when he had previously offered to assist her? He supposed, in some capacity, one could consider his opinion that same assistance. It certainly wasn't jealousy or some other ridiculous emotion. He didn't become jealous. One needed to take life seriously to experience the emotion. One needed to care.

He forced distance between them and leaned against the opposite wall. She'd looked startled when he first happened upon her, but now she appeared as lovely and intriguing as he always seemed to find her.

Something about Caroline soothed his restless soul, and for a jaded man such as he, a man with too many knots to untangle, she posed a danger indeed.

He intended to bid her goodnight and continue up the stairwell, but when he opened his mouth different words came out. "You bewitch me, Caroline."

She didn't reply, and in that silence, as the words hung in the air, he admired the glow of candlelight on her skin and the pearly sheen it lent to her pale silk wrapper. He noticed the way her hair spilled over her shoulders, down her back, and wondered what she wore to sleep. Something ethereal and lovely, no doubt. Arousal sharpened to painful need. His fingers itched to touch her and, agitated in their uselessness, he clenched his coat in frustration before folding it through the balustrade to free his hands.

"I should let you go," she whispered in a confiding tone.

The words were easy to misinterpret if he allowed himself the foolishness of the task, but why search for meaning in what was likely a careless turn of phrase?

Besides, her expression betrayed her and lacked true conviction.

"And here I am already looking forward to seeing you again." One side of his mouth curled upward. "Good night, Caroline. I hope you find what you're looking for."

She bit her bottom lip before she replied, "Have you no other advice for me, Jonathan?"

It was her use of his name that gave him pause, regardless he'd already requested she use it. And too, the attention she brought to that lower lip, all plump temptation and deserving of another bite. His, alone.

He stopped one step below her, her mouth perfectly aligned with his. They stood that way quietly and he imagined it was so their hearts could synchronize their beat and their breathing could even before he gathered her into his arms.

He knew it was wrong.

She was a young idealistic debutante in want of a staid husband and secure future, and he had nothing to offer on either account.

But it was only a kiss.

One kiss in the dark.

One kiss.

Just one.

* * * *

Caroline went into his arms, her will no fortress against the delicious desire pulsing through her veins, strong and insistent she take haven in his strength, just as when he'd lived so vividly in her thoughts earlier this evening. She promised herself it would be but a minute's respite. Only one minute. Nothing more.

But when he gathered her close in his embrace, his hands firm through the thin silk of her wrapper, the heated pressure enough to reach her skin through her night rail, she knew that promise was nothing more than foolish placation.

His lips crushed down on hers before she'd released her gasp, his hungry kiss met with equaled ambition. His mouth fit perfectly to hers, his beard like rough velvet against her cheek. Sensation wove a languid path through her, and she melted against him. He growled his pleasure, a rumble low in his throat that somehow rippled against her as much as him. And it was as though he lit a fuse to her fantasy, every secret desire and naughty dream come to life. She wanted to thread her fingers through the thick glossy waves of his hair, experience the heat of his broad chest pressed to her bare breasts, know the taste and feel of his muscular body.

He angled her head to deepen the kiss, slanting his mouth over hers and she opened to him, allowing him to taste and explore, to stroke deep. Her body tingled from the inside out, some unknown coil of intense awareness unfurling in her lower belly to create sensitivity everywhere he touched. The tips of her breasts ached as they rubbed against warm silk, and she restlessly clenched her thighs, shamelessly aware she grew damp. She inhaled again, wanting to know the scent of him better, aware all too soon she would need to break their kiss. Things couldn't go further than they had already.

Perhaps he knew the same. In the next instant he pulled his mouth from hers, though he kept their faces aligned, his breathing as heavy as hers.

"What you do to me. What to do with you."

His mouth was only a whisper away, his words indecently seductive, and she reveled in them. To know she affected him so made her heartbeat thunder in her chest.

She searched his face. His eyes flashed molten velvet, but he allowed no time for her to answer, or think, for that matter, before he captured her mouth again. This time his kiss wooed and tempted. Gone was the rash impatience of their first embrace, and instead, this kiss promised decadent pleasure and forbidden indulgence.

He tasted as he appeared. Powerful and virile, terribly handsome. Though she doubted any of her observations made sense. His fingers pressed through the flimsy silk of her wrapper, clasping her back with tight insistence, reminding she wore next to nothing. The hair on his forearm rubbed in sensual suggestion against her wrist as he released his hold to clasp her chin, tilt it slightly, and murmur his approval. Then he licked into her again, the heat of his tongue, stroke after stroke, coaxing her to join with him. The very idea sent another sharp pang of longing humming through her body.

It was wrong in so many ways to allow these liberties, but she couldn't bring herself to stop him, the pleasure too new and intense. Her pulse skittered with an irregular beat and she clung to his upper arms, the flex of hard muscle beneath further tinder to her desire. She fell further from grace, lost to a kiss composed of contradiction, strong enough to make her weak, enveloped in warmth that caused her to shiver, an offer of safety which threatened illicit danger. Yet her stomach rioted, her emotions awhirl, as a tremor of decadent pleasure swept through her so acutely it left her powerless to object.

He moved his hands to her waist, bracketed on either side as if to hold her firmly in place. Then he slid one palm over her ribcage, higher, until he skimmed over her breast, the few thin layers of silk no barrier to the heated strength of his touch.

"Caroline," he murmured against her mouth, and deepened the kiss with matched sensual pressure as he cupped her breast. He held her that way, his palm against her heartbeat, and she trembled beneath his caress. "You're so very precious."

It wasn't what she'd expected him to say, but then she couldn't think straight for the scandalous liberties she allowed him with her body. Still, she didn't stop him.

He kissed his way across her cheek, near her ear, where his hot exhale tickled a riot of gooseflesh beneath her clothing. He continued his exploration and offered a teasing nip to her neck, an enticing lick to her clavicle.

His breath was hot against her skin, and she leaned her head back against the wall, her eyes closed tight as his mouth traveled lower, somehow finding skin where she'd believed her wrapper kept her covered. Temptation and desire tunneled through her, settling low in an unfamiliar ache. She had no idea what he planned. The exquisite manner of each touch assured it could be altogether wicked. But no, not here in a stairwell where they might be discovered. At least, that was the lie she accepted without question.

He took her breast into his mouth, silk and all, wet from the stroke of his tongue as he held the tip with his teeth and suckled. She trembled, the sensation too intense to bear. A whimper of consent and surrender escaped. A sound of encouragement, dare he stop when it felt so very good. She'd never experienced such powerful pleasure.

Was this how one fell in love? Was this turbulent rush of emotion what she yearned for all along? Or was she making a serious mistake, allowing what might be nothing more than a convenient indiscretion to a man as unscrupulous and jaded as the Earl of Lindsey was reputed to be?

She couldn't say.

She hardly knew him.

And yet somehow, she did.

"Jonathan." She drew a tight breath and he broke away, leaning in to do the same.

"Yes, Caroline?"

She'd heard her name voiced countless times, but for some unnamed reason when he said it, the word sounded special.

He traced a fingertip over the tip of her breast, sheathed in damp silk, and she shuddered, that same tight coil of longing an echo through her lower half.

"I shouldn't be here with you." Her hushed whisper was both admonishment and guilty pleasure, an excited revelation concealed as misdeed.

"But you are." He answered as matter of fact. "It's only a kiss."

His words were the exact tonic needed, and she pulled from his embrace and backed to the wall. Pity he thought so little of it. *Of her.* "Yes. Only a kiss."

Heat stole up her neck to her cheeks, and she was thankful the stairwell remained dark. She'd be every kind of fool to believe their embrace meant more to him than a casual dalliance. She couldn't bring herself to continue their intimate interlude even though her body sang with the glory of his caresses. "Good night, my lord."

"And you, Caroline." He slipped past her shoulder and up the stairwell, the echo of his boots on the shallow treads in rhythm to her thundering heart.

* * * *

Dawn broke with unrelenting sunlight, brilliant and unapologetic as it streamed down from the heavens to dry the morning dew. It was the perfect day for a fox hunt, and the back lawns were crowded with riders and horses, grooms and servants, all in chaotic disorder as they arranged for the sport.

Lord Henley had cultivated an outstanding reputation for hosting the annual event and, as expected, no matter the change in date, every gentleman worth his snuff was out in his finest attire at the ready to prove his horsemanship and superior ability. The ladies were ornamentations. Little more than decorations, really. At least, that's how Caroline viewed her attendance. Females weren't allowed to ride or participate in any manner.

Instead they were instructed to cheer, tie ribbons to the manes of their beau's horse, or wait patiently for a group of riders to pass. At the day's end, it was considered the highest honor to be presented with the foxtail, but Caroline wanted no part of the cruel ritual. The fox was obscenely outnumbered by the horsemen and overpowered by the hounds running it to ground. While she enjoyed the atmosphere and opportunity to mix with the ton's most select members, she disliked how a striking animal would be harmed for the sake of masculine boasting privileges.

Oblivious to Caroline's defense of the fox's welfare, her mother stood beside her on the balcony completely enthralled in watch of the goings-on.

Beyond their position, a wrought iron fence edged a gravel path leading to the western field where the fox would be tracked and pursued. At the moment everyone waited, tension and anticipation thick in the air. Lord Henley hadn't addressed the crowd to signal the start of the event, and in the surround Caroline heard chatter and laughter, savvy speculation, and pretentious braggadocio of every variety.

She had no trouble locating Lindsey and Mills in the fray, her eyes drawn to the earl as if he cast a spell of hypnotic power. As she expected, he looked masterful atop Infinity. Whatever one observed about the sleek Arabian horse could be echoed in the man who served as the animal's master. Lindsey looked magnificent. Potent and virile. If all the men around him were hounds, Lindsey was the fox. A man who led with innate ease, while the others followed. He was clever, wily, and extraordinary in nature. She smiled, pleased with the image as she continued her perusal.

The earl wore snug buckskin trousers tucked into black top boots that caught the early light in their sheen. His perfectly tailored coat hugged his shoulders and tapered neatly to his trim waist. Last night's interlude rushed back with startling clarity, her palm pressed against the wall of his chest, the determined thrum of his heartbeat. She shook her head. Still, he cut such a fine figure she found it hard to look away. Her mother noticed, unfortunately.

"Is that Lord Mills talking to the Earl of Lindsey, Caroline?" Her mother strained beyond the intrusive adornments of her velvet-lined bonnet in an effort to see through the crowd moving toward the far field. "I hope you're encouraging his suit. He's taken a special liking to you."

"Do you think so?" Caroline skimmed her fingers across her left collarbone, the same place Lindsey had nipped through her wrapper the night before. Her skin still bore a reddened shadow from his teeth, the slightest rub of whisker burn alive beneath her skin. The secretive sensation fascinated her. It was scandalous and dangerous that she'd allowed him the intimacy, and yet her pulse skittered whenever she relived the moment, as if eagerly suggesting she let it happen again.

"You should pay Lord Mills special attention. My acquaintances suggest he intends to find a wife this season. If he's in a hurry, he may not be as particular as other gentlemen." Thankfully, her mother stopped short of expounding on the subject.

Happy for an excuse to stare at Lindsey again, she followed her mother's line of sight and landed on the two gentlemen in the same spot. Mills had his back to her now, but Lindsey scanned the field until his eyes locked with hers in return. He touched the brim of his top hat and she stifled an immediate smile. Then she cast her gaze down to her gloves, happy she'd chosen the navy-blue riding habit and heeled black boots. When she raised her eyes, he was engaged in conversation with a cluster of young bucks who fawned over Infinity.

A short blast from a trumpet sounded and Lord Henley exited the house on the slates below the terrace where they stood. As host, he would ride out first. The master of foxhounds followed him to the blocks where Lord Henley mounted a dappled grey, its mane woven with bright ribbons.

Caroline and her mother moved to the edge of the balcony for a better view of the proceedings. Once the riders set off, they would join the promenade on the garden path and beyond to a clearing where the ladies gathered in wait.

"Lady Caroline." Lady Henley waved up to them. "Do come down and join us. I'd like to continue our earlier conversation while we await the fanfare. After the men set out, we'll have a good amount of time before the hunt is called at an end."

* * * *

Lindsey aligned Infinity beside the other horses at the threshold to the forest near the west of the estate. If he continued through the wood and crossed the rolling hills there, he would reach his property border. Kingswood Manor was his favorite of all the Lindsey holdings, although a few manors and their acreage were tied up in litigious legalities until he produced a trio of paintings and a legitimate heir. His father had created a complicated tangle of demands for the inheritance. Worse yet, Lindsey suspected there were others who waited on his actions. All the while, time clipped past.

This fact needled him further. How dare his father threaten others' happiness and future solvency by making Lindsey's legacy so bloody complicated. Capitulation seemed inevitable.

And he now had a bastard brother to contend with. He hadn't believed his opinion of his father could sink lower. But it had. What further complication would be laid in his path?

An endearing image of Caroline on the balcony chased away his annoyance. How had it come she held power over him? In all his personal relationships, he'd maintained control. He'd decided how far he would proceed with affection and attention. He'd made the unavoidable break when he'd tired of his mistress' company.

But Caroline was an anomaly. Barely out for the season, young and idealistic, she intrigued him, invading his thoughts whenever he dared allow it.

How prim and proper she'd appeared on the balcony moments before, her navy-blue riding habit a complement to her creamy skin and lovely long hair. The fashionable ensemble hugged her bodice where a hint of frothy lace peeked out from the collar to remind of the unexpected intimacy they'd shared in the stairwell. How far would he have gone? That question remained unanswered.

Three sharp horn blasts signaled the hunt was to begin. Every inch of open grass filled with riders and a copious number of hounds, yipping and yapping in their hurry to be off the leash.

Mills pulled into position at Lindsey's right at the same time Powell approached on the left. Were Lindsey a more suspicious man he would accuse the men of colluding against him. Instead he acknowledged them both, aware they more than likely wished to keep pace with Infinity. His Arabian would leave their horses in the dust.

"Let's sweeten the stakes." Mills leaned over to smooth a turn in his horse's bridle. "I've an eye on Lady Caroline, and I'm not so conceited to believe she won't become distracted by your performance in the hunt or, worse, smitten despite your insincerity. You have a way of disturbing the intended course of things."

Lindsey listened closely, his friend walking a thin line with his unflattering description. Yet he waited, holding his response until Mills completed his proposition.

"If I win the hunt and trophy the tail, you will refrain from socializing and dancing with her at the masquerade this evening."

"You're aware I'm riding Infinity and have no interest in terrorizing the fox. It's a foolish wager with a foolish request." He bit back the words he most wanted to voice. That no one warned him away from a woman, most especially Lady Caroline. But he knew better. He needed Mills' help in recovering the paintings and therefore couldn't alienate the man. As to the hunt, he had no intention of competing with sincerity. Each year he joined the race and then gallantly stepped aside so another could claim the victory.

"Does that mean you won't accept my terms?"

"Where is the benefit for me?"

"I will locate the last painting and deliver the Morta to you."

"You know of its whereabouts?" He shifted on the saddle and his horse sidestepped with impatience, causing a separation from Powell.

"We've no time to dither in details, but you have my word."

"Not a forgery, mind you, Mills."

"The authentic art piece as verified by my associate."

Lindsey chuckled low, sly enough to know how Mills' mind worked. There was flawed thinking involved in the wager, and yet what did it matter? He would clear the field so another could win the hunt and this conversation would all be for naught. "I accept."

Mills broke away without a sideways glance and Lindsey hadn't another moment to consider it before Powell caught his ear.

"We have further business."

"We established that last evening."

"You have something that belongs to me."

"Not that I'm aware." Lindsey watched as Henley trotted to the front of the grouping. "I have no ability to turn back time, Powell. Had I the power, I'd be too busy fixing my own past to interfere in yours."

"We'll see when this is over."

That last bit was ambiguous at best, but Lindsey had no time to reply as a long trumpet blast fired everyone into action.

Impeccably trained and loyal to a fault, Infinity galloped into the fray, anxious to please his master.

Chapter Seventeen

The ladies were assembled on a lawn near the finish. Servants bustled about with food stuffs and refreshments for anyone who cared to picnic. Thick blankets covered the flattest grassy areas and hampers of bread, cheese, and fruit were available. Caroline stood with Teresa Henley in the shade of a pyramidal hornbeam tree. Her mother was seated on a bench a few strides away, engaged in animated conversation.

"How fortunate the weather turned out fair," Teresa commented. "I don't know what I would have done if rain kept everyone indoors."

"I marvel at how perfectly you've arranged this event considering you're—" Caroline hesitated as she searched for the right word. Her gaze dropped to the subtle swell of Teresa's rounded belly.

"Moving slower than usual." Teresa laughed lightly. "We've hosted this event for several years and aside from a review of the guest list, it practically plans itself now. Of course, there's the exception this year that we're holding the party earlier in anticipation of our child." Teresa paused as her smile grew wider. "I suppose everyone will be able to discern who I am at the masquerade ball this evening."

"True, although with each guest's face concealed and the woodland theme dictating elaborate costume and mask, the event is set to be a festive success. It all seems so mysterious. I might dance with a stranger or promenade with a friend and I'd never know. It certainly makes the evening more exciting. I'm looking forward to it." *And the chance to finally share a waltz with Lindsey.*

"I see that wistful gleam in your eyes. You're thinking of someone in particular. A certain gentleman *has* caught your attention." Teresa touched her arm fondly. "Is he riding in the hunt this morning? Perhaps he'll win and present you with the tail."

"My affection won't require such a grand gesture. A dance would be fine. Just one, dare I wish for two."

"You seem especially smitten," Teresa continued. "I'll do everything in my power to see that your wishes come true, although I can make no promises. Even I won't know who is who, their identity concealed behind a mask or domino. Revealing one's name is against masquerade rules."

"It doesn't matter. I'll know him." Caroline nodded with confidence. "For no reason I can explain, whenever the gentleman is near it's as if..." Her voice trailed off.

"You needn't explain further. I understand. It was the same for me when I met Lord Henley. Fate dictated it would be so, and we were useless to resist."

"Hopefully tonight I will decipher his feelings toward me. I've shared his company, but his actions have left me puzzled. And yet, other times..." She stalled in her explanation, unsure how to interpret Lindsey's attention. He embraced her fervently and yet broke promises to meet, sometimes sacrificing the opportunity to kiss her hand in greeting or walk beside her. To have it her way, she would grasp every chance to know him better. Certainly, in the stairwell, they'd shared an intimacy like none other she'd experienced. But Lindsey was a notorious rakehell. Could it be what she interpreted as sincerity was nothing more than distraction? Her high hopes plummeted.

"Since you're interested in finding a match this season and have this gathering to better acquaint yourself with the gentlemen in attendance, I hope you won't squander the time pining for one beau in particular. When you meet the right person, you'll know without a doubt."

This bit of advice, unlike mother's vague and often misguided contributions, rang true to Caroline's heart, and yet in that the contrariness of Lindsey's attention intensified. Her pulse leapt whenever she thought of him. Did he feel the same attraction? She had little aside from flirtation to cause her to believe so. With him being older and more worldly, perhaps she was nothing more than a passing fancy.

* * * *

The fox was a wily devil on the run. The hounds were fast after. And not ten paces behind, Infinity gave chase. Lindsey maneuvered the Arabian with skill, skirting shrubbery and rocks which jutted into the forest path, riding flat against his horse's neck whenever low-lying branches intruded to easily maintain a lead over the pack of riders atop inferior horseflesh.

He had no wish to win the hunt for a variety of reasons. Caroline's disdain for the sport served as the strongest impetus, but too, he'd only participated the past few seasons as it was expected, and then pursued the fox *because it was expected*. His father's interference in his future and demand he find not one but three paintings to reestablish solid fiscal security before he marry and beget an heir drove whatever misgivings he might have harbored straight to hell.

He was bloody sick and tired of doing what everyone *expected*.

While the ton viewed his lifestyle as an endless string of indulgent freedoms, he often played a role, one which was once daring and interesting and now paled greatly, the roguish portrayal difficult to abandon although he desired to do so.

He longed for a fresh beginning. Caroline represented everything he hadn't realized he wanted until he tasted her kiss. Noticed the light in her eyes. Lost himself to frequent distraction, where nothing else mattered beyond the next words that would pass from her honey sweet lips.

Foolishly, he'd given his word not to interfere in Mills' courtship and yet the thought of his friend placing a hand on Caroline or tasting her delectable mouth lit Lindsey with fury, an emotion he needed to keep in check at the moment.

Infinity whinnied and Lindsey shot his attention to the path. A lone rider intersected his progress. It was Powell. *Goddammit*. He could only have cheated and taken another route. But it appeared his half brother wasn't interested in chasing the fox.

Powell raised his arm, revealing a pistol in his hand, and with a sharp jerk of his head indicated Lindsey detour into a nearby copse of trees.

Infinity obeyed this redirection swiftly and soon became hidden by a cluster of hornbeam and juniper. Other anxious riders raced by and Lindsey's slick maneuver went unnoticed.

"What the hell is this about, Powell?" Had he not been so lost in thoughts of Caroline, he might have avoided this situation altogether.

"Ironic, to confront you here so close to our father's most lavish holding." Powell nodded in indication to the east of the property. "But as the legitimate heir, it's yours now, isn't it? You were the chosen son. The one who signified. I was the bastard, the ugly truth kept hidden." He hardly paused. "I've tasked myself with making things right when all I really need is to make things mine."

"If this is about greed, we can remedy the situation," Lindsey scoffed, his mind fast at work. "If this is about our father, then it is out of my control. Bitter and spiteful, wasn't he?"

"I wouldn't know beyond a few brief encounters. Still, I want what I should have had always. Reputation, financial security, and a proper home. He stole my mother's virtue and in return left us with nothing but hardship. Kingswood Manor is a fine beginning to a long overdue compensation."

"Kingswood Manor is mine." Infinity whickered, the horse impatient, and Lindsey held him firm with a tug on the reins. "Do you want all of history or just the spoils? Our sire was neglectful and abusive. Were he alive I'd gladly support your petition for what you believe you deserve, but I can't resurrect the old bastard." *Nor do I have funds to spare.*

"I'm after a rightful share of recognition and a large sum of money." Powell waggled the pistol still clenched in his right hand. "You'll deal with me sooner than later."

"You won't kill me." Lindsey held his half brother's stare a long minute before he nudged Infinity forward. As he turned his back on Powell, a gunshot sounded in the distance. Across the acreage, someone had cornered the fox and won the day.

* * * *

Caroline made her way upstairs, intent on having time to herself before she readied for the evening's masquerade ball. She'd enjoyed her conversation with Lady Henley. Teresa was easy to talk to and possessed an optimistic outlook likely due to the upcoming birth of her first child. As much as Caroline's heart ached with fear and remorse concerning her own future and ability to have a family, she found joy in their new friendship. Mother's unsolicited advice and close companionship were something else altogether. Deep down Caroline knew her mother meant well, but for all the archaic and misguided instruction Mother spouted, Caroline found she behaved in the opposite manner. Whether subconsciously or not, the unsolicited input urged her to rebel.

She made for the hall stairs now, anxious to rest her eyes and sort her thoughts. The finishing field where Lord Mills had regaled everyone with his triumph over the fox had left her feeling unsettled. How anyone could congratulate an armed and intelligent man for cornering a defenseless animal was beyond her comprehension? And what had happened to Lindsey? He'd all but disappeared. For all the talk of his horsemanship he was nowhere to be found. Foolishly she had hoped for a bit of conversation. She would have settled for one of his piercing stares that never failed to set her blood to boil. But as with other times when she'd expected to see him, when he'd promised her otherwise, disappointment proved the victor.

She reached the landing and moved swiftly toward the hall, then came up short. She'd almost collided with the same man who occupied her thoughts. Perhaps she'd conjured him by sheer willpower.

"Jonathan."

He approved of the familiarity with a flash of his smile. Damn the man for being so handsome. It distracted her from purpose.

"Caroline."

Her name rolled from his tongue like an endearment, his voice low, meant for her ears only.

"I thought I might see you outside at the end of the hunt."

"Were you disappointed?"

"That's terribly arrogant of you to ask." Her lips crept upward to soften the admonishment.

"I'm here now." He leaned a little closer, a note of mischief alive in his voice. "And where are you off to?"

"I hope to rest before tonight's masquerade." She matched his eyes. "Will you attend?"

"Far be it from me to miss the pinnacle event of the entire gathering. I rather like to dance," he mused. "And I wouldn't miss seeing you dressed as an ethereal fairy nymph or endearing wood sprite for all the world."

Her smile broke free despite she shouldn't appear so delighted by his words. "You still owe me a waltz, my lord."

"Tonight, I will give you all my dances, my lady."

"How very daring." She warmed from the inside out. "But you court scandal with that promise and will cause every tongue in attendance to wag with gossip. Propriety dictates we dance no more than twice."

"Propriety be damned. Life is full of inconvenient complications, isn't it?"

A door opened and closed down the hall and she slid her eyes to the right, unwilling to turn her attention away but equally concerned their moment would be lost.

"You shall have all my dances, Caroline. That is my vow."

All teasing abandoned, he spoke so sincerely she was tempted to believe it true.

"There are no dance cards, and everyone will be masked. I hardly see how—"

"Have faith this time, love." He took a step away and bowed. "Until this evening."

* * * *

Lindsey walked away, cursing himself as a fool. What nonsense had he spouted, charmed by a mere slip of a girl almost a decade younger than himself? Had life and the lessons found there taught him nothing of wisdom and caution? Apparently not.

She would be hurt in the end. No matter he saw his future in her eyes. No matter his heart beat with enthusiasm and desire whenever he thought of her, he could never offer her the lifestyle she deserved. Oh, he had reputation and status. He'd likely have money enough in the end.

But loyalty? Honor? Love? He wondered if he were capable after so many years of avoiding emotional attachments. He had been raised in a home as cold as the winter wind. He doubted he knew much about tender emotion. He wasn't composed of the traits needed for a lasting marriage. It could only be that she presented a reprieve from his regular schedule of indulgence and discontent. Besides, he was supposed to be advising her on the better candidates of the season, not conjuring ways for their paths to intersect. How despicable.

Still, he wouldn't disappoint her in this. He would have each of her dances if she desired it so.

With the decision made, he forced his concentration to his bastard half brother. Hadn't the man any sense? Confronting him with a pistol during the hunt was a sly, if not dramatic, ruse. Had Powell wished to finish him off, the gunshot would have been dismissed as nothing more than a participant's attempt to win the day and kill the fox.

Bloody hell, not this fox.

Perhaps his father, *their father*, had placed impossible demands upon Powell as well. Lindsey experienced a beat of guilt at the suggestion. While he had endless resources at his disposal, Powell would have a more difficult time. Still, Lindsey couldn't be distracted by whatever unknown conditions existed. He needed to find the two remaining paintings and be damned with begetting an heir. His father had proven a failing example, but the earldom belonged to him. Rightfully. And no one would deny him that power.

Chapter Eighteen

Caroline twirled in front of the cheval glass, pleased with her appearance. Her hair was arranged in a simple style, pinned atop her head with a few soft curls near her nape, where her maid had woven a satin ribbon with seed pearls and peridot gemstones that glinted in the candlelight. Her costume was composed of a flowing gown made of a shimmering silk the color of rich emeralds. The neckline exposed a modest portion of skin, though her shoulders were bare. Her satin slippers were adorned with ladybug shoe clips. She looked every part the enchanted fairy who lived in the forest's flowerbeds. Would the fox find her this evening?

She certainly hoped so.

A tremulous shiver raced through her. What was this game she played with Lindsey? Would he truly attempt to collect her for every dance? The scandalous idea was both reckless and enthralling.

Still, a shred of her mother's unending advice managed to penetrate her giddy anticipation. *A lady must always present herself as the epitome of decorum. Not a hair out of place. Not a laugh too loud or smile too wide.*

Whenever Lindsey spoke to her, looked at her, her pulse tripled, while anticipation developed a maelstrom of emotion that swept through her from head to toe, squeezing her heart and leaving her breathless. What did any of it mean? As of yet she'd squandered every opportunity to converse with other gentlemen, instead spending her time seeking Lindsey or, worse, woolgathering about their conversations.

Reality intruded to remind she was determined to find a husband who would accept her as an equal, despite the possibility she could never bear children. Despite she was *less*. The smile fell from her face and she blinked back the threat of tears. With a deep breath she regained her composure.

All the more reason to enjoy a little excitement away from London. A rare thrill of forbidden pleasure. Who knew what the future held?

Louisa had cautioned her that men often behaved a certain way to obtain the wife they wanted and then adopted entirely different habits once the vows were spoken. Couldn't the reverse be true? Couldn't a rake suddenly decide to settle down?

When had she begun considering him husband material?

With a sharp wag of her head she pushed the questions from her mind and made her way downstairs. Unready to remain alone with her conflicted thoughts, she rushed toward the ballroom. The estate hummed with activity and a tangible sense of excitement, the festive mood contagious and more than invigorating.

Summoned forward by the melodic notes of an orchestra spilling from the large doorway, Caroline crossed the threshold and gasped. The interior of the Henleys' vast ballroom had transformed into a captivating wonderland. Featherlight gauze adorned with fresh flowers and leafy bouquets draped from every cornice and molding piece to create a magical woodland aptly described at the end of a child's fairy tale. Musicians played otherworldly tunes, the light notes of a flute and piccolo accompanied by a harp and the tinkling sounds of bells and chimes.

Each floor tile glistened like a mirror to reflect the crystal chandeliers overflowing with candles overhead. Refreshment tables brimmed with sugary desserts, marzipan sculptures, and crystal goblets with a variety of beverages all set upon intricately laced tablecloths as fine spun as gossamer webs. Guests milled about, their jovial conversation and laughter adding to the fascination. Everyone wore a mask or decadent domino with their costume. A few ladies wore sheer fairy wings, others donned brilliant crowns, whereas most every gentleman appeared some kind of animal, whether bear, wolf, or hound. Servants wore charcoal-grey livery that ensured they blended into the background and didn't detract from the festive interior.

Caroline scanned the room, her eyes wide with wonder. Where was Lindsey? What disguise had he chosen? She glanced to her white satin gloves decorated with tiny ribbon rosebuds. Would he approve of her costume? How silly to wish it so.

A goddess dressed in flowing white drape with a coronet of sage leaves atop her head approached Caroline's elbow.

"Teresa, the ballroom looks beautiful. I'm transported to an absolute paradise," Caroline said.

"Thank you." A smile grew below Teresa's half mask, trimmed with ornate feathers to conceal most of her face. "It's a wonder the staff manages such a dreamy experience every year."

"I know the gentlemen attend your annual event for the fox hunt competition, but surely the ladies must live for this masquerade."

"Oh, yes." Teresa laughed. "The expectations of the season can become so weary, I think everyone enjoys dressing in costume and pretending to be someone else for a change."

A wealth of knowledge was encompassed in those words, and Caroline eyed her new friend pensively.

"I've had several themes through the years, but this one might be my favorite. Now, let me see you." Teresa laughed as she took a step backward. "Why, you embody the perfect woodland enchantress. All you need is a diamond tiara and I'd believe you were queen of the fairies."

"It was easy to choose from the assortment of lovely costumes you provided. I've never seen such fascinating fabrics. The seamstresses who worked tirelessly to adjust the fit should be rewarded. How they managed to make the appropriate alterations in the span of a day or two is amazing."

"Oh, don't doubt they charge me a scandalous amount, but it's worth it."

The two ladies turned their view to the dance floor as an energetic tune began. A whirlwind of green, umber, and honey swirled past as couples moved to the music, their clothing a riot of earth tones in the candlelight.

"It's odd to see animals scampering about a ballroom." Caroline accepted a glass of champagne from a servant's silver tray, her attention snared by a man in a peacock mask with long teal plumes.

"I don't see anyone who resembles Lord Mills in height or stature, though it's near impossible to tell one guest from another. He won the day and the fox tail, and I'm anxious to see to whom he presents the prize. He's made no secret he wishes to find a wife this season."

Caroline remained quiet, unsure if Teresa would pursue the subject with an attempt at matchmaking, most certainly after her friend had discouraged any further interaction with Lindsey. But then the conversation took an unexpected turn.

"I wonder what became of the Earl of Lindsey. He wasn't present at the finish of the hunt and it seems unlike him, although now that I reflect upon it, while he garners everyone's attention, he's too clever a fellow to ever be cornered."

For no reason she could name, Caroline turned her attention toward the entrance of the ballroom and no sooner than her eyes settled on the doorframe, Lindsey walked through. Teresa followed, her attention drawn by Caroline's.

"As if my words reached his ears." Teresa glanced in Caroline's direction and then back again. "I'm not sure if I should be charmed or angry. He's the only guest who has chosen to eschew the masquerade and attend without costume. I'm rather disappointed."

"As am I." Caroline caught the forlorn note in her voice and hurried to continue. "Though it may be he doesn't plan to stay very long." In her mind this made the situation worse, though she tamped down any show of disappointment.

Still, reality reminded, with the earl unmasked and his identity revealed, there would be only one chance to share a dance. She amended the thought, aware even if he had come in costume she wouldn't have been able to accept his partnership repeatedly. She shook her head, angry with herself for allowing hope to muddle her thinking. He'd said he would give her all his dances, but that was impossible now. Why had he offered her that foolish promise? Should she feel honored he would offer her his solitary engagement of the evening, or slighted that as before he wouldn't keep his word? Perhaps *all his dances* referred to one in number.

She chastised herself further. Lindsey was an experienced and worldly man of the realm and she behaved as a naive ingénue, hanging on his every word as if he meant even one of them sincerely. Still, with knowing this, she couldn't tear her attention away.

"No doubt he wishes to distinguish himself from every costumed creature in attendance."

Good lord he looks dashing. More wicked and wild than any disguised gentleman at the masquerade.

Curiosity licked through her. No, not curiosity. Desire? Was that it? She couldn't label the emotion that kept her mesmerized but never had she been so vitally aware of another person.

Perhaps she'd become enchanted. Unable to look away. Outlined by candlelight, from his black eveningwear to snowy white cravat, he looked more the fairy tale villain. His eyes, with their glittering depths and long lashes, promised forbidden pleasure, not salvation.

And then his gaze locked with hers and no matter the distance, despite the elaborate wigs, costumes, and masks, it was as if he knew exactly where she was and delighted in peeking into her soul.

"He's walking over here." Teresa's hushed whisper caught Caroline by surprise and she startled. "You're hidden behind a mask, silly. There's no reason to feel nervous."

"I'm not nervous." She gave a giddy laugh that revealed the opposite.

"Ladies." Lindsey bowed politely before them. "Your costumes are intriguing. I daresay there isn't another guest in the ballroom who compares to either one of you."

He might have meant the words to be shared, but his attention was riveted to Caroline and her heartbeat thundered in response.

"Ah, I see a stag on the other side of the ballroom who looks unmistakably like my husband. Excuse me, will you?" Teresa didn't say more and slipped away before Caroline murmured a soft goodbye.

"My lady."

"My lord."

"Caroline."

His deep tenor made her name a caress as sensual and inviting as warm velvet.

"How did you—"

"I would know you anywhere."

"Why?"

"There are too many reasons to name and, besides, I'd rather dance."

"But I don't understand." And she didn't. She didn't understand her attraction to the earl or his returned interest.

"Nor do I, but that makes it no less true." He smiled and she delighted now in the fact he wore no mask. "And so, may I have this dance, my lady?"

* * * *

Lindsey intended only to enter the ballroom and confirm Powell was among the guests before he went upstairs and searched his half brother's rooms. With everyone running around in disguise it would be virtually impossible to pinpoint a specific culprit if he donned a mask and was seen near the man's quarters. More importantly, any information concerning the Decima, its whereabouts, or Powell's current address would prove useful. Then Lindsey planned to return to the masquerade, make his presence known for the obvious reasons, and pursue his promise to dance with Caroline.

But one glimpse of Caroline in costume and his entire plan went awry. Lust, insistent and visceral, conveniently blanked his brain of thought, while his blood heated, anxious to pursue this new avenue of interest.

She looked otherworldly tonight, dressed in sheer silk, layer upon layer, all of which he'd prefer to tear away with his teeth. He itched to run his lips over her silky smooth skin, breathe in her light fragrance, taste her lips, and kiss her, kiss her again in hope he'd elicit that same soft wanting whimper of rebellion as he'd done in the stairwell. His cock twitched in his breeches and he forced himself to exhale.

His entire existence narrowed to one objective only.

He escorted her to the dance floor and gathered her close in time for the first waltz of the evening.

"Are you enjoying the masquerade?"

"I am now." He looked into her searching gaze, her eyes a-sparkle to their crystalline-blue depths.

"Lady Henley mentioned you didn't show at the end of the hunt this afternoon."

"Mills was the victor. He won the day."

"Hardly a feat to be proud of, at least in my opinion."

"You are too goodhearted, Caroline."

"And you, too jaded."

His mouth quirked in a charming half-smile. "You've put me in my place."

"Someone has to. It may as well be me."

Their dance continued and neither of them spoke for a time, each revolution winding the tension between them tighter.

"If you didn't finish the hunt and you dislike masquerades, what brings you here, Jonathan?"

Her use of his Christian name made his heart lurch. So few people became personal friends, familiar enough for him to allow it. Or maybe it was more hearing his name in her voice that made his pulse thrum with desire. He met her eyes and replied. "You do."

"Ah, so the charmer has returned."

She smiled up at him and he unwillingly lost a piece of his heart.

"What else then?"

"Kingswood." He stated confidently. The property was the one place on the planet he cherished. "Kingswood is Lindsey heritage. The manor and property have passed through decades of generations. People believe I attend Henley's annual event for the festivities and accolades which accompany the hunt, but at the core is the truth: it provides me another opportunity to visit the family's oldest holding."

"It's important to you then."

"Immensely." He wouldn't share how it was the only place that held pleasant memories of his childhood, more importantly of his mother. A woman who endured the same wrath and scorn from his father but chose to plant roses instead of rebel. He'd visited in the past only when his father remained out of house. Now, he needn't concern himself with the complication.

The dance forced them to take a turn nearest the orchestra, and for a few moments conversation was impossible until they were once again ensconced in agreeable position beside two costumed guests, a scruffy bear and sparkling sapphire dragonfly.

At her curious glance he added, "My mother held an interest in horticulture and had extensive gardens planted behind the estate. In summer, it's a sight to behold." Almost as beautiful as the lady in his arms.

"The property sounds lovely."

"Indeed it is."

"I would like to hear more of Kingswood."

I would like you to see it.

For a moment the deliriously reckless request almost left his tongue.

The music ended on a quiet note and she looked slightly dejected.

"Pity that our dance is done."

"You said you would offer me all of them, and I suppose you have kept your word even if *all* was equal to one." Where had that objection come from? Her mother wasted time with her abundance of advice.

He bowed over her gloved hand and nodded.

Then, when he was sure she watched him, he winked and took his leave.

Chapter Nineteen

Caroline stepped away from the dance floor, her emotions in disorder. She rejoiced in having shared a waltz with Lindsey. Better still, an unexpected revelation to the evening. Yet another part, perhaps more than she'd admit to herself, reminded it would be their only chance. Without a disguise, a repeated dance would proclaim a public interest even she wasn't beguiled enough to believe existed.

She schooled her features into polite contentment and aimed for the refreshment table, quick to nab a glass of champagne. Her earlier anticipation paled. The masquerade would extend into the wee hours. Still, she would enjoy herself despite she couldn't share Lindsey's company further.

With a quick scan of the room and the assortment of costumes, she released a wry laugh. This truly was the worst environment for identifying husband candidates. She turned away and lingered near the tables in an attempt to quell a sudden wave of emotion. Lindsey was an elusive man who protected his personal life with vehemence. She'd learned that much in the short time she'd kept his company. Any scant info she'd gleaned was hard won and often achieved through a third party, and yet he'd openly conversed about his ancestral home while they'd danced. Pity the music had ended so soon.

She returned her attention to the ballroom as the notes of the next musical arrangement rent the air.

"May I have this dance, my lady?"

A tall gentleman dressed completely in amber, from his flocked velvet domino to his flowing robe, bowed deeply in front of her. He extended his hand in wait of her answer.

Caroline eyed his elaborate mask, fashioned in the likeness of a fox with pointed ears and long whiskers. His eyes were partially hidden in shadow, their outline dark.

"Of course."

He took her fingers in his, tightly held, warm and insistent, and she followed. The heat of his grasp sent a shiver of delight to the pit of her stomach.

Something about the gentleman's husky voice caused her to peer more closely as they took position on the floor, but the music began before she deciphered a clue. It was a lively country number, not conducive to conversation, though as soon as they joined he spoke to her directly.

"What else is it that you wish to know?"

Her heart tripped with recognition.

"About Kingswood." His mask moved the slightest and she wondered if beneath his familiar half-smile had hitched it upward.

"Everything, my lord," she said with a catch in her throat. The way he looked at her now had her melting like candlewax. Perhaps she was falling in love. Just a little bit.

"You must call me Jonathan." It was a command. Not a request.

"Everything, Jonathan. I wish to hear all about your home."

"Perhaps not that much."

He might have chuckled after his last remark. She couldn't be sure, as the arrangement forced her to move away.

Regrettably, the song ended before they discussed the subject further, and she watched him depart after he pressed a kiss to her glove. The heat of his mouth was perceptible through the satin as it lingered in kind to her anticipation.

Her next dance partner was a black bear, his hooded collar accompanied by a capelet. She scrutinized him from head to boot tips. The gentleman's face was completely concealed, but she needed no clue this time. His eyes held a familiar sparkle. No one would have dared suggest it was Lindsey in disguise, but Caroline knew it as surely as she knew her own name. She'd memorized his gait. Understood the honorable slant of his chin and broad strength of his shoulders. He would keep his word and offer her all of his dances, and not one of the two hundred guests in the ballroom would be wiser.

Etiquette be damned. The Earl of Lindsey was a sly and clever devil. One who'd undertaken an extravagant inconvenience to ensure they would dance all evening.

"Caroline."

Her name in his voice produced a heady reaction, a swirl of delight quick to skitter through her and settle low in her belly. They were dancing a quadrille just as they'd done all those weeks ago.

"Yes?" She had trouble catching her breath.

"Are you pleased?"

"I am." She paused for only a moment. "And impressed by your extravagant ruse."

"Coincidence takes a lot of planning."

"Indeed." He led her through the turn, their bodies perfectly tuned.

"Have you solidified your husband list? Tell me how your hunt is progressing."

His growly demand was in keeping with his ferocious attire.

"Aren't you the wily one to advise and pursue simultaneously?"

"Indeed."

"I have eliminated several gentlemen and continue to thin the field."

He tugged her closer in what others would interpret as a movement in the dance, yet she knew differently. He might ask her about possible suitors and negate her suggestions concerning candidates to wed, but deep down he disliked the conversation. She guessed he persisted only because he *needed* to know. That idea tickled her decidedly.

Her lips were a scant few inches from his chin, the only skin exposed by his mask, and she wished to press her mouth there, lick over the deep indent in a sensual caress that sent a shiver of naughty anticipation straight to her core.

"Is that how you view my intentions?"

"How could I not?" She forced herself to exhale. "I remember our kiss in the stairwell."

"As do I." His hand tightened on hers for the briefest moment.

"Is this your idea of courtship, my lord?"

"Is that what we're doing?"

She might have heard him chuckle, though the movement and music made her unsure.

"Why don't you tell me more about Kingswood. I enjoy hearing of your home."

"Perhaps you should see it for yourself."

She didn't know what to make of that, but a spark of excitement reverberated along his veins, chased too quickly by a shock of impropriety. Dare she be so bold? His hand gripped hers more firmly and he released her just far enough to lead in a full turn before he gathered her close again.

"I would like that."

"As would I."

The music ended with a flourish and she pressed her lips together in disappointment, knowing their conversation had ended too abruptly.

He stepped back and the swelling crowd of festive garb and chattery guests swallowed him. Hopefully he would reappear in yet another disguise so they could continue what seemed an abrupt end to their negotiations.

But that was not to be.

Her mother found her not a beat later and chased the threat of disappointment away.

"I rejoice in seeing you on the arm of so many gentlemen this evening. You've partnered for every dance. Accepting this invitation was a good idea, Caroline." Her mother gave a thoughtful nod. "Surely you'll come away with future opportunities from the evening. Remember, a gentleman's conversation is most important. Be demure. Listen attentively and dare not speak your mind. I know you understand the importance of making a fortuitous match. No matter the circumstances, do your best to remember all we've discussed."

Caroline dismissed her mother's contrary advice as she watched her walk away. The ball continued and she politely accepted invitations to dance from three guests who were not Lindsey. As the hour progressed, she began to wonder if perhaps he had no other disguises, no other ideas to place himself in her path.

"Don't look to your left, but a lion is watching you as closely as if he hunts his prey."

Lady Henley came up beside her, two glasses of champagne in hand. Caroline welcomed the distraction of her friend's conversation, though she politely declined the beverage, her stomach too knotted for the sweet refreshment.

"I'm afraid I've danced too much already." Caroline dared a slight peek over her shoulder in hope she could identify Lindsey in the vicinity, but the thick crowd prevented it. "I was contemplating whether or not to retire for the evening. These slippers have pinched my toes terribly for the past hour." She glanced downward and silently apologized to her footwear for the exaggeration of what was nothing more than a lack of desire to remain at the event now that her earl had gone.

"Ah, but not quite yet. The musicians are beginning another waltz, and it would appear the king of the jungle means to claim your hand." Teresa laughed softly as she stepped away, and Caroline looked up into a pair of familiar eyes, their long dark lashes as beguiling as the lion who stood before her.

"My lady."

If only she was.

The startling thought that this wasn't just a whimsical game of flirtation, that she would very much like to mean more to the Earl of Lindsey than a distraction from his boredom, rose up and snared her attention.

They fell into step and spent the first minute of the dance in utter silence. Her mind spun with the gravity of her realization. She had no idea what Jonathan contemplated.

"Your fragrance is enchanting, my lady."

He wasn't given to frequent compliments, and her smile curled at his kind words.

"Thank you, my lord." She glanced up, into his enigmatic gaze, far too beguiling behind that mask. So many masks he wore in real life. How ironic to discover a touch of the true man while he was disguised.

"Meet me in the garden after the next musical arrangement." He turned her, the pressure of his palm on the small of her back insistent she pay heed to both his words and movement as they neared the rear wall of windows adjacent to the marble terrace. "I have a gift to share."

He chuckled at her questioning stare, the throaty sound evoking a race of shivers across her bare shoulders to warm her blood and cause her heart to join the chase. And then he released her from his hold and exited the ballroom through the French doors, vanishing into the night. She might have stood there, motionless, blindly watching after him, if the orchestra hadn't begun a high-spirited number, as if to remind she had limited time to execute her plan. With nothing more than a shallow smile, she excused herself and hurried away.

Chapter Twenty

Caroline slipped through the rear doors of the estate, discarded her mask into the forgiving fronds of a nearby potted plant, and ventured out onto the same walkway she'd traversed the day of her arrival. At that time she'd wanted another glimpse of Lindsey, at best a chance opportunity to converse with him again, but now she escaped the masquerade for a clandestine meeting. A whisper of fog swirled over her ankles to remind she wasn't dressed for strolling through a garden. Overhead, diamond starlight studded the sky but otherwise, aside from the few oil lanterns that crackled and flickered as they adorned the doorframe, she'd stepped into complete quietude.

Her heart beat hard in her chest. Was it nervous anticipation or a thrum of her conscience which reminded no good could come of her actions? Mother's abundant advice poked at her brain. *A lady knows her place and never endeavors to venture beyond society's strictures.* How about beyond the garden wall? It was both scandalous and daring. Her mother would suffer an apoplectic fit if Caroline were discovered.

But she yearned to learn more of Lindsey, his enigmatic allure most certainly a mask for a man of sincere thought and emotion. He'd gone to great trouble this evening, changing into multiple costumes to dance with her repeatedly. Hidden beneath all those layers of rakish charm was a loyal heart of gold. She was sure of it.

And now, she would have the opportunity to know him better. Without worry or interference from society and its restrictive rules. Perhaps then she could satisfy her curiosity and put it all to rest.

She walked across the slates with unwavering certainty this was what she wanted to do, needed to do. If she didn't take advantage of the earl's invitation, she'd never forgive herself and never hold a thought for wondering if she'd mistakenly chosen timidity instead of adventure.

But what of Lindsey? She'd fallen under his spell and likely fallen in love along the way. What of his interest? Was she yet another diversion? What gift could he possibly mean to share with her in the darkened gardens at this late hour?

The steady thud of horse hooves interrupted her conflicted deliberation. Shadows shifted against the curtain of night sky and she recognized Infinity first, because there was no disguising the regal animal, even in the velvety darkness.

A moment later, the stallion slowed to a stop.

"You're here." Lindsey looked majestic dressed in eveningwear atop his bewitching mount.

"You told me to come to the gardens," she whispered, though there was no fear of being discovered. She'd walked far enough from the estate that she couldn't be detected by sight or sound.

"I asked you," he corrected, a note of teasing in his voice.

"Was there a question? I don't recall."

"It doesn't matter. It's more important that you're here."

He slid from the saddle and stepped beside her. His horse retreated, swallowed by the darkness, as if the animal possessed equal manners to its master, a misty cloud of lingering breath the only proof the scene wasn't an aberration.

Everything fell silent except her pulse. The heady scent of night blooms and gardenia added perfume to the air. He closed the distance between them in one stride and stared at her intently.

"Is this what you want, Caroline?"

His voice moved over her; each syllable brushed again her skin. He leaned in, a covert smile at play across his face. Then with hardly any movement at all his lips possessed hers, his tongue brushing into the hollow of her mouth in a sensual bid for attention. He broke the kiss before she could register all the pleasure it offered.

"Are you asking permission?" Her words sounded breathless. She willed her pulse to slow, her heartbeat to steady.

"I would never harm you and despite the late hour, night sky, and foolish masquerade, I would never risk your reputation or respect without your full consent to step beyond society's strictures."

"Very prettily said, my lord." She moved her mouth closer to his in case he desired to kiss her again. "My answer is yes."

"You will be ruined if anyone discovers you've left the party to sneak away with me to Kingswood."

"My answer is still yes."

She heard him exhale. Was it relief or contentment which caused his reaction? She didn't have time to decide, as he let out a low whistle and Infinity reappeared, his huge form separating from the night like black magic. The gravity of the moment caused her breath to catch. She hadn't ridden sidesaddle or otherwise since her accident. She didn't fear horses. She admired them actually, for their beauty and strength. But likewise, her mother's dire warning rang in her ears. Nevertheless, she trusted Lindsey and knew his reputation as an excellent horseman.

Lindsey mounted in a graceful movement that belied his broad stature. Once settled, he extended his arm. She stared at his hand for a beat and then with surety placed her palm in his firm grasp.

* * * *

The short ride to Kingswood would be the death of him. Every nudge and nestle of Caroline's firm backside against his groin provoked wicked images he'd rather contemplate alone and not astride a horse. It was an uncomfortable pleasure-pain, but still he couldn't vanquish the happiness she brought to him with her trust and eager acceptance of his invitation. He had only a vague idea of what the night would hold. He wanted to show her his estate. Wanted to separate her from all duties, distractions, and responsibilities and keep her locked away all to himself, at least for a good hour or so. He needed to spend time with her for reasons he wasn't yet ready to examine.

He'd hardly sorted his thoughts and intentions before they turned onto a wooded trail that connected the two properties. He hadn't visited Kingswood since his father's passing and the solicitor's unsettling reading of the will. Not wishing to exhume the ugly, often violent memories his father had instilled here, Lindsey had also neglected his mother's memory. Kingswood was her home more than anyone's. She'd persevered and endured by pottering around in her gardens when others might have succumbed to their husband's tyranny in an altogether different manner. He supposed she alone was the reason a few strangled childhood recollections survived here among the soft scent of so many roses.

He slowed Infinity and maneuvered his horse around a bend which led to the rear entrance of the estate. Sallow moonlight lent a burnished tone to the limestone stonework, and as he nudged Infinity closer his eyes followed the pathway straight to the back door. A soft glow shone in the lower-floor windows, while few of the second-floor windows were lighted. He'd sent word ahead he would make use of the property this week, although he hadn't informed the staff of exactly when he would arrive. Now, as he approached, he wondered at the wisdom in his decision to bring Caroline here. In one of many poor habits, he hadn't thought beyond the moment. Beyond the desire to have Caroline all to himself.

Here.

Now.

"It's lovely." She twisted her neck in an effort to be heard and he moved closer, bowing his head so her lips nearly brushed his cheek. Her scent was quick to settle in his soul.

"I love this property and despise it just the same." Not wanting to pale the evening, he didn't explain further. It wasn't the time to complicate matters with his unhappy history. If only they could spend hours here in the daylight instead of the dead of night. Night hours revealed all kinds of unpleasant memories. At least in the new sun, his mother's gardens promised a shred of hope.

He'd underestimated his staff, as a footman readily opened the rear door and signaled to another servant, who took hold of Infinity's reins. Lindsey nodded, no words necessary, and after he slid from the saddle he turned and lifted Caroline down with great care. The footman, a man of discretion, as were all his servants, viewed Caroline warily and then just as quickly cast his eyes away. Aside from the lady's beauty, which would cause any male to take notice, she remained dressed in costume. Coupled with their unexpected arrival, the man earned his startled lapse.

Another beat and they were once again alone.

"Were it daylight, I would take you into the grounds." He canted his head and she viewed the direction he'd indicated. "My mother planted roses."

She returned her attention to him. Did his tone give away too much? "I see."

"No, you couldn't possibly. But I hope someday you will." Her brow furrowed at his cryptic remark, but she didn't question him.

His parents had shown little affection. His father withheld any approval or fondness, and his mother was too consumed by her own sadness to spare him gentleness. "My mother planted flowers whenever my father troubled her. And be assured I use the word troubled in the broadest definition. He drank and spewed vitriol. She planted roses. He raised a hand to her. She planted roses. He brought whores into our home and she planted roses. Were it daylight you would see hundreds, if not thousands, of blooms in every color imaginable. Not just some cutting garden where the staff collects blooms for the hall, but endless beds in a riot of colors that form a tapestry of pain and abuse. As their marriage endured, her gardens grew in proportion. And yet however bittersweet, I didn't realize how much I missed the remembrance of her in this place until we rode onto the property."

"I'm sorry, Jonathan." She hurried to continue. "I can smell their lovely fragrance despite it's so late."

He met her eyes, stared into the depths, and any further consideration of his disgraceful father and miserable upbringing evaporated like mist in the night. Yet at the root of it, he knew it was why he never dared open his heart to love, never took an interest in the women who'd warmed his bed in the past. It was a convenient habit he believed hurt no one. What a fool he was after all.

"Come." He reached for her hand, clasping her fingers tightly. "Let's go inside."

* * * *

Caroline placed her hand on his forearm after they'd walked over the threshold. The flex of his muscles beneath his coat caused a shimmer of excitement to sweep through her. Either that or she'd caught a chill from their spontaneous jaunt across the countryside. She couldn't explain it and didn't try, because whatever Lindsey meant to accomplish by bringing her here was important to him. She could tell in each of his deliberate movements, each carefully spoken word. This man who shared so little of himself.

They'd entered through the back and were met with immediate warmth. She glanced briefly into each room as they accomplished the hall, first the service kitchens, where several fireplaces kept the rooms aglow, and then farther, past the decker's room and dining room until they reached a cozy parlor. Undulating shadows cast by an eager flame danced across the hall. She was surprised to see a fire burned here as well, more startled when he closed the double doors and turned the key in the lock.

"Had you already planned to visit Kingswood this evening?" She couldn't keep her curiosity at bay any longer.

"I think so."

His puzzling answer left her confused, not for the first time since they'd arrived at Kingswood. "This is a lovely room. Your mother must have enjoyed greeting guests here." She wondered of his history, his upbringing. The few words he'd spared as they'd come across the property border left her aghast at how solitary and sad his childhood must have been.

"She rarely took callers. Aside from the distance to London, my mother was often in need of quietude. Whether it was an abundance of emotion she wished to disguise or the evidence of my father's mistreatment, I shall never know. I was sent off to school as soon as I was of age."

She measured his reply, unsure if she should comment. He wouldn't want her pity or sympathy. He was far too proud for either, though she longed to wrap her arms around him. The usual devil-may-care attitude that served as his mask was gone, replaced by a haunting expression of disappointment.

"I'm sorry, Jonathan." She couldn't resist the slightest comfort. "It must have been difficult growing up in a house with so little kindness. My parents are a loving sort and I find myself equally giving of gentle emotion."

"My father and I did everything we could to avoid crossing each other's path. It was a simple task to accomplish. The house is large and meant to be filled with the sound of laughter. Instead my father considered me..." He paused and drew a deep breath. "Useless in all but one purpose, which was to carry on his name. I will never give him that satisfaction, even in death."

She touched her stomach involuntarily, his harsh words a hammer blow to her heart. How foolish, really. She didn't even know if she could bear children, and yet to hear Jonathan vow never to father a child affected her with fatalistic impact. She should be happy. Perhaps a future together would not be such an impossibility if the earl cared little for creating a family. Yet her heart twisted itself inside out, turbulent emotion the cause.

He turned then, his eyes piercing her with such intensity it was as if he looked into her soul and searched for peace. Then just as quickly his expression changed.

"I didn't bring you here to bore you with maudlin tales."

"Why did you bring me here?" She stepped closer, wanting to gauge his reaction and at the same time regain her equilibrium.

"I thought that was obvious." He smiled, all evidence of earlier sorrow gone. "I intend to ravish you. I'm a despicable scoundrel, as you know. A wily fox too clever for the hunt. A reprehensible rakehell who preys on unsuspecting ladies foolish enough to trust my charming conversation and run away with me into the night."

His self-proclaimed pride in reputation should have sent her sprinting toward the doorway, but instead a spike of intense pleasure spiraled through her.

"I've heard the same spoken of you. A man of many masks. So tonight, you are the fox who devours whoever crosses his path." She met his eyes and did her best to flatten a sudden hint of smile.

"And yet you're here anyway. Despite I'm not recommendable husband material."

He leaned closer to whisper and his voice held a lovely calm to it. He knew exactly what he was about.

"Indeed I am looking for a husband." She didn't elaborate and turned away to walk toward the hearth and steady her nerves from his disarming charm. Instead, the heat of the flames aided the sparks of desire that simmered through her veins. She forced herself to focus on the painting above the mantel. Something about the work was familiar. Had her father made a point of showing it to her when they'd visited a gallery in Italy? But then, how was it here in Bedfordshire? Before she could decide, his voice drew her attention away.

"Would you like a glass of sherry?"

"No, thank you."

He left off the sideboard and moved to stand beside her, his attention on the same artwork she'd studied moments before.

"It's a priceless original. My father collected a series of paintings, interested in their value more than their composition. It was not unlike his bearing of a son. He needed an heir but took little pleasure from possessing one."

"It's a pity he was blind to the admirable qualities I see so readily."

She detected surprise by the slight lift of his brow, but he did not reply. Instead he turned to face her, the space between them diminished to the width of an exhale, the air charged with a heavy undercurrent of desire.

"There is no need to gild my unsuitability. My father left me quite a legacy. His cruelty shaped me into the man I am today, wary to ever care too much, look too deeply, or dare to trust."

"That isn't true, Jonathan."

He drew a long breath in answer, and she waited for him to elaborate, but when he remained silent she forged on. "So you perpetuate this charade, this uncaring character of roguish indifference?"

"Not a charade, more a distraction." He stared into her eyes as he continued. "I would never ruin you, Caroline." His words held a startling vehemence.

It was her turn to be surprised. Not for the words but the sincerity found in them.

"I know." Her answer came out in a hushed whisper as longing winnowed through her.

Time stretched. His gaze dropped and he focused on her mouth. Her heart pounded in her chest. Still, she held her breath in wait. It was as if this single moment meant more than all the trifling conversations and amusing flirtations they'd perpetuated the last weeks. All the contrived coincidences and manufactured excuses, coy glances and tempting half-smiles, were insignificant compared to the way he viewed her now. His dark lashes lowered in sensual attention and the weight of his stare was unlike anything she'd experienced before. Decisions were being made silently as their hearts communicated. Mayhap their souls.

She played with fire. Even one ember of desire was too dangerous. And yet one tiny spark, small and insignificant, given enough air to breathe could create an inferno.

Would he not kiss her and allow her to breathe again?

Chapter Twenty-One

Emotion gripped him without warning. He wasn't thinking, and yet he was never so sure in his decision. He stared into the sparkling blue depths of Caroline's eyes and lowered his mouth to hers. Her breath caught, nothing more than a sigh of relief perhaps. But she melted into their joining, and the heat of her body matched his despite layers of inconvenient fabric separated them.

It was a claiming kiss.

An unspoken promise.

He needed to hold her.

Wanted to keep her.

Mine.

The word streaked through his brain, fierce and unyielding.

She might bandy about the idea she sought some other gentleman for husband, but lest she make that mistake he would kiss her into oblivion and remove any such illusion.

Caroline was his. Even if he wouldn't admit it.

She opened beneath the subtle pressure of his mouth and that was all it took to release his barely constrained ardor. Their tongues touched, rubbed, tangled around each other in an erotic dance. He breathed deep and the delicate scent of orchids assailed him, causing his cock to grow hard in his breeches. He gathered her close, quick to lift her effortlessly and deposit her atop the overstuffed chaise near the corner of the hearth. She fit his body like a key in a lock. Perfectly formed to counterbalance and complete him, to open dark secrets he thought never to confront.

He shifted, lowering her gently so she aligned with the purfled pillows at her back, and then leaned in without breaking the hold of her eyes, sharp with curiosity and wonderous just the same.

He was done for.

Rubbish.

A besotted fool.

He'd tried to fight it and failed miserably. There was nothing more to be done, but so much more yet to do. Otherwise he'd go on wanting her forever.

He cupped her face in his palm, her cheek silky smooth, her ripe lips parted as if she couldn't decide on what to say. Tilting her chin, he captured her mouth in a deep lingering kiss. She tasted like everything he wanted and never dared to allow himself. A share of happiness. A chance to begin again.

Possibility.

How foolish to think that when he had no choice at all. Heat pumped through him, scorching hot, firing his veins to settle in his groin where he grew harder still.

She set her hand upon his chest and the tremble of her fingers against his heart was his undoing. He shut his eyes and inhaled, summoning the courage to harness control.

Where to begin? Anywhere. *Everywhere.*

He nuzzled kisses down the length of her neck. Her soft-spoken murmurs of appreciation added tinder to his conquest. His mouth hungered to taste every inch of her, nip at her pale smooth skin and laze caresses to each of her full breasts. Her costume was composed of countless layers of gauzy fabric, so light and barely there he could feel every soft curve beneath with little effort.

She smoothed her hands inside his coat, her fingers outlining his tensed muscles as if she counted the ridges, hesitant at first but then more determined. Could it be she'd never touched a man's body before? The idea gave him pause despite it instigated a surge of possessive pride.

He would be her first. The knowledge brought him considerable satisfaction despite it was a selfish irrational thought. Long from now, when he was gone and she lived a different life, she'd still have reason to remember him. If for no other reason than he was her first.

He wanted her, all of her, still he'd never ruin her. He wasn't so selfish as that. So then kissing would suffice. But as delightfully exquisite as it was, it could never temper the raging storm of desire licking at his heart, or quiet the one-word litany roaring through his brain.

Mine.

* * * *

Caroline closed her eyes and melted against the cushions in shameless invitation. Somewhere between him sweeping her from her feet and capturing her lips in a deep open-mouthed kiss, she'd abandoned all better sense and embraced reckless emotion. Her gown was no barrier to his heat, the delicious friction of his muscular thigh against her hip a forbidden yet enthralling pleasure. She dropped her head back and savored the rush of sensation he ignited with each caress. The sensual brush of his whiskers against her neck was a foreign pleasure-pain. How many liberties would she allow? She'd already compromised herself, her future, by slipping away into the night. But when it came to Lindsey, she found she hadn't an ounce of resolve.

There was no denying he called to her heart, that the mere sight of his dark gaze and tempting smile left her undone. But what were his intentions beyond this moment? He composed a perplexing riddle and she refused to quit the solution, though her thinking grew increasingly more muddled.

He paused, and his exhale sent a shiver of anticipation skittering across her shoulder. Was he caught in the same half-mad musings, wanting the unthinkable and at the same time refusing to end their evening?

Still, this wasn't something as elemental as physicality. She enjoyed his company, replayed their witty conversations, and pursued any opportunity to place herself in his path. She wasn't so foolish not to realize they shared an attraction that went beyond the boundaries of the chaise where she now reclined. But what would become of it? If they progressed much further, their relationship would take a marked shift. She sensed his hesitation, his careful touches and restrained position.

Hadn't she already reassured the earl she wanted his attention? Perhaps she would have to show him.

"Jonathan." Her voice sounded tentative.

He exhaled deeply and murmured a response against her neck as he nuzzled another kiss, his thick hair tickling the underside of her jaw.

She smoothed her hands over his chest and up to his shoulders, forcing him to pull back and meet her eyes. His face looked severe, so tightly held, for a fleeting moment she wondered if he was angry with her for interrupting him.

But no. His expression immediately softened. Another breath and he appeared more at ease.

Deciding against words, she tugged at his cravat, her fingers as unsteady as her voice only moments before. She would show him this was her decision, and not his, to make.

He placed his hand over hers, ceasing the action. "I've braved more than I'd expected, forbidding myself from spoiling your beauty, but, love, there's only so much I can endure."

"So I'm not to touch you?" Even to her own ears her response sounded petulant. She bit her bottom lip, aware she played with fire. And too she saw that same acute awareness, not unlike a desperate longing in his eyes that likely matched her own.

"There are ways I can bring you pleasure that won't ruin you, Caroline." He searched her face as he spoke. "Would that suffice?"

His question prompted her to smile, and she thought to answer, but in that instant his mouth was already on hers in a hard hungry kiss that promised he told the truth. He broke away just as quickly, once again practicing control though his eyes held a wild gleam.

Under his avid attention, she reached for the ties at her neckline, loosening the ribbons that held it in place, the costume no match for her determination. He watched her fingers at work. Indecision quirked a wrinkle in his brow. And then he seemingly discarded whatever vow he'd made to himself.

Pushing away her hands, he slid her sleeves down and adjusted her position so she rested more firmly against the cushions, his body slanted over hers, a fierce look of carnal desire on his face.

He exhaled deeply, as if he tempered his ardor further, and then set to work lowering layer after layer of silk and linen until he reached her chemise. His gaze was heavy-lidded now, his jaw set tight before he lowered the fabric and brought his mouth to her breasts, first one, then the other.

And oh, the glory of the feelings he wrought, so sensitive and intense, more erotic than her wildest imaginings. Her nipples pebbled harder with each stroke of his tongue. The clever caress of his fingers as they cupped and stroked reduced her breathing to stilted sighs.

He pressed his thigh between her legs and she welcomed the heated strength. Inside, her awareness gathered and pulled, tugging at every point of sensitivity to settle lower at the exact place he pressured. She wriggled, wanting relief, and he grunted his approval, nudging his leg farther between hers.

The costume still surrounded them, each brush of gauzy tulle and lace accentuating sensation against her skin until a rush of cool air met her calves, the firm hold of his bare hand on her knee almost too much to bear as he collected fabric and pushed it aside, all the while never breaking contact. He teased her breasts, nipped her shoulders, and explored her mouth, his tongue after every secret she kept hidden.

He slid his hand higher to the tender flesh of her inner thigh and she quivered, all thought beyond irrepressible pleasure abandoned. His fingertips traced the edge of her stocking, a teasing graze that made her more impatient. She was wet and aching with want, all at once forgetting herself, lost to the Earl of Lindsey's intoxicating charms. Anxious to fall headfirst into the abyss of potent pleasure he'd conjured with nothing more than a kiss.

He stroked a fingertip across the lacy opening of her pantalets and she nearly lifted off the cushion, aroused and alert, frantic for relief from the wanting. He chuckled against her neck, the deep throaty sound reverberating through her until he stroked again and the result skewered her in another pleasure rush.

"You're so wet for me, Caroline. I want to drown in you, taste you, bring you to glorious climax. You're so very lovely, and tonight you're completely mine."

She slid her hands through his hair and down to grasp his shoulders, anchoring herself and waiting. Wanting. She tensed with anticipation and again he stroked, featherlight, barely touching her skin. To her mortification she moaned in disappointment. It seemed no sooner than he began then he stopped, the fleeting pressure of his caress already gone.

"Again." The word came out ragged and harsh, and she swallowed before she continued. "Please." She clenched her eyes closed, too aware he watched her. When had she become so wanton? Her begging no better than every sin and accusation made of the earl. Her existence reduced to no other thought than the pursuit of relief.

"What is it you want from me, Caroline?"

Oh, he was a wicked, wicked man to force her to put it into words. To give voice to her fantasies and speak her darkest desires. She struggled for clarity from the haze of sensation, her breathing none too steady. Forcing her eyes open, she saw his held a devilish gleam that dared her to answer. "Touch me there again."

"Like this, love?" He stroked slower and pressed his fingertips past the lacy edging of her underclothes to delve farther into her wet warmth. "Yes."

He found her mouth again and swallowed her answer, their tongues tight as he pressed his fingers to her core and rubbed, coaxing her to cry out, eyes clenched, as a shower of sparks danced behind her lids.

* * * *

Lindsey pulled Caroline into his arms as she reclaimed her composure. With her decorum and innocence, he'd never have predicted she'd display such uninhibited pleasure. He could barely wait for next time they—*no*. Foolish thought. He couldn't allow it. Because next time, he would never be able to stop. As it was, his erection strained painfully inside his breeches, the opportunity for release all but impossible. Somewhere buried within in him, a shred of conscience survived. He wouldn't ruin her and abandon her, nor take her innocence and offer nothing in return. He couldn't hurt her as his father misused and shamed his mother.

He knew his boundaries. Touching Caroline again and listening to those breathy little moans without stripping her bare and devouring every inch of her beautiful body was impossible. And he'd wouldn't destroy what was never meant to be his.

She sighed against his chest and nestled closer. His heart, that traitorous organ, continued to pound and taut it was able to do more than pump blood through his veins. Caroline deserved someone without a broken history and complicated future. She deserved predictability, stability, and a domestic fellow who didn't need to chase after stolen paintings in order to afford the most basic necessities for a secure future.

Barlow's latest missive had turned the screws tighter, and a part of him wondered how far the solicitor would go in refusing funds. His father must have set exacting boundaries. Would the old duke and his grim man of affairs allow Lindsey to sink completely? The idea was debatable. His father had had no use for him in life and seemingly enjoyed the last laugh from his cold dark grave. He couldn't expect Caroline to wait indefinitely while he sorted out the mess.

And where had *that* thought come from? He sounded the besotted fool. She wasn't meant to be his, no matter his brain demanded he pay attention, that single word a mantra as loud as his heartbeat in his ears.

Mine.

What had he done to himself? He would go mad with wanting.

"Jonathan?"

He jerked to awareness as Caroline wriggled backward and set to work adjusting her gown. She hadn't looked at him yet, and he wondered now if shyness claimed her. The idea amused. She would prove an amorous lover in the bedroom. A spike of bald jealousy caused him to clench his teeth.

"Thank you." She met his eyes from beneath lowered lashes, and it took every bit of his remaining strength not to kiss her again.

"How have I earned your gratitude, my lady?" He couldn't help but tease her into a deeper blush. Lord, she was beautiful with her hair mussed and skin glowing.

"In many ways." An impish smile curled her lips. "For bringing me here to Kingswood Manor and allowing me into your home."

"And?"

"I didn't know I could feel this way." Her voice held a note of fascination. She drew a deep breath and met his eyes with unnerving intensity. "I feel newly aware, every cell of my being alive and sensitive." The words tumbled out one over another until she paused and her gaze somehow reached his soul. "I…"

Don't say something foolish, Caroline. Don't say words you hardly mean.

She hesitated, and the silence brought with it an uncomfortable ill ease. She was no ingénue, inexperienced and prone to dramatics. Intelligence lived in her lovely blue eyes. Only a fool would mistake innocence for ignorance.

He knew not to dally with her feelings or body. Still, at this moment, he felt punched in the heart.

"Indeed." He stood from the chaise. He needed distance from all that emotion and nodded toward a crystal decanter and glasses on the sideboard across the room. "Would you like something to drink?"

Her brows lowered, as if deliberating a difficult decision. "No. I'll need to return shortly."

"Already?" He moved across the room to pour two fingers of brandy. If he wasn't going to ravish her this evening, he needed fortification. With her poised atop the velvet chaise, a tempting mixture of rosy skin and frothy gown, he had to keep his wits about him.

What was he thinking, bringing her here? Too many answers demanded to be heard.

He wanted her alone.

He didn't want to come here alone.

More than anything, he wanted to see her in the house he would someday call his home.

And why had she agreed to accompany him? Curiosity? A foolish quest for a taste of wickedness?

The reason didn't matter. He would return her tonight as if nothing happened, and that would be the end of it. Their lives unchanged. He swallowed the rest of the liquor in his glass knowing he didn't believe his own lie. Something sliced through him sharp and indelible, perhaps the notion he was making a mistake that he would regret, the idea he was ending something that was meant to continue.

He glanced in her direction. That same awkward silence pervaded the room. Did she already regret what had transpired between them? He may be older, but for all his life experience he didn't know what to say. Previous interactions with females had required little conversation afterward. He certainly couldn't tease her about her husband search when he'd just had his hands—

"What are you thinking?" She rose from the chaise and drew nearer. "Your scowl could scare the fire from the grate."

"This evening is impossible."

"How so?"

He advanced as he spoke. "I'd like nothing more than to carry you upstairs into my bedchamber, which reflects sadly on my control at the moment. The Devil knows I have little to offer you beyond that."

She returned a slight smile, which again surprised him. He'd worried he would shock her, and yet she hadn't batted an eyelash.

"You're lovely, Caroline. Far too lovely. Yet as black as my soul and the sins I've committed, I could never ruin you. One lucky man will someday take you for wife and the mother of his children. That's how it should be. I was selfish this evening, and for that I'm sorry. Forgive me."

"No. Please don't apologize." Her smile had fallen away while he spoke, and she dropped a hand to her stomach, as if his words upset her. "That very well may be how it *should* be, but I doubt my future will follow that plan. I—" She stammered and recovered in too short a span for him to interject, though she sounded slightly defeated. "I can't have children, Jonathan. Circumstances being what they are, my chances at motherhood are narrow indeed."

He touched her shoulder lightly, unable to understand fully and yet unwilling to pry for details that would cause her pain. Still, he couldn't ignore her discomfiture. "Are you ill?"

"No." She turned and his hand fell away. "Recovered from an accident. Well enough. But now I'm less because of it."

He waited for her to elaborate, his hand curled into a fist at his side.

"I was thrown from my horse and something inside me was damaged, or so the physician told my mother. I only knew the pain and aftermath. The internal injuries left me..." Her whisper trailed off, lost to a rude hiss from the fire. And then she sniffed valiantly and reassembled in the next beat. "Despite your angry declaration earlier, I know you need an heir. Every earl does, doesn't he?" She turned again to face him, the shimmer of unshed tears in her eyes. "You deserve a house full of sons. And daughters too. I've come to terms with my future. I'll need to find a husband who'll accept me despite the sadness that likely awaits any attempt at childbearing." She rushed on now, with hardly a breath in between. "Or, as my mother suggests, I should find an older gentleman who already has the family he desires and needs pleasant companionship in his twilight years."

"Caroline. You are so much more than a man could hope for in a wife." Anger overrode the kinder emotion in his voice. Too many fierce objections crowded in at once and he remained wholly unprepared. He drew her close and tucked her head under his chin, her cheek against his heart. "Any fool who dare label you as less will feel the point of my blade."

She gave a slight nod but said nothing else. The moment wanted for no more words.

Chapter Twenty-Two

They returned to Henley grounds soon after with sparse conversation between them, though they'd formed another unspoken bond. First with their intimacy and then afterward, with candid conversation. It was well into the morning hours when he dismounted, quick to lift Caroline down, but hardly ready to release her.

"Thank you for tonight." The moon bathed her face in pearly shadows that emphasized her beauty, the crystalline sparkle in her eyes as reflective as diamond dust. "Thank you for listening."

"And you in turn." He thought better than to tug her into his embrace, aware any guest unable to find sleep might choose to gaze at the stars and discover them instead.

So he stared at her only a moment longer before he stepped back into the darkness to watch her scuttle safely inside.

The return ride to Kingswood was fast and direct. He reentered the house, took the stairs to the upper level, and stalled outside his father's bedchamber. How many years had passed since he walked these halls, since he stood in the same room as his father?

Too many. Yet still not enough. He'd visited Kingswood to hear the solicitor read the impossible conditions of the inheritance but Lindsey hadn't stepped beyond the drawing room, at first not wishing to exhume painful memories, and then afterward too consumed with volatile emotion for clear thought.

Tonight he was no better. Except it wasn't Barlow who disturbed his peace, but Caroline in the most opposite manner. He already missed her smile, her light scent still in his lungs, her tempting kiss branded on his lips.

He'd held back. Refused himself. Not a habit in his usual nature. But he had a heart, no matter he ignored it more often than not. Because to take all she might offer in the heat of the moment would ruin her beyond anyone's repair. Only the Devil would demand Lindsey need produce an heir as soon as possible and then put the tempting lady in his path.

This conclusion ceased his pacing and with a long hard stare at his father's bedchamber door, Lindsey strode away.

* * * *

Caroline fairly floated down the stairs the following morning. Her mother's gay chatter beside her went unheard as one thought monopolized Caroline's mind. *Jonathan Cromford, Earl of Lindsey.* She'd fallen asleep reliving his blissful touch and her body's reaction. Never had she imagined the simmering passion he'd elicited. She couldn't wait to see him and inspect his face for any evidence he was as shaken as she. Would he behave any differently for the secrets they'd shared? Would she? It wasn't only their intimacy that caused her heart to thud a heavy beat. She'd confessed her deepest fear and he'd reacted with a fierce statement of possessive protection. That one condition could not be overlooked. Meandering through these thoughts, she crossed the threshold to the breakfast room with her mother at her side.

"Caroline." Lady Teresa met them and together they moved to the sideboard.

It was the last morning of the gathering and while footmen milled about at the ready to assist guests, a casual ease claimed the room. Conversation and laughter intermingled with the sound of utensils on china.

"How quickly the days have passed," Lady Derby began. "Thank you again for your kind invitation, Lady Henley."

"It was my pleasure. Making your acquaintance and becoming fast friends with your daughter has been the highlight of this year's gathering for me."

Teresa glanced her way and Caroline returned the smile. She had many reasons to feel gratitude. Darting her eyes to the dining table, she noted the guests who'd already begun breakfast.

"Still husband hunting, I see," Teresa teased. "You won't find many gentlemen about at this hour. Most of the men played cards into the wee hours after the masquerade concluded. It's an unwritten tradition every lord has one last chance to best the other as our annual gathering comes to an end. The hour grew late. Lord Henley didn't return to our bedchamber until after three."

"I see." Lady Derby's tone expressed concern for those who rabble-roused at such late hours, but Caroline knew Lindsey was not included in the group.

"Indeed," Teresa continued. "And too, others have already left for London. Prolonged fresh air and pastoral nature is seemingly unfavorable for their health."

They shared a light laugh, after which Caroline made her plate and overtly searched for Lindsey in the pockets of guests around the room. Could he still be abed? He wouldn't have left already. Most especially without saying goodbye.

"Caroline hasn't had the advantage of mixing in London society to great extent, as we've only recently returned to England," her mother supplied. "Your invitation proved ideal. I often remind her, when a lady comports herself in the most respectful and congenial manner, the best gentlemen will take notice. Now, who was the handsome lord who assisted me when I misplaced my fan the other day?" Her mother turned toward her in wait of an answer, and Teresa did the same.

"I'm certain Lady Henley would prefer to speak of more interesting topics than my quest for a husband, Mother." Caroline restrained her tone, but a touch of amusement leaked through. They settled at the table with their food and she lent her attention to arranging her napkin.

"Ladies, good morning." Lord Mills approached in greeting. "Is this seat taken?" He indicated the empty chair across from Caroline.

"No, please join us."

"Indeed I will." Mills shared a glance to both Lady Henley and Mother. "I wondered if Lady Derby and her daughter desired an escort for the return trip to London. I'm prepared to leave at whatever hour suits your plans. Though the weather appears fair, one can never be sure of the roadways."

"How thoughtful." Lady Henley's tone sounded curious.

"You're very kind and generous to offer your time," Lady Derby quickly continued. "My daughter and I have you to thank for introducing us to this lovely gathering. We would be honored to accept your escort."

And like that, without a word or acknowledgement from Caroline, the plans were set.

* * * *

Lindsey paced a hard line at the foot of his bed, his mind muddled. He hadn't returned to the Henley party and he wondered what Caroline would make of his absence after the intimacy they'd shared. Struggling to rationalize his desire to see her again, he couldn't stop thinking about her kiss, her body strained against his, the lovely and sensual sound of her breathy gasps as he'd brought her to completion, and the insistent litany that she should be his and his alone.

Still he rebelled.

It was a game.

It wasn't a game.

Then he'd label it a distraction. A much needed one from the unholy conditions forced upon him by his father. Who wouldn't prefer to think about a beautiful tempting woman when the reality each day saw his coffers lighter with no easy solution in sight? Not to mention he'd acquired few clues for the maddening hunt of the Decima. Powell knew something and enjoyed leveraging that fact in an act of revenge against him. Lindsey was left waiting for his bastard half brother to make another move. Meanwhile, Mills' promise to locate the Morta depended on Lindsey stepping away from Caroline. The tangled mess made him furious. He was unaccustomed to having so little control. His father be damned.

He heaved a long exhale meant to expel his frustration, his thoughts quick to return to the one pleasantry he'd allowed himself. Caroline. Despite his every excuse, the image of her gentle smile and echo of her laughter demanded attention.

What did they share beyond a few scorching kisses? Kisses that made him feel as though he'd die without another.

Still, he didn't believe himself capable of love. At least not the love she deserved. His mother had hardly made an effort, too locked in her own despair to nurture in him tender feelings. His father saw him as an instrument to manipulate, no more than a necessary nuisance to preserve the Lindsey heritage.

Heritage be damned. He had no use for messy entanglements and deep emotional relationships that tied him in knots. Sex served as release, not attachment. He'd rather leave the lady than run the risk she'd tire of his company. Call it selfish, indulgent, but it was all he was willing to offer, and he wouldn't allow himself to behave otherwise. Vulnerability was a flaw he'd not possess.

He'd do well to purge Caroline from his brain.

It didn't signify whatever he'd experienced with Caroline was unlike anything he'd encountered before. That solitary realization terrified him more than any disinheritance or impending destitution. While he couldn't label it a courtship, whatever it was, it was dangerous. Caroline owned part of his heart.

Likely more than a part.

This was madness. He couldn't bear the thought of her wedding another when he already considered her his. A wave of self-loathing rolled over him. He couldn't afford any distractions, and Caroline was so much more than that. She caused him to forget his solitary purpose. He wouldn't become a forlorn soul crippled by emotion like his mother. Nor play the enamored swain, lovesick over a beautiful maiden. No, his energy was best spent chasing after Powell and finding the paintings needed to secure his wealth. It was pragmatic and practical, the exact opposite of tender emotion, not at all the decision of a coward.

At least, that's what he told himself.

* * * *

London no longer possessed allure. Its original promise of lively entertainment produced nothing but despair now. Caroline hadn't heard from Lindsey in over a week, and if she remained alone in her bedchambers any longer, reviewing the time she'd shared with him at the Henley party, she'd surely go insane.

What had she done? She'd given her feelings, *her body,* to a renowned rakehell. She'd allowed him to touch her intimately with not so much as the slightest hesitation, swept away by his handsome good looks and captivating charm. Believing their time together, the flirtation and innuendo, meant something special to him. *Something more than all the others.*

She should be appalled at her actions, and she would be if all emotion wasn't consumed by the unadulterated humiliation compressed beside intense anger and abject hurt, her bruised heart unable to withstand the lethal combination. She was every bit the naive ingénue to have been lured into thinking their relationship was lasting. She clenched her eyes closed. How could she allow this to happen? Hadn't she come to London to find a suitable husband? One who would love her unconditionally? As it remained, she'd added wantonness to her list of offenses.

She'd begun with her intentions set. Her future mapped. But that was before she'd found her way into Lord Albertson's study, soon after discovered by the Earl of Lindsey. What a fool she'd become. His very actions that evening spoke of his unredeemable character. Still, she'd allowed her perspective to become skewed, her carefully constructed plan upended, her life now divided into two succinct parts, *before* and *after* the earl.

Worse yet, she missed him. Literally ached for him. While her mind told her to rebel, her heart yearned for the sound of his voice, the breath-catching moment when he'd slant his glance in her direction and gift her with a disarming half-grin.

With few confidantes and even fewer friends, she dashed a note to her cousin Louisa out of distraught desperation. This was not a topic for Beatrice at tea, and she'd never become especially close with Dinah, who seemed to have the world perfectly sorted. But Louisa, yes, Louisa would understand.

Her cousin arrived promptly, and with little more than a meaningful flick of the eyes toward the terrace doors they escaped conversation with Caroline's mother, who had joined them in the drawing room as soon as her cousin was announced.

"What is it?" Louisa led them away from the house at a brisk pace. "You look wretched. Tell me the whole of it. Did something happen at the Henley affair?"

Caroline edited her retelling, but she harbored no doubt her tone expressed more than her words.

"I warned you away from the earl. I wish you had listened." Louisa's eyes filled with tears, and Caroline immediately knew there was more to her cousin's reaction than distress and empathy. There was, perhaps, painful regret as well.

"How foolish I was to follow the callings of my heart instead of the advisement of my brain."

"The heart is a traitorous organ. Its strength provides us precious life, and yet its fragility allows it to shatter with the slightest insult from the wrong person."

"I didn't think him so." Caroline sniffled herself into a semblance of calm. "But it was nothing more than a figment of my imagination."

"The reality of a rake's manipulation, dear cousin." Louisa let out a forlorn sigh, as if preparing herself for the worst.

Caroline shook her head, refuting her cousin's assessment, and they walked in silence for a long minute. "Have you ever had a connection with someone—"

"Yes." Louisa turned and clasped Caroline's hands tightly. "And you can tell me anything. I won't divulge a word."

Caroline couldn't bear to correct her cousin's misconception despite she'd spoken of her feelings for Lindsey. She knew in her heart they were connected, calibrated somehow, by an invisible and powerful force that brooked no refusal.

"You didn't..."

"No!" That was one assumption she wouldn't allow.

"Well, there is that. Women bear the brunt of societal censure when men are allowed every freedom. That's rich, isn't it? At least you weren't foolish enough to fall in love."

Caroline's face heated with a conflicted mixture of anger and mortification, though Louisa continued regardless of her embarrassment.

"Heartbroken is better than ruined."

"I rather think they're as close cousins as we are, Louisa."

"As we are." Louisa tugged on Caroline's hand and pulled her closer. "We'll see your way through this without one whisper of scandal and have you married by season's end."

Caroline remained silent. Louisa's idea of resolving the problem caused her heart to ache even more.

* * * *

Too many questions began and ended with Powell. His bastard half brother might not have the Decima or be aware of its location, but he knew something. Their conversation had been riddled with innuendo and insinuation when Powell intersected his path during the hunt. It might be a frantic grasp at clues, but it was all Lindsey had at the moment.

With Mills on the trail of the Morta, the matter could be solved sooner than later. Then, with the earldom once again secure, he would clear his mind and listen to his heart, because Caroline continued to speak to the useless organ no matter he attempted otherwise. Her pursuit of love and a suitable husband gave him pause. He hadn't made the effort to call on her, hadn't attended any affair where she might show, and yet she was his first waking thought and last nightly dream. What did she think of his careless abandonment? Had her fond feelings turned to disdain? Did she pursue her goal with invigorated zeal? With Mills? And how many candidates did she have on that list anyway?

Not that he should be one of them. She deserved better. But if she would have him...

Bloody hell.

His wants didn't matter if Barlow held firm with the conditions of his inheritance. Lindsey needed an heir, and that complicated things extrinsically. Still, Caroline's health concerns sounded possible, not permanent. Certainly not absolute. Damn it all, it would be no hardship to attempt to get her with child.

And then if nothing came of it, if Caroline couldn't conceive or carry a child, and if Barlow insisted Lindsey fulfill his father's stipulation, then the earldom be damned. He'd find another way. All this second-guessing and speculation was enough to make him senseless. But for now, he'd continue his attempts to recover the remaining paintings and secure financial freedom. That problem needed to be settled before any emotional matters could be explored.

With that decision made, he at last closed his eyes and as sleep rolled over him, he thought again of Caroline's kiss.

Chapter Twenty-Three

Caroline sat beside Lord Mills in his high-perch phaeton, mindful to keep her hands in her lap and a proper amount of space on the seat. He'd called on her three times this week and she'd agreed to each outing. Partly at her mother's insistence she cease pacing about the drawing room, partly to distract from self-loathing and behavior unbefitting to a lady—to be so forlorn was an embarrassment and testament to her foolishness—but mostly due to the slimmest chance the Earl of Lindsey would intersect their path or happen upon their outing. Lindsey was a close friend of Lord Mills, and without a word from the earl in the past two weeks, she selfishly hoped the coincidence would occur.

Oh, it wasn't to peer at him calf-eyed and lovestruck. Quite the opposite. She wished to empty her spleen of all the anger, indignation, and hurt that replaced her admiration. Seeing life through her heart had always been her downfall. Why hadn't she paid more attention to her cousin's knowing advice? Still, no matter regret haunted her, it took a great deal of effort to keep her emotions focused on anger above all else and enjoy the present moment. It wasn't that she disliked Lord Mills, it was more so that he wasn't Lindsey.

"Allow me." Mills extended his gloved hand to assist as she disembarked. He'd managed a spot adjacent to the walking path in St. James Park, and they intended to stroll and take some air in the late afternoon weather.

Mother had become enamored of Mills' recent attention, and further smitten when he'd arrived in his toplofty two-seater phaeton, so she'd allowed Caroline's maid to stay behind. Caroline wondered at the propriety of it all. Had Mills purposely orchestrated the arrangement to guarantee them privacy? She didn't wish for anyone to draw the wrong conclusion.

"Thank you." She released his hand and looped hers through his elbow.

"Did you enjoy the time spent away from England?" Mills politely steered the two of them onto the walkway.

"Italy was fascinating. My father is an avid art enthusiast, and we spent many an afternoon in the extensive galleries." It was a safe enough topic, though her mind spun in search of a way to work the earl into their conversation.

"I have admired the works of the Italian artists as well. It's a pity London offers a thimble's worth compared to the masterpieces showcased in Rome." He smiled down at her, and she returned his attention. "It will be agreeable to travel again someday, but for now I've plans to settle my future with more domestic arrangements."

"So you are serious about finding a bride?" How was it possible that their discussion strayed to the farthest possible topic? How could she recover?

Mills answered without pause. "Most definitely, my lady. When one is young, it seems the whole world will wait on each and every decision. Intelligent men realize the flaw in this manner of thinking before it's too late. Others never do. Lindsey is a prime example of someone who lives in the moment without a care for later days."

She disliked the disparaging remark. Not so much because her heart was still woefully entangled with feelings for Lindsey, but more so since Mills couldn't truly be a friend if he so churlishly expounded on the earl's flaws. Besides, while others considered Lindsey reckless and self-serving, she knew he possessed finer qualities beyond his roguish attitude. He was a man of many layers, complicated, complex, and deeply emotional. She found him charming, his kisses disarming.

"I suppose the world would be a rather dull place if everyone shared an identical viewpoint. I haven't seen Lord Lindsey at any recent functions. Perhaps he's taken your advice and abandoned qualities you perceive as flaws." They neared a curve in the path, and for a few moments Mills remained silent. When he finally replied, there was a dubious note in his voice that hadn't existed before.

"He's involved in a chase that has him distracted to no end."

"A chase?" She drew a deep breath in an attempt to dispel her ill ease.

"He's turning London inside out in search of an elusive woman."

Mills kept his attention straight on as he replied, and his arm tensed beneath her hand. Meanwhile, each word of his answer was a hammer blow to her heart. What did she expect by nosing around in an attempt to discover information? It served her right. Twice Mills had shared Lindsey's interest in an unnamed female. Who was this woman who'd captured his devoted attention?

"To that point, I'm more of a traditionalist," Mills continued. "I've noticed you're an amenable lady who respects the commitment of marriage and seeks a congenial relationship."

"Thank you, my lord, although I suspect that describes a great many ladies of your acquaintance."

"How true." He looked at her warmly. "And naturally, I'd like a future family. I'm not so traditional to only care for an heir and second son. A daughter would also be acceptable."

Caroline needed to strengthen her resolve. Perhaps this conversational bend offered her the ideal opportunity to discourage Mills' suit. Yet he continued before she'd assembled her reply.

"A wife should love, honor, and obey." He rambled on. "Although I suppose there's nothing wrong with a little independence now and again."

"I'm afraid I'd likely disappoint you." She dared a chuckle.

"I don't see how. From what I've observed, you possess the finest qualities."

"Thank you again, though extensive travel and the experience I've gained causes me to thirst for continued learning. I can't imagine being confined to a preconceived depiction of my wifely role."

She heard him exhale deeply, as if choosing his words with care. "You've a more progressive view of things. Not in kind to a bluestocking, mind you, but more of an adventurous spirit." He said the last words as if they puzzled him.

"I believe females should enjoy most all the same freedoms granted males."

"Indeed, there's the Orphans Betterment League." He paused, as if he sought for even one more example. "Although avocations outside the home should never overshadow those within. Surely you dream of children someday."

"I dream of them, yes." She bit her lip, disallowing herself to say more and saddened all the same. Like a wish granted, a cloud moved over the sun and she leapt at the convenient excuse to return home.

"There's a sudden chill in the air, and with your open carriage I'd prefer not to be caught in the rain."

"By all means, my lady, let us leave at once."

* * * *

Lindsey stood beside a soot-dusted wall, lost in the shadows outside the dimly lit tenement where Mills had led him weeks ago. If Powell possessed the Decima and needed cash as badly as he'd let on at Henley's gathering, this fencer served as an ideal solution. Honest men went to galleries and auctions to buy and sell, but men like Powell sought the most illicit deal. It was difficult to rationalize how Powell had managed the invitation to the fox hunt in the first place, but then Lindsey hardly knew the man and didn't care to learn more.

Regardless, he needed the Decima and whether or not Powell showed this evening or when he confronted the fencer, valuable information was to be gained. And so, he waited.

In time his mind wandered to Caroline and a pang of regret clutched his heart. He'd made a muck of things. Would she understand when he finally explained? He couldn't know. What he did recognize made her reaction to his absence intrinsically more important, because now he knew affection outweighed the possession of any missing painting. Caroline had not only found his heart, she'd stolen it. That was a miracle in itself.

He'd taught himself not to care, to turn off all emotion, and it hadn't been a particularly difficult task to complete. His upbringing had enabled it. Still, despite his flaws and otherwise misplaced predilections, he'd developed feelings, some he still didn't understand, though he labeled them as unlike any he'd experienced before, made richer by the absolute fury igniting him whenever he considered her as someone else's wife.

At first, he'd worried she'd become a distraction, and she had, a distraction made stronger the longer he attempted to ignore it. In hindsight, he wouldn't have it any other way. She was meant to be his from that first moment in Albertson's study.

Would she have him remained the question to be answered.

Across the street a hansom cab pulled to the curb, nabbed his interest, and forced his attention to the present. A stout fellow dressed in shades of brown stepped out onto the pavement. He held a slim rectangular package wrapped in paper. Even from the considerable distance Lindsey discerned it most likely contained a work of art.

The gentleman hadn't turned, and even with his hat pulled low on his brow and the late hour Lindsey could tell he wasn't his half brother, although a note of familiarity accompanied the thought. No doubt their paths had crossed at his club or some innocuous social affair.

Lindsey crossed to the opposite corner, anxious for any opportunity to gain entry. He allowed the unknown man to pass and then stepped away from the wall and shadowed him, his brain a beat slower to realize it was Lord Derby and not some nondescript stranger. What business could Caroline's father have here in Seven Dials? Did he wish to sell a painting in clandestine fashion, unbeknownst to his family? Could it be he suffered from financial concerns? Surely, late night assignations with questionable art brokers in the worst area of London didn't bode well for a logical explanation. Still, life had a way of causing one to make impetuous, sometimes rash, decisions.

As proof, Lindsey had fallen victim to the same logic. In consideration of his own impending penury, he'd reasoned a viable solution. He could breed Infinity and collect a stud fee, along with several other prize Arabians in his stables. He hadn't planned on becoming a livestock breeder. A wry grimace accompanied the thought. But neither had he anticipated a somewhat dire need for funds and a chokehold on his rightful inheritance.

But what of Lord Derby?

Lindsey followed the man to the door and waited a good distance not to incite detection. The same scamp who'd previously permitted entry appeared and Derby followed the lad, the door fast to fall shut until the very last second when Lindsey caught the latch.

* * * *

Less than an hour later, Caroline returned home. She entered the drawing room and found her mother alone, an expression of worry marring her face.

"Is everything all right?" Caroline approached in time to see her mother effectively conceal whatever had troubled her moments before, but Caroline wasn't fooled by her mother's newly donned look of inscrutability.

"Nothing for you to concern yourself over." The slightest tremble rippled through her mother's reply.

"Where's Father?"

It was after hours, and while her father often frequented his club or met with associates, a prickle of apprehension told her something wasn't as it should be. Her mother's tightly laced fingers and pursed lips confirmed her suspicion.

"You needn't worry, Caroline." Her mother's reassurance sounded dreadfully unconvincing. "Your father will set things to right."

"But what is wrong?" She tried to suppress a beat of panic. Why was her mother behaving so secretively? "Is Father unwell?"

"Nothing of the kind. It's not a matter for discussion. Ladies never speak of indelicate subjects." Seemingly at a loss to say more, her mother took a seat on the velvet-covered divan.

It was the wrong thing to say, a spark to tinder actually, for Caroline had only just endured Lord Mills' insulting denunciation on the limitations of the female mind.

"That's ridiculous. I will decide what's appropriate, and you will tell me now." Her voice held a sharp edge that dared her mother to argue.

"What has come over you, dear?" Her mother's distress caused Caroline a wave of remorse. "First with your insistence to attend the Henley gathering and now with your sharp tone. I did not raise you to display such defiance. A refined lady should always quiet her—"

"Mother." Caroline gentled her tone and took the opposite seat. "I've no need for any further advice. I've my own mind and heart." One glance at her mother and she buffered the words. "Thank you for sharing what you glean as important lessons in decorum, but I'd much rather know what has you so distraught. Did something happen? Is Father..." Her voice trailed off as she followed her mother's glance to the far wall of the drawing room. "Oh, you've changed the painting over the writing desk."

"Caroline." Her mother hesitated, her voice laden with dismay.

"Yes."

The silence stretched, but she dared not interrupt her mother when an understanding of the tense atmosphere might be imminent.

"Living abroad and returning to England, maintaining our lifestyle, has taken a toll on our finances." Each word was muttered softly, as if her mother feared someone would shame her for speaking of domestic finances. "Once you're married, I'm certain these worries will all be for naught, but in the meantime, there's your dowry and the expenses to see you properly wardrobed..." Her mother didn't seem inclined to say more and left her sentence unfinished.

"I didn't realize." Caroline tried to remember the impetus that took them from Italy to England in a hasty rush. While she'd expressed a desire to return to London and participate in the season, she'd always believed her suggestion was secondary to a more important issue. Her father had returned one day from an outing with a sense of urgency about him. He'd declared unexpectedly they should pack and prepare to travel. She hadn't questioned him, as she'd always been a dutiful daughter and his purpose aligned with her own. But now, upon reflection, she wondered what spurned his sudden assertion they leave as soon as possible.

"Was there a particular reason we left Italy, something more important than my wish to reenter society?"

"Nothing that should concern you, dear. Besides, once you marry Lord Mills—"

"Marry Lord Mills?" She sprung from the chair as if the cushion caught flame. "I'm not going to marry Lord Mills. I may never marry at all." She realized she sounded irrational. But everything had changed. After Lindsey entered her life, she couldn't focus on finding a suitable husband, because all thoughts and emotions were consumed by him.

And where had that gotten her?

"Oh, my." Her mother's expression looked more forlorn than before.

"Just tell me, Mother. Please. Tell me all of it." She moved beside her mother and placed her hands within her own. Her mother's fingers were unusually cold, the skin thin and soft. She didn't want to add to her parents' distress, but if she understood the secrecy that surrounded their present predicament, she could find a way to assist in the resolution.

A sigh escaped and her mother's mouth drooped into a disapproving frown, but at last she began to speak.

"As you know, your father enjoys the arts. So much so, he fancied he might try his own hand."

"Buying and selling paintings?"

"Yes, although there's more to it than that, and if you'd like me to explain you must allow me to do it all at once, without question or interruption, otherwise I doubt I'll be able to give it voice. It's a secret I've kept for so long I'd rather have it out in one breath." Her mother tugged at her hands in an attempt to remove them from Caroline's clasp, her words filled with emotion.

Quieted by the impact of her mother's confession and adversely startled by the sudden sprint of her pulse, Caroline released her mother's hands and settled her own in her lap. What could possibly deliver such despair to her parents?

"It all began innocently enough. Your father was at a gallery with his easel, painting a replica of one of the works displayed, when a stranger complimented the likeness. Your father and the stranger continued the conversation, and the man offered a handsome sum for the painting whenever it was completed. At first, your father declined. He was hardly as good as the stranger declared, and furthermore he saw art as a creative pastime, not a means to make money." Her mother expelled another long sigh before she went on. "But the stranger became insistent, and I suppose the compliments may have turned your father's head. He agreed to finish the painting and deliver it to the gentleman's home in return for a handsome sum. No sooner had he accomplished that than the man insisted upon another, and then another. It became a habit, one your father believed harmless until a disturbing nuance came to light. He discovered the stranger was selling his reproductions as originals, and when your father objected the man claimed he'd ruin our family's reputation by exposing what Father had done, casting him in a poor light and accusing him of actively participating in forgery. This culprit demanded more and more paintings and, instead of sharing the money gained, withheld payment whenever your father showed reluctance to participate. He beggared us with blackmail, manipulating your father into a most indefensible position."

"This is horrible." Aghast, Caroline could only shake her head in dismay.

"It is." This time her mother gathered Caroline's hands and stroked them in reassurance. "We fled Italy not to hurry you back to the season, although we want you to have every happiness, but more so to escape that despicable man and the threat he held over your father. His influence was too great, and we were visitors in a foreign land. Despite your father's reputation, he would have been powerless against the web of thieves and criminals involved in the dishonest forgery scheme run by that terrible thief." The anguish in her voice was unmistakable now.

"I'm so sorry. I had no idea."

"Of course you didn't. We're your parents. Our purpose is to guide and protect you. We couldn't have you worry, but needless to say this has taken its toll on your father and me. The household finances are in a shamble, and there's significant debt that's come due. We can't risk slander or poor reputation. It would mar your chances of an advantageous future."

"If only I had known, Mother. The fashionable gowns and accessories purchased in Rome, the excursions to museums and galleries, the restaurants…" At a loss to reverse those decisions and spare her parents' further expense, she stopped speaking.

"Caroline." Her mother's voice was stern. "We almost lost you once. We knew your spirit suffered as much as your body, and we wanted to give you everything a young lady could ever desire. The promise of a happy future with a responsible and well-heeled husband has always been our greatest goal."

"At least it's over now." She swept her hands over her face to wipe away all unpleasant emotion and turned to her mother with a valiant smile.

"It will be soon, dear."

"What?"

"The unfortunate experience has left our funds depleted, not to mention the expense of our relocation. With your interest in marriage and the expected dowry to attract the most select suitors, I'm afraid your father had to act."

"What has he done? He's not still involved? Not still producing forgeries?"

"I'd rather not continue this conversation. He'll be angry with me for divulging so much already. You know how much your father loves you, don't you?"

Caroline didn't reply, her mind already awhirl, determined to find a solution to make everything right again.

Chapter Twenty-Four

Frustrated and unsure how to proceed, Lindsey walked his way through the maze of dank alleys and shadowy streets until his boots found pavement outside of Seven Dials. He promptly hailed a hansom cab and directed the driver to his town house on Orchard Street overlooking Portman Square. His home was fashionable enough to be considered highbrow, and yet detached from the limestone façades of Brook and Davies Streets, beyond the alluring status of Grosvenor Square. It was a private residence and he rarely entertained, content to find amusement elsewhere.

Without a doubt, tonight he was in want of quiet. His experience inside the fencer's lair had been anything but successful. Lord Derby had disappeared into a room not unlike Lindsey's first encounter at the address and had exited emptyhanded. Unwilling to lose his own opportunity to secure information concerning the Decima, Lindsey had allowed the older man to walk out unconfronted, and yet when he'd finally managed to locate the bloke who'd confirmed the authenticity of the Nona, he'd met with belligerence and distrust no amount of money or haughty aristocratic influence could change.

Momentarily defeated, he dropped his head to the leather bolster and closed his eyes, quick to summon an image of Caroline as she'd reclined on the chaise at Kingswood, the frothy gauze of her masquerade costume billowed around her as if she were perched upon a cloud, an otherworldly goddess that may as well live only in his imagination. He possessed strong feelings for her. He could no longer deny it, nor attempt to persuade himself she was nothing more than a lovely distraction. But what to do about that realization remained a riddle.

Unquestionably overdue, he needed to make amends for his behavior. A gentleman did not share an intimacy of their magnitude and promptly neglect the lady straight after. It was his worst mistake among many, yet the intensity of their moment together shook him to his soul. She must thoroughly despise him now.

He also needed time. Time to sort his feelings, organize his life, and produce the words necessary to convince Caroline to forgive him. He'd ignored the situation because he hadn't the courage to admit she'd found his heart. He'd avoided her because he hadn't the trust to believe he would ever be enough. It was fear and a healthy dose of undeniable emotion, both of which he'd little experience. And while the latter frightened the hell out of him, it persisted nonetheless.

The hansom jerked to a stop at the curb, interrupting the determined path of his thoughts. He paid the driver and took the steps, confident with his newborn plan. With the right amount of deliberation, soul searching, and time, he hoped he could win her back—if he was lucky enough to have ever possessed her admiration in the first place.

He produced his key, but Hobbs, his butler, opened the door before he could fit it into the lock.

"You've a visitor, my lord."

Damn it to hell. He wanted peace and quiet.

He wanted Caroline.

"Have Mills wait for me in my study, Hobbs." He hadn't expected news about the Morta so quickly, but perhaps his fickle fate had changed and things would resolve before he'd need worry about penury.

"Pardon, my lord, but Lord Mills is not here."

"Then who is it?" Lindsey stepped into the foyer, a beat of annoyance turning his question sharp as the bracket clock in the hall chimed the hour.

"The lady hasn't given her name."

"Lady?" Lindsey heaved a breath of frustration. If Lady Jenkin chose this moment to rail at him and further complicate his life, he'd toss her out on her dainty arse.

"She insisted, my lord, and said it was a matter of great importance. I believed her, as she was visibly shaken. I could not turn her away."

"Of course not."

"She waits in the silver drawing room, my lord."

"Thank you, Hobbs."

"Shall I arrange for refreshments?"

"No, that won't be necessary. Whatever business poised to present itself will be expediated. You may close the house for the night, Hobbs, and take your rest. I'll see the visitor out."

Lindsey strode briskly toward the drawing room, his patience on a short leash. Damn it all if his life wasn't one inconvenience after another.

He cleared his throat to give Lady Jenkin forewarning he was on his way in, and started speaking before he fully entered. "It doesn't matter what reason you think you have to be here, you need to leave at once." He pulled up fast as his gaze landed on the lady, her back to him as she startled and spun at the sound of his rude pronouncement. "Caroline."

He was shocked, inordinately pleased, and completely at a loss for words. "Jonathan."

He stood silent, drinking in the sight before him. He couldn't understand her visit, and yet the sound of his name in her voice was the calm his soul had searched for since the last time they were together. He regretted the clumsy way he'd handled that situation. Still, the lady was dangerous. She made him think about things he would prefer to ignore. Most markedly, the future.

"Do you want me to leave?" She didn't move, her lips pressed together in a frown of disapproval.

"No." He stepped closer, still gathering his wits. "I misunderstood my butler." Seeking to gain a modicum of time, he moved to the sideboard and reached for the brandy. "Would you like something to drink? I have wine or sherry if brandy doesn't suit."

"No, thank you." She shook her head and a few loose ringlets dropped across her ear.

His fingers itched to sweep them back, tuck them away, before he covered her face with kisses. His eyes fell to her velvet cloak draped over one of the Hepplewhite chairs. "Tell me you brought a footman or other servant with you this evening."

"My maid is in the kitchen, if that abets your anger. Your housekeeper was kind enough to offer her tea and biscuits."

The mixture of indignation and regret in her voice caused him to proceed with care, though he couldn't decipher exactly which emotion claimed victory.

"I'm not displeased." He poured two fingers of brandy and moved toward her beside the hearth. She appeared more skittish than she sounded, although he still hadn't the slightest idea why she'd arrived at this hour of the evening. Again he was struck by the fact Caroline was out unescorted, with no heed of her personal safety aside from one slip of a maid. She must have assumed his displeasure, as she continued without prompting.

"I left my parents a note so they wouldn't worry. They believe I've gone to visit Louisa. I told them not to wait, for I'll be returning late."

He stopped several paces away and stared, hoping to understand and at the same time wanting the moment to last. She looked as beautiful as he'd recalled only this evening in the hansom cab. She wore a silky gown of cobalt blue, modestly cut but all the more appealing for what it concealed from the eye. "I didn't expect to find you here."

"Why would you? You made it clear you had no need to see me again." Her chin rose a notch and her eyes blazed as she faced him. By damn, she was glorious in her temper. "Be assured I wouldn't be here if it wasn't imperative."

Her voice, strong and composed, was betrayed by the delicate tremble of her lips.

"Are you well?" He'd much rather she tell him directly whatever troubled her, but he had the good sense not to press.

"I must be mad to appeal to you, given your lack of—"

"Caroline—"

"It doesn't matter." She hesitated, as if she wrestled with her reply. "My situation is dire, and I have nowhere else to turn. My aunt and uncle must never know. They'd be mortified. We'll all be ostracized." She blinked hard and drew a shuddering breath before she continued. "My family... my father is in trouble."

Perhaps his first assumption proved correct and Lord Derby was in Seven Dials to sell artwork in an effort to gain quick access to funds. Lindsey groaned inwardly at the irony of the situation. Were Caroline to ask him for money, he had little to spare.

"How can I help?" He stepped near enough to see the glisten of unshed tears in her extraordinary blue eyes.

"I recalled Lady Henley's comment that you're interested in the arts. She mentioned you were seeking a painting, and I assumed you might know someone who could assist me."

"In what way?" He almost reached for her; his fingers curled inward against his palms to tamp down the urge. He wanted to offer comfort but didn't know if she'd welcome his touch. "You'll have to explain further, no matter how difficult the telling, but be assured, love, I'll employ every resource in my power to solve your problem."

Her eyes shot to his at the use of the endearment, or perhaps he looked for forgiveness where there was none. Chances were she merely sought the information he could provide.

"I don't know how to fix this." Her voice broke on the confession and at the risk of earning further scorn, he surrendered to temptation and pulled her into his arms.

* * * *

She despised herself for seeking refuge in Jonathan's embrace. Still, when his strong arms encircled and supported her, she relished the heavenly comfort he offered. She burrowed against his chest, the thick wool of his coat soft beneath her cheek, his scent an instant balm to the onslaught of emotion churning chaos within. Another minute and her tears evaporated, her upset abated, though anger was fast to replace it.

She disentangled herself and he let her go without hesitation.

"I'm not here for personal reassurances."

"I want you to know—"

"Don't. It doesn't matter. I'd rather we discuss the situation that prompted me to seek you out."

He continued despite her attempt to deter the conversation.

"It does matter. I didn't call on you after our evening together because—"

"Because I'd fallen so easily under your spell. You'd needn't say more." She struggled to keep the bitterness from her voice. She wouldn't add another humiliation to the list.

"No. You have it turned about. I was the one who'd become enchanted, Caroline."

"So I'm to believe a renowned rakehell, one with worldly knowledge I can't even imagine, became taken with me after a kiss or two and therefore ignored me right after?"

"Yes."

She glared at him in lieu of answering.

"Yes," he repeated. "Because the connection we shared was like nothing I've ever experienced. The intensity of my feelings and the power you held scared the hell out of me. I didn't contact you because you mattered too much and in that, I was powerless."

She inhaled deeply to guard against his words, refusing to allow the slightest vulnerability.

"You affected me to the depths of my jaded soul. Still, I couldn't ruin you. I'm not *that* selfish. To that end, I couldn't tolerate myself if I did, and yet I couldn't have you. You deserve someone who will offer you every dream of your heart." He reclaimed his brandy from the end table and finished what was left in the glass. "Not a world-weary earl on the cusp of poverty."

"What?" Had she heard him correctly?

"My life is complicated, and a sad story to tell, but be assured, all matters aside, I wanted you then and even more so now."

"I don't understand, but I do know you should have called on me or sent me a message. Anything to reassure me your immediate absence wasn't my doing. I was warned abandonment was in your nature, and yet I naively chose to believe otherwise."

He set down his glass and advanced, until they stood so close she could see candlelight reflected in his midnight eyes.

"It was never your doing. I accept all fault."

She searched his face and found sincerity there. Beneath the unmistakable regret of his words she heard tenderness and affection. Her heart relaxed though the circumstances hadn't changed. If she had come seeking his help, she may as well confess it without further delay.

"Somehow our conversation has strayed the path." She shook her head in admonishment and reordered her thoughts. Mustering the courage to tell what she knew, she prayed trusting him wasn't another mistake. She hemmed her bottom lip. Lindsey was a peer, an honest, noble gentleman who wouldn't harm the smallest animal, no matter he was painted as a scoundrel. Would he view her family poorly for her father's dishonesty, or understand the conditions of the situation? Would she lose whatever respect he held for her?

"Your visit is unexpected, but also opportune." Lindsey exhaled, his expression serious and resolved. "I'd like to tell you something that may change the way you view me. Will you at least listen, Caroline?"

"Yes." Caught in ambivalence about her own troubles, she welcomed the chance to wait a few minutes before telling Lindsey about her father. She watched him closely, desperately trying to decipher the emotion in his eyes.

"My father was a plague." Lindsey swallowed audibly. "As I already shared when we visited Kingswood, he made my mother's life a living hell. The only way I escaped his tyranny and abuse was to stay out of his path until I was able to leave permanently. Upon his death, when his will was read, he attached contingences to my inheritance in the form of a legacy. He has particular demands, despite he's buried in a cold grave. He's tasked me with recovering three specific pieces of artwork, as they constitute a bulk of the earldom's wealth."

"Artwork?" She didn't want to interrupt, and yet the similarity in subjects was too uncanny.

"Yes." He stepped closer, his eyes narrowed by the forlorn grimace on his face. "And there is an additional condition as well."

She waited, though each second stretched unbearably.

But something changed in that moment. A decision was made. His forehead cleared and his eyes grew sharper as he matched her attention.

"I haven't located the paintings, so the second task hardly matters." He reached for her hand and drew her up from where she sat. "I can hardly offer you a future when my present is chin-deep in chaos."

She wouldn't add to his misery. She'd find another way to help her father. Still, her emotions were strained, and she yearned to feel close to someone. Not someone. Only Jonathan. "I'm sorry."

"It's not for you to worry over, love." He stroked a fingertip down her cheek. "I just needed you to know that my every decision has been forced. Now, how can I help you?"

He already carried the burden of his own future. She wouldn't add her troubles to the list. Rising up on her tiptoes, she pressed a kiss to his mouth. She needed comfort. That was all she would accept from him right now. And from that strength she'd find a way to salvage her family's honor.

She didn't object when he gathered her into his arms. She'd called herself a fool a thousand times for believing there could be something lasting between them, yet when she looked into his eyes, she saw her heart reflected. Whatever reason he'd had for neglecting to contact her hadn't come without a cost. But could the reasoning he'd supplied be the truth? Could he care so much for her?

She turned her face toward his. His thickly lashed eyes, dark with secrets and intent with ardor, held her captivated. For several moments they didn't move. His gaze mesmerized her. Their breath mingled while the air became fraught with undeniable longing. He brought his palm up and cupped her cheek. His touch possessed a gentle, trembling restraint that nearly stopped her heart, as if she were precious, fragile, and he barely able to control his desire.

Chapter Twenty-Five

He couldn't solve all her problems, deeply entrenched in a series of complications of his own, but he could offer her comfort, and from there work to free her from worry. He hadn't lied. He would employ every recourse to assist in extricating her father and family from whatever concerning scandal threatened them. He would work to clear the flash of indecision in her eyes, and when she was ready to share the details, he would do everything in his power to spare her family the embarrassment she feared.

But there was more to it than social responsibility and access to resources. His feelings were involved. Whether he liked it or not, and he liked it more than he should, he cared for Caroline deeply. Dare he label it something more? It wasn't as though he'd ever experienced anything akin to love and could recognize its symptoms.

"I will assist you in every way possible, love." A shiver ran through her and he imagined her relief too great to measure. He wanted her despair to vanish, her emotions to calm, at least for one evening. "Caroline."

Her slender brows twitched with curiosity and her eyes traveled down to his mouth in wait of what he would say—or do.

"You've turned me inside out." He had no other way to explain the longing that settled all the way to the marrow of his bones whenever he envisioned her and relived their intimacy. "I want you."

Words failed him; they sounded more clumsy than eloquent.

He smoothed a wayward tear away with the pad of his thumb, her rose petal skin soft beneath his touch. She didn't pull from him. He stroked across her cheek, his fingertip trailing to the corner of her mouth, her lush lips ripe and tempting, so close to his.

"I have no control over my emotions when I think of you with another gentleman. But it isn't jealousy, at least not completely. It's more that I consider you mine. I have since that very first evening in Albertson's study. I know I have no right to these emotions, and I've treated you poorly. For that I apologize." His voice dropped low, his next words more a wish than a command. "Tell me you feel the same. That you have feelings for me as well. Otherwise I'll never speak of my misplaced affection."

"I do."

She needn't say more. He brought his mouth down on hers. It was a hungry kiss, anxious and forceful, but as he licked into her sweetness, he never knew such immense pleasure.

He still wore his coat, unprepared to find Caroline in his drawing room, unprepared for the intensity that gripped him. He couldn't bring her close enough, taste her deep enough. He pulled her against him, as if by some sleight of hand he could bring her into him, every pure and innocent quality into his dark heart, not to ruin or exploit her, but so he might begin again, so that he might be renewed, like the earth drinks the rain and flourishes.

She slid her arms around his middle, roamed her palms over his back, surveying every muscle and ridge. Her shy yet bold touches aroused him like nothing he'd ever experienced. He wanted to lower her to the rug before the hearth and undress her, worship her endless legs and luscious breasts bared to him, all silky skin and velvet blush.

Blood surged to each cell in his body. His cock twitched, every muscle invested in the thought, despite he knew he could never expect such a gift.

He broke from their kiss and she whimpered, her mouth following after his for the slightest moment before she blinked her eyes open.

"I've missed you. I didn't know what to believe."

"I'm a fool, Caroline. A fool who has fallen in love, something I doubted would ever come to pass. A condition I never wanted but now realize I can't live without because you're worth any risk."

Emotion gripped him, his chest all at once too tight. He should tell her to go home before he said something scandalous and ruined the moment, before he succumbed to his basest desires. Yes. He would send her on her way and pay a proper call tomorrow, that way she'd never doubt the sincerity of his confession. "Come upstairs with me. Do you want that, love?"

Damn his tongue for not listening to his brain.

"No matter how heavenly your kisses, I can't go upstairs with you." Her mouth hinted at a smile.

He released her and strode to the door, closing the latch with a snap echoed by the clock in the hall as it chimed the midnight hour. "That was the correct answer, of course."

He removed his coat as he returned and took her hands, her fingers fast to lace with his before he tugged her down to the overstuffed divan.

"So what are we to do now?"

He rather hoped she wasn't still discussing the problem that brought her to his door. "I can suggest a few things."

Her throaty laughter had his body screaming with desire. His mouth hungered to taste her skin, trail kisses down her neck, and laze caresses across her full breasts before he caught a pale pink nipple between his teeth.

"We can begin like this." He turned his body so they faced each other, and with their eyes matched he kept his mouth above hers in anticipation of another soul-searing kiss.

Her breathing hitched and he growled his pleasure before closing the space between them. This kiss was unhurried. This kiss spoke more clearly than any words he'd tried to assemble earlier. He nibbled across her plump lower lip, his tongue at play near the corner until she opened and allowed him to delve into the sweet hollow of her mouth, their tongues tangled in a sensual rub. He released her hands and lowered his palms to her hips. He needed to anchor himself, all the while in want of more.

When he finally broke away, they remained nearly nose to nose, their breathing matched, and he suspected the thunder of their hearts as well.

"Jonathan." Her breathy entreaty caused his whole body to pay attention. "I think of you all the time."

"And I, you." His whispered confession sounded far too intimate for kissing in the drawing room. Still, happiness welled in his chest for having heard her admission. "You've kept me awake too many nights."

"I'm sorry."

"Don't you dare apologize." He almost smiled.

"You visit me in my dreams."

"At least one of us is getting sleep." This time he grinned.

"But I don't want to sleep."

"Nor do I, love."

"But…"

She sighed and he tensed, all of a sudden unsure of what she would say.

"What are we?"

Silence answered her question, the definition of their relationship still mutable. He wanted her. That much he knew. Despite their age difference.

Despite his impending financial crisis and conditions of inheritance. Or her health concerns. Despite it all, he knew one thing with certainty.

"We are…inevitable."

He didn't allow her to comment, practically finishing his answer on her lips. She could only have agreed as she returned his attention with equaled fervor. Though she hadn't spoken of love as he had. She'd never said the words.

He deepened the kiss, relishing her intoxicating fragrance, treasuring every little whimper and sigh, her delicate gasps and the stroke of her tongue as sensual as warm velvet, embracing the heat that seared him from the inside out.

This time they came apart more slowly, each reluctant to withdraw. She brought her palms up over the planes of his chest, her touch incendiary even through layers of linen and wool. She didn't speak but instead played idly with his cravat, loosening the knot and slipping the neckcloth free to discard over his shoulder.

"I want to touch you the way you touched me." An impish smile played on her mouth, ripe and swollen from their kissing. "To bring you pleasure."

"Minx." He swallowed and drew another shaky breath, cautious not to read more into her words than intended.

She repositioned so she was partially draped over his thighs and he finished the task by tugging her onto his lap.

"I want all of you at the same time. Climb up, love, and trust me." He moved so her knees bracketed his hips and she straddled him. "That's it. The same way one would ride astride."

"Astride? Women hardly—"

"You know what I mean."

She settled on his thighs, her skirts gathered and separated. "I've seen horses mate."

"Have you now?"

"This isn't how they do it."

"Indeed." He closed the distance between their mouths, all the while his fingers at work on the laces and ribbons that kept her concealed from him.

* * * *

He gave a growly chuckle, a low rumbled sound that reverberated from his chest and chased away the thunderous beat of his heart against her palm. When she looked at him, he wore that legendary half-smile, the one that caused a bevy of butterflies to take wing in her stomach and tickle her knees into mutiny. But she was seated now. *Across his lap.* And then they were kissing again. And kissing again. They kissed until she wasn't sure if she drew her own air or just breathed him in with each inhale. It was a never-ending kiss.

Her palms were still flat on his chest. His heart had resumed its fierce rhythm and she was intoxicated on the heady pleasure, sitting astride his powerful thighs, her skirts parted and her body responsive to his every touch.

She didn't object when he unlaced her gown and lowered her bodice. Nor when he slowly peeled away layer after layer, until only her short stays and chemise remained. She wanted him to see her, revel in her, the same way she yearned to explore his body and taste his skin.

She broke their kiss and watched his expression as she nimbly set to work on the laces binding her breasts. His Adam's apple bobbed. His jaw pressed tight. For a renowned rakehell and infamous scoundrel, he seemed to struggle to keep his desire on a leash. A rush of pride swept through her at the victory.

"Caroline." His voice had gone husky, and the rasp cut through the heated air between them. "Allow me."

He placed his fingers over hers and continued to untie the laces. Her heartbeat pounded in approval, and down below a distracting ache, an insistent longing, caused her to wriggle in impatience.

"You'll bring about my untimely death if you do that again." He may have tried for a stern tone, but the devilish look on his face defeated the effort. "And I cannot die before I've tasted every inch of you."

The manner in which she sat was naughty indeed. Beneath her skirt, with her thighs draped over his, she was open to him. Completely exposed, the slit in her drawers hardly a barrier. Were he to move his hand beneath her skirts and find her, stroke her, she would come apart at his first touch.

She didn't know how to define their relationship. Oh, she knew in her heart she loved him, and he had just tonight confessed the same, but could they have a future together? Perhaps, perhaps not.

Lindsey was a complicated man. He'd agreed to help her without the slightest hesitation. He was reputed to be a rakehell, a waster of women and an arrogant libertine, and yet he was the first gentleman to ever treat her as an equal.

Not to mention his kisses.

She gloried in his kisses, each one delicious and skillfully adept at offering unending pleasure.

They might not have forever, but they could have this evening. It wasn't as though he could truly ruin her. She was already ruined. Barren. Incomplete. Lost in these thoughts, she startled when he spoke again. A muscle flexed beneath his sleeve and desire rippled through her.

"I've kept myself closed off for so long, my emotions inaccessible, it became a comfortable habit." He released the laces he held and brought his fingers to her chin. "Then along came you, and every defense I believed kept my heart unreachable was breeched, plundered and ruined without my permission, done so quite permanently." His voice held an intensity she'd never heard before. "You've caused my complete undoing, and yet I can't feel a whit sorry for it. If I could go back in time, I'd find you sooner, Caroline."

She smiled, her pulse thrumming. "So where do you envision yourself in the future?"

"Much the same as right now."

He answered immediately, and she forced herself to remain silent. Once an unrepentant scoundrel, always one, she supposed. Another comfortable habit, no doubt. He continued, no matter disappointment pierced her heart.

"Beside you." He stroked his thumb across her lips, holding her silent though she didn't dare interrupt. "With my arms around the woman I love."

His answer surprised her. Thrilled her as it shot a shiver of anticipation to her core.

"I love you too." Her words were whisper-soft and spoken from the heart.

"Caroline." His voice sounded strained, though his gaze smoldered.

"Yes."

"I already told you I love you, but damn it, I need you too."

His words undid her more than his kiss. These words were easy to understand, and from there on all conversation ceased and instinct took over.

Chapter Twenty-Six

He was a jaded, unrepentant rogue. At least, that's what his reputation declared. But now, in his drawing room with Caroline atop his lap, it could have been the first time he ever touched a woman, his physical reaction so intense. Emotion was the cause. He'd suffocated any kind of tender feeling in his need to remain indomitable and inadvertently walled up his heart. But no longer. He loved her. He loved Caroline. The thought unnerved and enthralled him. It was both an invigorating and paralyzing realization. But now was not a time to examine his discovery.

His cock strained painfully against his falls. His body hummed with radiant energy. His mind blanked and his fingers became clumsy. He managed, with her help, to undo the inconvenient trappings of her underclothes, and her breasts bared in front of him caused him to clench his teeth so tightly his jaw ached. The simple task of undressing her had proven spellbinding, but the sight of her delicate, creamy skin convinced him he dreamed. Longing squeezed his chest, making each breath difficult, a piercing pleasure, the notion he could touch, taste, arouse, fast to remind she waited for him. He struggled to maneuver his shirt free, the linen thrown over his head and discarded so they could connect skin to skin, the plush velvet at his back a ready buffer for the force of their joining.

He cupped her breast, the silky weight naturally formed to fill his palm, and her eyes fell closed as she relished the contact. She was exquisite, all willowy grace before him and unyielding strength beneath. She was perfection.

He brought his mouth to her breast, laved his tongue across the ruched tip as hard and eager as his cock beneath too much cloth, presently nestled against her bottom. He suckled and she whimpered, a broken moan of pleasure-pain, and he smoothed his fingertips over her shoulder, memorizing the curves, reveling in the sweet softness of every dip and arch from her clavicle to her shoulder blades. She threaded her fingers through his hair, holding him against her heart, each indrawn breath an aphrodisiac.

She rose up as he caressed her and then resettled, each downward slide wicked torture to his erection, impatient and swollen within his breeches. She was a seductress. She'd beguiled him from the start and he never wished to let her go. They'd crossed a line now. There'd be no turning back and as if to solidify that realization, he grew harder still.

Bloody hell, he would spill himself in his pants like an untried green lad. He needed more, and she could only have read his mind. Too much fabric pooled between the two of them and she pushed it aside, all the while he worked to loosen the buttons of his breeches. They fell into another kiss while the seductive skim of her nipples across his chest urged him to work faster. The friction of skin to skin, heat pressed against heat, was maddening. He leaned back against the divan cushions and swept his palms beneath her skirts, smoothing upward over her shapely knees trapped by the thin fabric of her drawers, wanting to bring her to climax, her head thrust back, eyes closed, and hair mussed, falling silently about her bare shoulders. A graceful goddess of seduction and beauty. An enchantress who'd stolen his heart.

Next time they would be gloriously naked, nothing between them but sweat and desire. Next time they would be in his bed.

Her muscles tensed beneath his touch and yet she did nothing but still in his lap. He spread his thighs, which in turn widened hers. One hand found her bottom, holding firm, the curve of her derriere as perfectly formed as every part of her, while the other traced along the sensitive skin of her inner thigh, slowing as her heat increased until he stroked with the lightest pressure along the slit of her drawers.

She jerked as if startled and then dropped her head to his, three lovely words whispered for his ears only: "Finally. Yes. Please."

He did as he was told and slid his fingers upward along her thigh to stroke into her wet heat. She clutched his shoulders, her fingertips biting into his skin with impatience, and he watched her face, never having seen anything so arousing or erotic as Caroline in the midst of pleasure. He stroked harder, deeper, finding the hidden pearl in her slick folds and rubbing with insistence, wanting to offer her relief and so much more. This he could give her. This moment belonged to the two of them alone and he wanted to make it last and last and last.

He knew when her endurance was spent. Her thigh quivered against the back of his hand, his fingertips drenched with her desire, and as she moved to squeeze her legs closed, he plunged his finger inside deep, her climax fraying the last threads of his control.

She fell forward, her breathing husky against his ear, and she nuzzled her face into his neck, the tips of her breasts again wreaking havoc with his grasp on control. But she possessed not an ounce of selfishness, and after the slightest pause, their bodies damp with sweat, she pulled back, her eyes aglint with mischief and mayhem as her fingers moved the placket of his falls aside.

His erection needed no encouragement. Freed from his breeches, he watched as her eyes widened, once glassy with arousal, now stark with a newfound clarity.

"I didn't expect you to be so big."

He chuckled. He couldn't help himself. "I don't know if I should be insulted or flattered."

"I'm…"

"You're ready, love. You're soft and wet and so very ready for me."

He wouldn't allow conversation to intrude upon their delicious joining, and with a kiss meant to reassure and ignite he gently brought her hand forward, wrapping her fingers around his erection. Her soft touch on his hard arousal sent unbearable sensation to every point of his being. He was tempted to rock back against the cushions, close his eyes, and fall into oblivion, but he wouldn't miss watching Caroline work him, ride him, find immense pleasure in their coming together.

She tightened her grasp, finding her way, instigating ache and at the same time soothing his raging desire. She'd donned a look of concentration and again he was tempted to chuckle, her earnest dedication to the task admirable, but a much more satisfying ambition came to mind.

He wrapped his fingers around hers, eased her hand to slow, releasing her grip, and gently positioned himself against her sex. They stayed that way a long moment until she raised slightly on his lap, their eyes matched, their hearts thrumming.

Then he came up off the cushions and crushed his mouth to hers. It was a hungry kiss that turned tender, a passionate quest that immediately became a gentle act of worship. He kissed her deeply, and as his tongue caressed hers, wrapped tight in her embrace, he guided himself in.

This was madness. This was lovemaking. This was pure joy and nothing else.

She settled atop his erection, though he could tell she held back. Her thighs trembled. His cock throbbed. Hot pleasure surged through his veins. He needed her. Wanted her. Couldn't wait a moment longer.

With as much care as possible, for he would never hurt her, he grasped her hips and sank into her snug heat. He nearly blacked out from the intensity of sensation. She was so tight. Her muscles held him still, stretching and squeezing, until he thought any movement would be the death of him.

But the lady had other ideas.

Achingly slow, she lifted herself and resettled. He growled in response, his breathing broken, as if he'd run a long distance and hadn't enough strength to draw another breath. It was exquisite torture. Unfathomable delectation. His mind emptied by the surge of sensual fulfilment, his body reduced to nothing more than primal gratification.

"Caroline," he rasped. "I can't…"

But his complaint was lost to her as she rose again, confident in her purpose, her fingers now at play with the hair at his neck, her thighs strong aside his hips, her body working his as if they were created for each other alone. She came down with surety, taking his full length, tilting her hips slightly to further her pleasure.

She kept on. Riding him, reveling in her ability to render him speechless, helpless. His pulse drummed. His fiery blood rushed within his veins. Her knees pinched into his hips, her fingers tugging his hair. She was close. He was closer. He couldn't wait, though he wanted it to last.

And yet, they fell into pleasure together, her cry overridden by his guttural groan. And then sated, amidst gathered silk with his boots still on his feet, he pulled her against him, skin to skin, heartbeats touching, and held her as he begged for his pulse to calm.

"How did you know to move like that?" He was glad her head rested against his shoulder and they weren't face to face as he asked.

"You said it was like riding a horse." Her whisper sounded sleepy, and he imagined her in his bed for the hundredth time.

"But you've never ridden astride. You said—"

"I'm cold." She shivered and pulled closer to his chest. He wrapped his arms around her tighter.

Devil take him, his body was on fire. Surely, several internal organs were scorched from their heated lovemaking.

"Let's get you covered." He was no better than a cad, a notorious rakehell. He'd stripped bare the woman he loved before a waning fire in his drawing room without a towel or basin of water in sight. He would do better next time. Next time he would cherish her as she deserved.

He reassembled himself and assisted with the wrinkled layers of her underclothes and gown to the best of his ability. They didn't speak more, though her cheeks remained rosy and a slight smile played at her lips the entire time.

"I'm sorry, Caroline."

Her head whipped up and she matched his eyes, her expression incredulous. "Sorry?"

"Never doubt I love you, but these conditions were less than what they should have been. Next time, it will be better. I will do better."

"Next time." A smile broke across her cheeks. "Better? I wouldn't change a thing."

He heaved a sigh of relief, anxious to replace his concern. Then he began to hunt for his shirt.

* * * *

Caroline eyed Jonathan as he retrieved his clothing. His body was magnificent, a work of art composed of sculpted muscle and hard sinew. Dark hair dusted over his ridged abdomen, downward in a kite string past his navel, where it disappeared into the waistband of his breeches. Now, as he raised his arms over his head and replaced his shirt, a spike of possessive desire lanced through her.

They'd made love. They were *in* love.

Still, she wondered what any of it meant, considering the circumstances.

She'd arrived at his home to seek help for her father and decidedly withheld the information. Lindsey hadn't offered more than words of affection. No commitment. And did that matter anyway? No doubt he would marry one day and need a successor. She couldn't produce the heir to secure his continued lineage. While she'd experienced unleashed freedom and joy a moment earlier, despair now stole the emotions away on a rush of insecurity.

"What is it?"

He was far too observant for his own good, but she was saved from explaining by a thunderous knock echoing through the hall. Jonathan glanced at the clock across the room, scowled, and turned to her, his brows raised in question.

"Stay here and I'll rid the house of whoever dares to arrive at this hour."

He unlocked the door and then closed it behind him as she dropped into a chair closest to the fire, her head filled with too many questions to consider.

* * * *

Lindsey hated walking out of the room. Short of an emergency, whoever bothered him at this time of night needed an urgent reason. He whipped the door open before a servant appeared, despite the house was shut for the evening. He shouldn't have dismissed Hobbs, but then he hadn't wanted anyone else on this floor.

"Mills? What's the meaning of this?"

Belatedly he remembered his friend had promised him the Morta. It was as if nothing really mattered anymore. He was lost to Caroline.

And yet he'd left her sitting in his drawing room after their extraordinary intimacy. Bloody hell, he'd abandoned her again. Albeit not the same, he turned a wayward glare toward his friend.

"Invite me in, will you?" Mills stepped over the threshold, a wrapped package in one hand. "For you, as promised."

Lindsey's attention dropped to the painting, and when he didn't reach for it Mills leaned it against the legs of the mahogany occasional table at his right.

"Invite you in?" His conscience smarted. He could be enjoying Caroline if not for his father's impossible demands. But there lay the rub, didn't it? Caroline claimed she wouldn't be able to bear children. It was a tricky knot, the conditions his father had placed on his son's inheritance.

"I promised you the painting." Mills eyed him as if he were mad. "After all, you did keep your word."

"My word?" Apparently, an evening of mind-altering lovemaking had turned him into a bloody parrot.

"Can't we move beyond the foyer?" Mills made to advance toward the drawing room doors and Lindsey stayed him with an upraised hand.

"It's late and I'm exhausted."

"Very well." Mills glanced around the foyer before he continued. "You kept your distance from Lady Nicholson. I honestly doubted you would be able to resist. I saw the look in your eyes whenever you glanced in her direction or heard her name mentioned. You were the fox and she, the little hen."

I saw her and my world stopped spinning. All the chaos and disappointment ceased. Life demanded I take notice.

"Is there a point to this conversation?" Lindsey straightened his shoulders to shake away the threat of ill-ease. He wouldn't like what Mills said next.

"But I suppose my concern was all for naught."

Wrong.

Although Lindsey would never correct him. True, he'd acted territorially, as if she were his, and he'd protected her fiercely when he'd spoken to Mills. Also true, jealousy tore through him every time he saw another man admire or pay her the slightest attention, but those were emotions he'd rather not examine. Jealousy and insecurity were traits of an inexperienced schoolboy, not a grown man. Unless, perhaps, that man had little experience with cherished emotion.

Still, none of it signified. At this very moment, Caroline waited for him in the drawing room, atop the divan which still held the musky scent of their lovemaking. His shirt still held her perfume, and his lips, the heat of her kiss.

"Turns out, the lady and I wouldn't suit," Mills continued, unaware of Lindsey's mental scrutiny. "She's too independent for my taste."

Lindsey refocused, but again he didn't reply.

"I wish to marry, but want none of the complications. Lady Nicholson doesn't seem the sort to remain sanguine while I perpetuate my unfettered habits."

"Indeed." Mills was a fool, but Lindsey wouldn't point out the flaw. If he ever decided to marry, Caroline composed his vision of perfection: rare intelligence, remarkable wit, and unmatched beauty. Why would a man want for any other woman?

"I'm leaving for Rome at daybreak. I've business there that needs attention." He indicated the painting with a gesture toward the tiles. "I don't know when I'm returning, so I thought to bring you the Morta."

"You've had it in your possession before this evening?"

"Why does it matter when I acquired it if I'm giving it to you now? Don't be difficult. It helps solve your problem, doesn't it?"

Lindsey searched Mills' face for answers. Had his friend supplied him with a forgery? Their conversation at the fox hunt still remained fresh in his mind. "Thank you."

"You look like hell, by the way." Mills turned to go. "You're right. You need to get some rest."

Lindsey saw his friend out and retrieved the package. Something was amiss. Was Mills involved with criminals? Lindsey would hate to realize that truth. Perhaps he jumped to illogical conclusions.

He tucked the painting away in the closet below the stairs and returned to the drawing room. He vowed to help Caroline. His own misery would have to wait, even if the two proved intertwined.

"Is everything all right?"

She stood before the fireplace, a portrait of loveliness, and for the slightest pause his mind blanked, unable to connect her question with a logical answer. She'd reclaimed her composure and appeared only slightly mussed from their lovemaking. He had the sudden urge to start all over again and do a more thorough job.

"Yes. Mills." He shook his head, not wanting to explain further. "We should get you home." He gathered her cloak from the chair and wrapped it tightly around her shoulders. "Not that I want you to leave." He kissed her forehead as he straightened her hood. "But I'm certain nothing good will come of keeping you locked in my drawing room at my decadent disposal day and night."

He backed far enough away to see her eyes widen, her cheeks stain with color, that same impish smile at play on her lips.

"You really are incorrigible." She slipped her arms out from under the cloak and wrapped them around his middle.

"I will call on you tomorrow, love." He couldn't resist pressing a soft kiss to her cheek, inhaling her sweet fragrance one last time. "If you're ready to share your distress, I mean to help ease your mind."

Chapter Twenty-Seven

It was barely half nine when Lindsey entered Edward Barlow's law office on Wigmore Street. He didn't have an appointment this morning, nor did he have patience. His father had left behind an impossible task with an imposing time frame, and Lindsey was no longer tolerant.

He hadn't wanted to say goodbye to Caroline last night. He'd lived his entire life without her, burying his heart and refusing to experience emotion because every waking moment of his childhood he'd seen how much damage love could wreak. But somehow Caroline had managed to revive the useless organ in his chest, and now he didn't wish to spare a single moment apart from her.

When the carriage had whisked her and her maid away last evening, he was altogether bereft. Not with worry; he'd sent additional footmen to follow and secure her safe return, although that hadn't made parting any easier. No, it wasn't until a good hour later when sentiment cleared and he'd begun to think matters through that he realized he needed to have a conversation with the solicitor, and not just for the legalities of a special license. He needed to set the present chaos into order.

This morning he would resolve his father's foolish legacy and begin to look toward the future instead of cursing the past.

Enacting his plan, he strode briskly past the young clerk stationed outside Barlow's office and entered without pausing to knock. The older man looked up with a startle, though he waved Lindsey forward without hesitation, simultaneously dismissing the anxious clerk who'd followed at Lindsey's heels.

"Good morning, my lord. What brings about this unexpected visit?"

Excellent. Barlow wished to proceed straight to the heart of the matter.

"I've decided to marry." Peculiar how what he once considered undesirable and downright inconceivable now prompted him to grin.

The solicitor extended his hand for a hearty shake. "Well done, you. A productive step toward fulfilling the legacy."

"No." Lindsey's smile dropped away. Any mention of his sire ignited years of unresolved anger. "I'm marrying for love, not some daft contingency and deathbed ultimatum. I wouldn't give my father the satisfaction or allow him to continue his manipulation from the grave."

"Still." Barlow exhaled, as if he deliberated carefully on his next words. "Your marriage will serve a dual purpose."

"Not actually. I haven't acquired the missing paintings, and I don't give a damn if I propagate the line. The earldom can die with me. Or as happenstance, I may produce a houseful of daughters." He'd protect Caroline's pride and reputation until he drew his last breath. Taking a chair in front of the solicitor's desk, he waited for Barlow to shed further light on the subject.

"Surely you understand the consequences, Lindsey. You'll throw away your future if you fail to—"

"Rather the contrary. I'll finally have a modicum of peace." And it was true.

"Whether or not you're decided on this course of action, you should know your choices have far-reaching repercussions for others." Barlow's face puckered as if he disliked saying the words aloud.

Lindsey considered this news. It was the first time he considered with earnest how his actions bore negatively on others. He'd become so angry after hearing his father's last wishes, he'd never considered the extended impact. "And whom would that be?"

A formidable conclusion stabbed his brain. *Powell.* Bloody hell. He'd suspected correctly when they'd spoken at Henley's fox hunt. His bastard half brother was connected to this mess.

"I'm afraid I'm not able to reveal more." Barlow nodded in the negative to emphasize the point. "At least not at this juncture." The solicitor lost his congenial expression and appeared uncomfortable by degree.

"Is that so? Then tell me in what capacity my actions will impose on others." His voice dropped lower, his anger tantamount to his curiosity.

"Again, my lord, your father was extremely specific with the details of his legacy and how it could be discussed, and with whom." Succumbing to temptation, Barlow snuck a glance at the clock.

Lindsey was done playing guessing games. He slammed his fist down on the desktop, and the sudden vibration caused the lid of Barlow's crystal ink well to jiggle loose and drop to the wooden slats below.

"How dare he interfere in so many lives."

The solicitor had the good sense to remain silent.

"And if I don't fulfill these ridiculous requirements? If none of us do? Then what happens?"

His father was too selfish and vain not to have prepared for such an occurrence.

"In that regard, I've instructions to follow." Barlow stopped abruptly, as if about to say more and then deciding against it.

"What is it?" Lindsey stood and leveled a stare meant to intimidate. It worked. Barlow heaved a weary sigh of resignation.

"I regret to tell you the late earl anticipated your refusal to cooperate. He doubted your ability and assumed you'd fail. With all due respect, my lord, I don't believe you'll benefit from abandoning the task."

"Did he now? Bloody bastard." Lindsey's expletive caused the solicitor's eyes to widen. "This is maddening. I didn't survive day after day of the man's cruelty to be told I'm disinherited. I'll have what's rightfully mine, and to that end prove my father wrong."

He left without further discussion. There was nothing else to say. Determined to help Caroline, confront Powell, and fulfill the damnable legacy, he directed his driver to Kingswood. He hadn't visited the family cemetery, but he assumed the dirt on the grave was good and settled by now, and that was for the best. He had a bone to pick with his father.

* * * *

"Another frantic message and urgent visit," Louisa complained, but there was a smile in her words. "Your mother will believe *I* have something to hide instead of her reserved and obedient daughter."

"Shush." Caroline flared her eyes to further silence her cousin. "Wait until we're a considerable distance from the house before you land us both in trouble."

"I've little to worry my head about," Louisa replied as she hurried her steps.

Caroline cast a glance over her shoulder to see Louisa's beaming smile. "Well, it would be the first time I'm the cause of a stir instead of you."

They walked briskly, one after the other, deeper into the gardens until Caroline stopped beside a trio of Gallica rosebushes, their blooms in varying shades of pink. Lindsey had mentioned the extensive gardens at Kingswood, and she wondered if she'd visit with him soon and see his mother's labor of love, a work of art born from terrible pain. She couldn't imagine the despair Lindsey and his mother had experienced.

"So now." Louisa reached forward and squeezed Caroline's arm lightly. "Tell me why I needed to visit with expedience. Your note gave nothing away, and I'm anxious to hear what has caused that twinkle in your eyes."

"I'm in love." Saying the words aloud were magical. She'd mentioned the importance of a love match to her mother and cousins, and regardless of their attempts to persuade her against a hopeful search for romance, she'd found herself exactly where she wanted to be.

"In love?" Louisa's voice held a fair share of skepticism. "With Lord Mills? Certainly not Lord Tiller."

"No." Caroline smiled, a shimmer of excitement alive within her.

"What the heavens are you talking about?" Louisa folded her arms over her chest, a confused look upon her face. "You haven't mentioned a single gentleman with fondness, unless..." Her voice trailed off as recognition bloomed. "I don't know what to say."

"I'm certain that's never occurred before." Caroline couldn't keep from teasing Louisa. Her cousin was not unlike her mother, with a steady stream of advice and opinions, as if she alone understood the intricacies of relationships and could impart sage knowledge to Caroline.

"Honestly, you've done the exact opposite of what I've recommended." Caroline laughed. "He seems to bring out that tendency in me."

"I'd call it rebellion," Louisa surmised with a nod of her head.

"No," Caroline quickly corrected. "Freedom."

"Freedom? That's preposterous. Women have few freedoms, I'm afraid." Louisa scowled, her voice rich with unspoken regret.

"Freedom to choose, Louisa." Caroline approached and laid a gentle hand to her cousin's shoulder. "Freedom to choose who I fall in love with and how I spend my future." Despite her family's situation remained tenuous, she couldn't regret sharing her body with Lindsey. She'd indulged her passion and discovered fulfillment. With their exchange of a love vow, she knew Lindsey would see her family out of danger. She planned to tell him the all of it when he called later today. Things remained complicated, and she couldn't presume he'd offer marriage, but she refused to allow her mind to wander down that path until they spoke further. Naturally, she wished her body wasn't defected. Only time would tell to what degree the physician's diagnosis rang true. Likewise, she knew Lindsey would someday need an heir. And she still wanted a home, a husband...

"And does he return your affection?" Louisa sounded unconvinced.

"Oh, yes." The warmth of that divine statement flooded Caroline's soul. "We are very much in love. He listens to me and asks my opinion. He doesn't have a care about perceptions, as he's comfortable in his own skin, not like other gentlemen who wish to impress me, preening as they list their accomplishments. Lindsey considers me an equal, and that in itself is refreshing and utterly freeing." She couldn't stop the grin that spread across her cheeks. "It's as liberating as removing one's corset at the end of a long evening. It's as if, when I'm with him, I can breathe. Simply breathe and be myself."

"Then I wish you every happiness, dear cousin." Louisa hugged her tightly. "I didn't believe it possible, but you've certainly proved me wrong."

Chapter Twenty-Eight

The staff at Kingswood was of impeccable capability, and neither the butler nor housekeeper, who had the unfortunate experience of crossing Lindsey's path as he stormed toward his father's bedchambers, batted an eye. Lindsey's arrival was unexpected. His show of temper, not as much. Still, there was no questioning the fact every servant in the expansive manor house relished the silent tranquility left in the wake of the late earl's death.

Lindsey had no intention of following in a tradition of hell-raising and rabble-rousing, yet the irksome condition of the legacy, combined with his fervent desire to settle matters and marry Caroline, spurred his travel before sunlight splintered the sky.

Why? Why would his father attach such a farfetched condition to the inheritance? Could it be only financial in nature? He crossed the parlor and advanced to the newel post, each step surer as he took the central stairs two at a time, his bootheels hard on the treads. He aimed for his father's bedchambers at the end of the hall. He had no recollection of the last time he'd entered these rooms, too many memories of his father's backhanded abuse crowded in to pierce his brain and cloud distinction. Fueled by anger and another unnamed emotion that burned in his veins, he did not hesitate longer. Instead he flung wide the double doors, advanced through the sitting room, and entered his father's bedchamber. His father had slept there alone for over two decades, never having remarried after his wife chose death over a future of abuse and neglect.

At once a rush of scenes, all of them unpleasant, reached out in a painful snare determined to claim him, but he refused to allow it. He paced farther across the floorboards and raised his eyes to his father's portrait over the massive Tynecastle panel bed. It was nothing more than indulgent glorification, his father in profile atop his favored mount, a riding crop in his hand and obedient spaniel below. Lindsey stared in fury and contempt at the configuration of oil paint and brushstrokes. How petty and arrogant to sleep with one's likeness hung over one's pillow. He scanned the area in search of something heavy to throw and saw little of use. He needed to remove that painting if there was ever hope he'd find peace within these walls. A mere glance stirred repugnant feelings better left in the past.

Climbing atop the mattress, he lifted the ornate frame and dropped the portrait to the floorboards unceremoniously. What the devil? Its removal revealed a wooden cabinet. With no more than a quirk of his lips to acknowledge his father's perverse inclinations, Lindsey opened the narrow compartment.

He reached inside. It took a few minutes to empty the cabinet and bring the gathered contents to the inlaid marquetry table near the double windows, but drawing the curtains wider provided the light needed to discern exactly what he'd found.

Among the pile there were deeds and certificates most gentlemen kept in their study beside the ledger, but his father was a shifty distrusting bastard, and Lindsey had no doubt, like his portrait, he needed to keep his most precious papers close. There were tightly bound stacks of pound notes that couldn't be misconstrued as anything else, at least six similar piles, and when Lindsey finished counting he found it totaled a sum of four thousand pounds.

There was also a black leather canister fastened by a single cord. He unraveled the string and extricated the contents to find a rolled canvas inside. The dull thud of his heart told him what he would see even before his eyes assessed the work. True to his speculation, the Decima stared back at him.

Why?

Why would his father send him on a wildly redundant chase after a painting already in his possession when nothing more than an unattainable outcome could result?

He gathered everything together with a curse, heading for the door before he fully assembled the contents. He'd pay a call to the fencer in Seven Dials and confirm the authenticity of the Decima and the Morta delivered by Mills before he traveled to Caroline's house to assist with her concerns. It wasn't that he placed his problems before hers, but he knew in his heart he'd never be free to offer for her hand until his future was settled. And too, with the newly acquired funds from his father's secret cabinet, he could offer relief if, as he suspected, her worries stemmed from impending financial crisis. And yet to place his trust in a criminal left him perturbed. He needed a better plan.

He reclaimed Infinity from the stables and began his return to London. He rode like the devil, and in that his horse did not disappoint. He stopped first at the Duke of Warren's home and convinced his friend to lend him the Nona. It wasn't an easy conversation, but in the end Lindsey's skills of persuasion and sincere promise to return it posthaste won out. Now, with Warren's copy of the Nona inside his leather bag and both the Decima and Morta rolled and bound beside it, he set off to meet with the fencer.

He arrived with excellent time, the hour not quite half two. Seven Dials looked differently in the daytime. Still, it was no place for a gentleman, even one as rebellious as he. Narrow alleyways lit with shallow sunlight exposed conditions better left to the darkness, the streets and slummed tenements deteriorated and filthy. At least he'd had the good sense to wear the same pair of boots as when he'd visited with Mills. He wondered at Mills' loyalty. How had his friend ferreted out the Morta when Lindsey had had little success? Acquiring the painting had brought him one step closer to fulfilling the legacy and finding a modicum of happiness, but he wouldn't think of Caroline now.

He moved swiftly. While more people were about, the inhabitants displayed the poverty level at its worst. Women wore nothing but rags, several children at their heel, and men who'd already imbibed too much at the local gin shop despite the early hour littered the curb. Sympathetic to their plight, Lindsey spared coins for the children and polite greetings for their mothers, but likewise practiced caution, not wishing to use his knife to ward off a vagrant who might think to relieve the earl of his belongings.

He arrived at the fencer's lair, surprised to see the door ajar. Several men moved in and out, and without challenge Lindsey entered. He followed the dingy hall to the same room he'd frequented previously to find it emptied of its contents. The few scraps of canvas and burlap left behind were hardly evidence of a once-thriving business. He blew a breath of frustration, immediately alerted when voices rose in an adjoining room. He followed the sound, anxious to learn more.

"Pack the last of those. I'm expecting one last delivery, and then we'll be gone from this place."

Lindsey recognized the fencer's voice and pushed the door wide to enter the room. As expected, the man stood with another, his expression one of immediate anger, though he didn't approach.

"Have you come back for another appraisal?" The fencer nodded toward the stranger lurking at his side, and the hulk of a man nodded in answer. "You've caught me at an inconvenient time."

"Leaving?" Lindsey made of show of surveying the room's vacant interior. "Going out of town then?"

"I don't stay overlong in one spot. It's bad for business. We're set to leave, so I have no time to spare. Let's make this quick." The fencer approached, although his comrade remained stoically in the background. "What have you got for me, aside from a purse full of coins?"

Lindsey removed Warren's copy of the Nona and handed it forward. The fencer made no haste in unrolling the canvas and eyeing the painting.

"I've already confirmed the authenticity of this painting. Do you not believe me?" There was impatience and irritation in the question.

"One can never be sure in matters worth excessive funds."

"There's truth in that, although every painting that crosses my table is confirmed as authentic. Collectors wish to believe they hold a valuable investment, and I grant their wish. I provide a valuable service, and when a truly remarkable piece shows here that will make me a tidy profit elsewhere, I'm able to supply a forgery that's so unmistakable, no one is the wiser." The fencer held on to the Nona, a shrewd gleam in his eye. "Mayhap you don't deserve to keep this one. Mayhap you should have accepted my word the first time and you wouldn't find yourself in this predicament now."

"And that is?" Lindsey eyed the door, too far from where he stood to offer a plausible escape. The knife in his boot would come in handy, but the odds were against him, as the hulking man who'd remained motionless until this moment was all at once standing beside the fencer.

"Leave me with the painting and your purse and we'll part as men of business should." The fencer grinned. "I'd hate to have my man dirty those fancy clothes of yours when in the end the same result will win out."

All havoc might have ensued if Lord Derby hadn't entered at that moment. It was just the distraction Lindsey needed, and he launched himself at the muscled bloke, striking with surprise and knocking him unconscious as the man barreled backward and struck his head on the floorboards. Lindsey added a series of blows to ensure the blackguard wouldn't rise quickly. The fencer, who'd watched in awe, snapped into action, muttered a curse, and vanished out another door. Lindsey didn't follow him, although it was unfortunate the man had taken Warren's painting with him. Lindsey would have a devil of a time explaining the events to His Grace.

Lindsey turned toward Lord Derby where he'd retreated into the corner, the older man shaken and pale.

"Derby? What are you doing here?" He watched as Caroline's father removed a handkerchief from his pocket and mopped his brow. A rolled canvas lay at his feet, and when he seemingly recovered his composure, he stooped to retrieve the painting.

"Lindsey." Derby cleared his throat. "This is unexpected, although it seems I may have distracted from impending trouble."

"Indeed you did." Lindsey approached and extended his hand for a hearty shake, sparing a glance over his shoulder to confirm the unconscious hulk remained motionless. "Why don't we rid ourselves of this place? I'm certain we both have riveting stories better shared far away from here."

Derby nodded and joined Lindsey as he made for the door.

* * * *

Caroline paced the carpeting of the drawing room. Too many emotions rivaled for attention within her. She rejoiced in the sincere declarations of affection she'd shared with Lindsey and warmed with hope for the expectations of the days and nights ahead, but what of her family's plight? She'd chosen to keep her father's involvement in the forgery ring to herself, but now thought foolishly of her decision. If she hoped to have any place in Lindsey's life, he would need to know it all. If he decided to distance himself in caution of scandal, she certainly couldn't fault him.

More importantly, they must see her father safely removed from the threat of criminal involvement or, worse, prosecution. Her mind jumped to conclusion after conclusion, none of them good. She needed Jonathan to calm her anxiety and yet he hadn't shown as he'd promised. She glanced to the ormolu clock atop the mantelpiece. It was already past four in the afternoon. She believed he would have paid call by now. Was he having second thoughts?

As if conjured by her wishing alone, the knocker sounded in the front hall and she waited, anxious to hear Croft announce Lindsey's arrival, though she remained facing the fireplace with her eyes clenched closed against disappointment. At the sound of footfall in the hall, she blinked herself to awareness and turned to see Lindsey catch the doorframe and stop his entry. His eyes moved over her, his expression serious.

Her stomach knotted tight. Had he discovered her family's situation? She needed to abandon cowardice and tell him the truth. With her decision made, she hardly spared time for a greeting, and then rushed on in a flurry of words.

"Thank goodness you're here. I need to talk to you. My father is involved in a desperate situation."

"I don't like seeing you so upset, Caroline." Lindsey came forward and stroked his thumb across her cheek. "Everything will be set to right."

"No." She backed away from his touch, too afraid his tenderness would sway her from purpose. "I visited you last night with the intention to reveal my concerns and was too quickly distracted. Please allow me to speak. Let me tell you everything."

"There really is no need." He took a step nearer, and again she hedged back. "I love you. Nothing is going to change my feelings for you."

"You don't understand." She wrung her hands and implored he listen. "Please."

He nodded and opened his mouth, but before he could interject with another word, she hurried on.

"My father has long admired fine art. He acquired a talent for oil painting at a young age and practiced his craft religiously, often striving to reproduce the masterful work of the classic artists he studied. He became quite adept and his reproductions were nearly indistinguishable from the authentic pieces he admired." She glanced at Jonathan, quick to note his expression had become pensive, his brows lowered and jaw tight, as if he struggled to keep silent.

"While we lived in Italy, a stranger expressed an interest in one of my father's paintings. Perhaps it was a bit of misplaced vanity, or all along he thought only of my future and the monies needed to offer me societal introductions, but regardless, Father agreed to produce a particular work and leave it unsigned. My parents worried profusely after I survived my accident, and always carried with them a concern for my future wellbeing and the ability to find a husband who would care for me despite my health concerns. I can readily understand how my father was tempted by the large sum offered for his painting. I didn't know at the time our financial security was in peril. Females are kept woefully uninformed, never mind a daughter who believes her father infallible.

"But it became a slippery slope after that first exchange. The stranger demanded more artwork and paid less, extorting my father with the threat of exposure. Financial security was one thing to consider, but his daughter's reputation and future proved another altogether. Scandal is a debutante's nemesis.

"So, unwittingly at first and then later most decidedly, my father bowed to this horrible man's wishes, supplying painting after painting, suspecting or mayhap fully knowing they were being sold as originals. When at last he broke free, we returned with haste to England."

"I'm sorry your family has suffered at the hands of these despicable thieves."

"That's not all." She widened her eyes and implored he allow her to finish.

"Go on then, love."

"This net of dishonesty thrives in England as well. There's a dark market for paintings, whether authentic or forged, bought and sold to collectors and investors without anyone the wiser."

"Yes, I'm too aware." Jonathan's voice acquired a conflicting tone.

"I believe, due to financial crisis, my father may be courting disaster again. I should have wondered at why he seemed anxious to insinuate himself into art circles here after his experiences in Italy. I was too consumed with my own concerns." She shook her head against the burn of fresh tears and blinked rapidly, her voice thick with emotion. "I don't know how to help him, but you do. You know powerful, influential people. Please tell me you'll assist in this."

"I've no need." He approached and placed his palms on her shoulders.

"No need?" Her voice broke with distress. "But I—"

"Caroline, I know all this already. Everything you've just told me."

"You do?" She reared back, unable to comprehend what he was saying.

"Yes. I just came from meeting with your father. You've nothing to worry over. The matter is resolved. I was also able to supply him the funds needed to settle the overdue debts."

"But you told me your funds were—"

"I promise I'll explain every detail to you later. You needn't worry any longer." He changed the subject abruptly. "Besides, I wish to discuss a different matter altogether."

"Thank you. I don't know what to say except thank you." She paused, only a heartbeat, all fear and pent-up tension dissipating. "If you knew all this, why ever did you allow me to carry on?"

"You were quite insistent, and I wouldn't dare interrupt. I'm smarter than that. Besides, I believe you needed to say it aloud." Lindsey pulled her against his chest, and she relished the warmth and strength he offered. "You accomplished the most difficult task. I feared if I were the one to deliver the telling of your father's predicament, you might resent me as the bearer of such distressing news."

"Never. When you truly love someone, you hold nothing back, no matter how difficult or ugly the circumstances." She wriggled loose so she could stare up at his face. "So everything is truly resolved?"

"Not quite everything."

Chapter Twenty-Nine

He didn't lie. Resolving the issues with Lord Derby had required a bit of finesse but in the end progressed seamlessly. With the fencer relocating under the threat of exposure, Lindsey didn't anticipate repercussions. Instead, he'd insisted Lord Derby accept the four thousand pounds "found quite unexpectedly," though he didn't elaborate, to compensate for the extortion and duress Lord Derby had experienced at the hands of the miscreants.

At first Derby was reluctant to accept the funds, uncomfortable with the entire situation, but then reasoned the pound notes would be left to thieves and other criminal perpetrators. Lindsey knew debt was more a matter of honor than money, and Lord Derby's pride willed out. In the end, Lindsey's father's hidden cash had resolved a prickly circumstance.

Lindsey saw it as a small sacrifice, most especially as he'd asked Lord Derby for Caroline's hand in marriage shortly after. His status and wealth remained unsure, and there was the troubling matter of the legacy's second condition, but he couldn't survive another day without knowing Caroline would be his wife. He'd already lived too many days without her. Somehow, he'd find a way to keep them financially secure and keep her in the circle of his arms. Becoming a horse breeder seemed a small concession.

And now the lady waited.

"Caroline." Saying her name brought a wealth of joy to his heart. "There is something I need to tell you." He gathered her close. "Before I met you, anger was often my most dependable emotion. I learned to master life by pretending not to give a damn, but perhaps I fooled even myself and achieved too much success in the charade. The role of cynical libertine suited, as I cared little for anything lasting in my life. But you've opened my heart." He paused, unsure of how to proceed. His emotions could never be expressed by words. Words were too ordinary. He needed actions in equal measure.

She stared up at him, anticipation alight in her beautiful blue eyes, as if she measured the value of his declaration.

"Knowing you're not mine, that our hearts are not given to each other, is a condition I find unbearable. Will you marry me, Caroline? Will you be my wife?" He was greedy for her kiss, but he wouldn't do a thing until he had her answer.

And yet she didn't speak, her brow pleated with worry. His heart gave a constricted lurch. Hadn't she spoken of love? Had something changed?

And then, at last:

"Jonathan." She pulled away slightly and laced her fingers in his, palm to palm. When she looked at him tears had gathered in her eyes, her voice tightened, awash in emotion. "Heretofore I believed I could suffocate my deficits under a blanket of love and desire, yet I find it is those two qualities that insist I decline your proposal."

He began to object, and she reached up and silenced him with a finger to his lips. Her voice dropped to hardly more than a whisper.

"You'll need an heir someday. As much as I want a child, it remains uncertain my body will cooperate. I cannot knowingly accept." Her voice grew ragged. "I love you thoroughly. Please know that alone is my greatest joy, and refusing you is my greatest disappointment." Despite she'd barely managed the words, they were bold and fervent, two qualities that caused her mother to shudder, but Caroline had always chosen to speak her mind, and she wasn't going to stop now.

"I don't care about producing an heir."

"But you will." She regained clarity and her voice grew stronger for it.

"Just think of all the fun we'll have trying to prove the physician wrong." He offered her a shadow of a smile. When she didn't reply, he continued. "Producing an heir was my father's obsession, not mine. He had no right to add that condition to my inheritance, and I won't allow him to dictate my life beyond his own."

"You're angry and confused." She shook her head for emphasis. "Perhaps this is more about defying his wishes than falling in love."

"You can't possibly believe we aren't meant to be together. You won't accept my proposal?"

"I can't allow you to make a sacrifice you will come to regret in time. I'm thinking of your future, even if you won't."

"You're wrong. My future is all I think about, and you're the reason." His reply stole her breath away.

"I love you, Caroline."

"And I love you. That's why I could never deny you your heritage and the legacy you have yet to leave the world. Why struggle to complete the condition of your father's will if you'll throw it all away now?"

She moved from his embrace so she could find the strength to ask him to leave. She had no answer for their predicament, and while she'd known saying goodbye would be heartbreaking and anticipated the pain, there could be no mistaking she'd underestimated the impact.

"I think you should go." She took a deep breath and forced herself to continue. "I can't marry you, but I have no regrets. I will always remember you. You are my first—"

"I am your last." He pulled her forward, his words vehement as his mouth claimed hers. "I am your *only*."

* * * *

He punctuated that statement with a bone-melting kiss meant to sufficiently silence the ridiculous argument she waged, and for a moment he believed it worked. She softened under the pressure of his mouth. Her lips parted, and he captured her breathy little sigh. But just as quickly he felt her tense within his grasp.

"What are you doing?" She wriggled to free herself, but he held tight.

"Jolting your memory, because you love me and you seem to have forgotten."

"It's not that simple, and you know it."

"Isn't it?" He gave her a little shake. "It's what you told me you wanted above anything else. Love." He raised his voice, frustration getting hold of him now. "The most impossible gift that I never thought I could give, and yet here I am, offering you my heart, and you're refusing it."

"What's happening here, Caroline?" Lady Derby came through the doorframe, her face sketched with lines of worry.

"Your daughter and I are having an invigorating disagreement."

"Argument," Caroline gritted out.

Lindsey wouldn't allow Caroline to misrepresent the situation. Perhaps her mother would decipher the scene and offer meaningful advice. He would thank her for the favor later.

"Good heavens, haven't I taught you better than to disagree with a gentleman?" Her mother's admonishing tone was almost too much to bear. "Please excuse her behavior, my lord. At times, my daughter doesn't know what's best for her. My vigilant advice has brought her to this moment. I won't allow her to ruin it."

"Lindsey." Lord Derby entered the room and rushed forward to clasp the earl's hand in a hearty shake. "I thought I heard Croft greet you in the hall. What's happening here? Why is everyone looking so grim?" Her father moved his attention from Lindsey to his wife, and then settled at last on Caroline.

"Hello, Father." Caroline caught her bottom lip between her teeth.

"Dearest." Lord Derby's smile grew. "For a moment, with all the commotion, I feared your mother entered and found the two of you caught in an amorous embrace. Some scandalous act that would cause me to demand Lindsey propose on the spot to save your honor." Derby was beaming now, his brows raised in expectation as he eyed the earl.

"Indeed." Lindsey grinned. "What were you thinking? Something like this, mind you?" He yanked Caroline into his arms and captured her mouth in a kiss that went on longer than it should. She protested at first, but with hardly true initiative. They'd proven the point, settled the matter, and yet they didn't come apart until Lady Derby's insistent throat clearing cut through the haze of their ardent embrace. "There. That does it. I'll return with the special license and we can get on with the planning."

"You've tricked me," Caroline protested softly.

"I had to have you, love. I'm selfish that way." He squeezed Caroline's hand as he released her and turned toward Lord Derby. "She's a bit of troublesome baggage at times, but I wouldn't have it any other way. I love your daughter completely." Over Caroline's laughing protest, he bowed to his future mother-in-law, shook his future father-in-law's hand with vigor, and headed for the door.

Chapter Thirty

Two weeks later

The wedding gathering was small, ceremony brief, and the scrumptious celebratory breakfast afterward seemingly never-ending, but at long last Lindsey was alone with his wife. In bed, as a matter of fact. Without a single care. They were in a guest room at Kingswood Manor while the interior underwent a complete renovation, a decision meant to banish ugly memories and claim the estate as their home.

A murmuring among the wedding guests included the observation the renowned rakehell could only have abandoned his notorious habit for claiming the ton's attention. In that opinion, they were correct. All his devotion and dedication now belonged to his beautiful wife.

Thankfully, his newly acquired half brother hadn't shown up at the church to cause a scene or incite an argument, but Lindsey anticipated some type of altercation in the future. Powell had too much at stake to surrender without a fight and, like an unread chapter in a book, Lindsey sensed his father's legacy instigated the action. Nevertheless, Lindsey was open to establishing a better relationship with Powell, their uneasy truce a tenable solution for now. But those were thoughts left for another day.

He glanced across the bedchamber, where his distinguished charcoal grey Merino wool formalwear, embroidered in a design that would have thrown Brummell into a fit of jealousy, lay crumpled and discarded on the floorboards near his wardrobe. His bride's diaphanous wedding gown, an elegant design hemmed in silver-threaded seed pearls and frothy imported lace, billowed in a gossamer cloud where he'd divested her of the garment beside the mattress.

Now they reclined in blissful undress beneath the soft-woven linens, their bodies still damp and sensitive after an adventurous bout of lovemaking, and he couldn't keep from grinning. His wife was his to tempt, love, and spoil to his heart's content for the rest of his life. With all the frenetic planning, they hadn't managed more than a few stolen kisses and affectionate fondles. Tolerating that specific torture had proven unbearable. He planned to make up for lost time. Already his body burned for her touch once again.

"It all worked out in the end, didn't it?" She cast a glance to the far wall, where the Nona, Decima, and Morta hung in glorious display. "Those three little paintings caused an awful lot of trouble."

"Yes, but they led me to you. Thankfully, Barlow's appraisers confirmed their authenticity. I've no desire to look beyond the demands of my father's will, his legacy be damned." Snaking a hand beneath the sheet, he reached for his wife, only to stall at her next, most unexpected statement.

"You should have told me sooner about the second condition to your inheritance."

"And risk losing you? I might be reckless, but I'm not daft."

Lindsey knew this subject would arise sooner or later, and he'd wagered on the latter and lost. As a betting man, he still believed if there was even a one percent chance he could get his wife with child, he intended to win that gamble.

"I've better suggestions for how we might pass our wedding night than discuss ill-begotten edicts and ridiculous demands." Lindsey had discreetly confided in Barlow, who understood the situation with remarkable empathy. The second contingency was left unfulfilled and ignored for the moment, and while the monies and properties were all reordered to reflect Lindsey's endowment, there was no reason the matter couldn't be revisited in the future if need be. "I've received my inheritance, and that's all that matters. I'd rather not think about my father at the moment."

She turned on her side, keeping the sheet up to her chin as she propped to her elbow, her eyes sincere and thoughtful. "My mother advised that we keep no secrets between us, that the way to a happy future is by sharing every experience, whether good or bad." She darted an impish grin and waited. Her slender brows arched in expectation.

"Since when have you listened to your mother's advice? Besides, I'd rather keep her out of our bedroom too."

"Oh, there's no worry of that." She reached across the sheets and ran her fingertips across his chest, smoothing over the muscles as she was often fond of doing. "You've corrupted me quite thoroughly."

"Caroline, my love, you have no idea." He captured her in an effortless action that defied logic and rolled her neatly against his side. Reaching around her slender waist, he cupped her breast, the nipple already peaked and teasing against his palm. "Now, let's continue your scandalous education."

* * * *

Her husband smiled and her heart stuttered. Good thing she was already lying down, or that legendary grin would have caused her collapse. In truth, she'd fallen quite completely regardless. Jonathan's attention had that effect. Still, after a conversation with her cousin Louisa, Caroline had acquired a few ideas, dare she label it *advice*, for pleasing her husband on their wedding night, and she intended to put each and every one into effect, if for no other reason than to demonstrate her ability to weaken his knees in return.

She turned over, bringing them nose to nose, and slipped her hand between their bodies to take hold of his tightening arousal. He was hard and heavy in her grasp, and she reveled in the fact she could cause this reaction. She brushed her fingers over the tip of his erection and he tensed, his look of surprise both pleasing and satisfying. "Why don't you lie back and close your eyes?"

He did as he was told, though he kept his eyes open, focused on the bed drapery above them.

"You mean to torture me, don't you, minx?"

"I mean to pleasure you." She tightened her grasp to emphasize her intent and began a steady rhythm, each stroke a little smoother despite his flesh throbbed and jerked with every pass.

"Caroline." The word sounded strained. "I don't know how much longer, ah—"

Draped against his ribs, her hair might have tickled as she took him into her mouth, although the subsequent sounds confirmed it was more the intensity of her bold caresses, press of her lips, and lap of her tongue that had him uttering incoherent noises. She might have kept going all day if he didn't rally some strength and haul her up and atop him.

"You are a seductress, a sensual goddess intent on punishing me."

She hardly replied before he reversed their positions and she found herself beneath him, the press of his hard, heated chest a delightful contrast to the plush bedding at her back.

"Be warned, my lady wife, I am a scoundrel, an irrepressible rogue, and I've a thousand ways to bring you to pleasure."

She laughed softly, and the sound held every joyful wish for their future.

"I certainly hope so, my lord."

And then conversation became unnecessary.

Printed in the United States
by Baker & Taylor Publisher Services